The Right Kind of Wrong

By

Jillian Marie

I

Note to the Reader

Even though this book takes place in the same world as *The Wrong Kind of Perfect*, you don't need to read that story first to enjoy this one. That said, it does offer a deeper glimpse into Will and Natalie's past and how their story began.

Please be mindful of your mental health while reading, as this book touches on themes of divorce and single parenthood. Still, I hope you'll find that love, especially the imperfect kind, has a way of finding its happily ever after.

Trigger Warning:

This book touches on themes of divorce, infidelity, and emotional healing. While it's ultimately a story about second chances and love, some moments may be difficult for sensitive readers.

Cover design, interior design and layout by Aura Lewis.

ISBN: 979-8-9986254-2-8
First Edition

Printed in the United States of America

www.booksbyjillianmarie.com

For my dear friend Kristin,
who read my stories in their rawest form
and never stopped believing in them—
or in me.

Chapter 1

When the Gate Reopens
Natalie

The school year began as always, the chaos at the gate, parents juggling coffee cups and brand-new Stoney Clover and Pottery Barn backpacks, kids in crisp uniforms darting through the crowd like they hadn't seen their friends in years.

But as I stood there, smiling and waving, 8-year-old Bebe and 6-year-old James ran toward their classmates, I felt him before I even saw him.

Will.

I noticed him like a scent that clings to your clothes long after you've left the room. Unmistakable. Lingering. Something I hadn't prepared for.

I turned slowly, bracing myself, and there he was. Standing just beyond the gate, casually leaning against the car. His sandy blond hair caught the light, and he looked as infuriatingly good as I remembered. Maybe better.

Then I saw her.

She stepped out of the passenger seat. Everything about her made my stomach churn. She was effortlessly put together with sun-kissed skin, oversized Prada sunglasses, a black form-fitting dress, and Dior slides. She moved with calm self-assurance, smoothing her hair like she belonged in the spotlight. And then the real gut punch. Will's daughter Ivy got out of the backseat and smiled up at this living Barbie doll before racing into school.

Will glanced up, his eyes meeting mine with a pull so magnetic it almost hurt. Just a second—maybe two—but it was enough. The memory of us surged back, sharp and unwelcome. I wondered if he felt it too.

Just as quickly, his expression shifted. Hardened. He turned away, saying something to the woman beside him, as if I wasn't there. As if none of it had ever happened.

I forced a smile. Pretended I didn't feel the ache rising in my chest. Pretended I didn't want to run.

I hurried to my car and closed the door. My fingers trembling slightly against the steering wheel, adrenaline still pulsing through me.

I needed a lifeline, something to pull me back before I spiraled.

I grabbed my phone and texted my dear friend and neighbor, Camille.

Natalie: Emergency coffee after Pilates? Also, I want to hear everything about Europe.

Camille: Of course, love. I saw that blonde bitch get out of the car with Will.

I laughed, half choking on the frustration. Camille always had a way of making me feel seen. Still, the way Will looked at me, just for a second, before turning back to her. The way she moved so effortlessly, like she belonged there, like she belonged with him, made my blood run cold.

"Focus, Nat," Camille said softly from the reformer beside me. "Breathe. We'll dissect it all over coffee."

By the time we made it to our usual café, my emotions were simmering just beneath the surface. Camille ordered for both of us and we settled into a corner table, tucked away from the buzz.

"So," she began, narrowing her eyes, "what's the deal with Will and Blondie?"

I sighed, wrapping my hands around the warm latte. "I have no idea. I didn't even know he was seeing someone. I mean, of course he's seeing someone, but..."

"But you weren't ready for the visual confirmation?" she offered.

"Exactly."

She leaned back in her chair, crossing her legs. "What's her story? Did you recognize her?"

"No," I said. "What I do know is she's... perfect. Polished. The kind of woman who probably wakes up looking like that."

Camille raised an eyebrow. "You're no slouch yourself. Don't give her that much credit."

I smiled, but it was weak. "Thanks. It's not just that. It's seeing him with her. The way he looked at me, like I didn't exist."

"He's probably trying to save face," Camille said. "Protect whatever situation he's got going on with Miss Dior Slides. Doesn't mean he's over you."

I shook my head. "It doesn't matter. I ended it. I chose my family."

Camille tilted her head, her expression softening. "And how's that going? You and Jason? Is the divorce final? I feel like I missed so much while I was gone."

I smiled. "You kind of did. I missed you. And yes, it's final. That chapter has closed."

"I missed you too," she said, squeezing my hand. "Six weeks visiting family in France sounds glamorous until you're dying for your own bed and someone who actually gets your jokes."

I laughed softly. "Well, while you were off sipping Lillet cocktails and posting sun-kissed photos from Paris, I was figuring out life as a sort-of single mom."

"And?" she asked gently.

"It's... working. Surprisingly well. Separate lives, but we're aligned when it comes to the kids. The summer was smooth, no big drama, no tension. The kids are happy. That's what matters."

Camille gave me a look that was equal parts encouragement and caution. "I'm glad. Truly. You deserve peace after everything."

I nodded, taking a slow sip of coffee. Peace. That's what I'd been craving. So why did it still feel like something was missing?

Jason and I had come a long way since spring. After everything came out—his kiss with Shannon, my affair with Will—it felt like the end. But as the weeks turned into months, we found a way to coexist.

Jason moved into a condo a few miles away, and we agreed on a schedule that worked best for the kids. The arrangement turned out better than I expected. He adjusted his travel to be more present, and I worked hard to make the kids feel stable, no matter whose house they were at.

The holidays would be the real test. But for now, we were okay. I didn't resent him anymore. The anger I'd held onto had dissolved, replaced by something quieter. Acceptance.

Still, seeing Will again had shaken something loose, something I wasn't ready to face. I'd told myself it was over. What we had was intoxicating but fleeting. Something that couldn't survive the weight of real life.

So why did it still feel unfinished?

Camille reached across the table, snapping me out of my thoughts. "Earth to Natalie. You, okay?"

"Yeah," I said quickly, forcing a smile. "I'm fine."

She gave me a look but didn't push. "Good. Now, let's talk about something that doesn't involve men."

"Great idea," I said.

We moved into lighter conversation, including dissecting the latest episode of "Selling Sunset" like Chrishell was our best friend.

It felt good to be back into a routine. Summer had a way of taking over. It was nice to return to the simple stuff. After saying goodbye, I carried on with my day—grocery run, folding laundry, sketching ideas for a new design project.

But that night, after the kids were asleep, I found myself scrolling aimlessly through my phone. I had deleted Will's contact, but at that moment, I regretted it.

I tossed the phone aside and sank back into the couch. This wasn't who I wanted to be—a woman clinging to what was already over, torturing herself with what-ifs.

But when I closed my eyes, there he was again.

Unbidden. Unwelcome.

Will.

Always Will.

Chapter 2

Ramble On
Will

I knew I was going to see Natalie. What I didn't know was how I'd feel when I did. Turns out, all the feelings came rushing back—the magnetic pull, the emotions I thought I'd buried over the summer. And honestly? I set myself up for this. I'd given my colleague, Lori, Natalie's information so they could discuss The City Center renovation. So even if our girls weren't in the same class at school, our paths were guaranteed to cross.

Sure enough, she was at the gate this morning, and she looked sexy. Her long, thick brown hair, cascading over her shoulders and down her back, her ass looking perfect in those jeans and that damn cute freckle on her nose. Well, I need to forget about her.

I just thought I was making progress. I thought dating Blake would help.

Blake Jones. She's tall, blonde, and bold—a real go-getter in the real estate world. We met at a brokers' tour, both pausing in front of a peculiar painting of a pear, laughing at how its shape resembled something vaguely anatomical. By the time we walked through the house together, she handed me her card with confidence, "I noticed you're not wearing a wedding ring. I'm Blake Jones with Blake Jones Property Group."

I was impressed. She was a knock-out.

"I'm Will Parker," I said.

"I know," she chided with a pop of her shoulder. "Call me."

And then she walked out of the room with the pear looking vagina painting, leaving me a little shaken up. It was good to feel something again, like I could get back in the game.

When I told my best friend Evan about her, he said. "Get back on the horse—or at least take it for a ride." Classic Evan.

Blake wasn't a one-night-stand kind of woman, though. When I finally called her a week later, she said, "I was starting to think you lost my card. Glad you found it." I asked her out, and that was that.

It started casually. I didn't think I'd be ready to date anyone after Natalie, but Blake made herself a part of my world before I even realized it. She was assertive, always making plans, and before I knew it, she was asking about meeting my kids.

That felt like a line I wasn't ready to cross, but Blake had a way of pushing without being pushy. "It's not like I'm asking to meet the President," she teased one night over dinner. "They're just kids. I promise I'll keep it easy."

Maybe that's why I finally agreed. Blake *was* easy. She wasn't complicated or emotionally draining, and maybe that's exactly what I needed.

My boys, Chase and Carter, didn't seem fazed about the introduction, typical middle schoolers, with other things on their minds. Carter mentioned later she was "hot," which made me laugh and cringe at the same time. Ivy was instantly fascinated by her diamond bracelets and asked endless questions about what was in her fancy handbag.

But Madison? She barely acknowledged Blake, then threw out questions that made me wince. "Are you even old enough to drink?" Madison asked, crossing her arms.

Blake gave a nervous laugh. "Age is irrelevant when you're over 25."

Madison tilted her head. "Are you 25?"

Blake smiled tightly. "I'm 29."

Madison rolled her eyes. "Hmm. You remind me of that girlfriend from "The Parent Trap"—the one with Lindsay Lohan who plays a twin, and the sisters switch places. You were probably like three years old when it came out."

I tried to intervene. "Madison, that's enough."

"Whatever, can I be excused?" she muttered. I let her go, sighing as I watched her stomp up the stairs.

I apologized to Blake. "I am sorry for that childish behavior."

Blake chuckled, "Will, you're a great dad, doing your best. Daddy's little girl is just going through a lot of teenage hormones."

Later, I went to Madison's room to talk.

"Madison, that was inappropriate. You can't speak to adults that way."

"She's hardly an adult," Madison shot back. "You could be her dad."

"Madison, I'm forty-three. I could not be her dad."

"Whatever. It's gross," she said, flopping onto her bed.

"Look, you don't have to like her, but you do have to be respectful."

She rolled her eyes again. "Sure, Dad. Whatever."

I walked out, shaking my head. I was in for it.

I remembered Natalie's words from months ago. "No matter who you date, Madison's going to hate her." Natalie wasn't wrong. Madison's reaction was proof of that. And maybe it was why I hesitated to bring anyone else fully into my life.

It was the Sunday before the first day of school, and we were finishing up the last of the school prep. Ivy was labeling her supplies while Chase and Carter argued over who was moaning loudest about school tomorrow. I put on a playlist to drown them out—mostly classic rock, the kind of music that always helped me focus.

"Dad, why do you always listen to old music?" Carter asked, wrinkling his nose as Led Zeppelin started playing.

"Because it's the best," I said, smirking. "When you're older, you'll thank me for giving you good taste."

"Whatever," he muttered, but I noticed he didn't leave the room, moving his fingers to the beat like a little drum. I smiled to myself.

Ivy started humming along, and I felt a rare moment of peace settle over the house. The kids were happy, the music was grounding, and for a few minutes, I let myself believe I was getting the hang of all this; divorced, single dad. I started singing right along with Robert Plant. "Leaves are falling all around."

The doorbell rang, breaking the calm. I wasn't expecting anyone. When I opened the door and saw Blake standing there with takeout bags and her perfect smile, I felt a mix of wonder and unease.

"Surprise!" she said, holding up the bags. "I thought maybe you could use a little help with dinner tonight, since you have a big day ahead of you tomorrow."

I forced a small laugh and invited her in.

She went into the kitchen and held up the In and Out bags. "Anyone hungry?" she asked.

"Me, me" said Ivy with a big grin. The boys mumbled something and said sure. All I could think was I was glad Madison wasn't here. She would have gone ape shit knowing Blake showed up unannounced. Madison had insisted on staying at Kelly's tonight. She preferred my ex's for nights like this. The first day of school, I guess, is a big deal to girls, especially teenage girls; they care so much about how they look. She wanted her mom's help. The plan was for Kelly to see Madison off in the morning and meet us at the gate. Kelly was a great mom; she would show up for anything important for the kids, even if the kids were with me.

During dinner, Ivy talked excitedly about the first day of school. "You should come with us, Blake!"

Blake laughed. "I'd love to."

I wasn't prepared for this. The idea of her at school, with both Kelly and Natalie there? It made my stomach turn.

But Blake was different. Or at least, she wanted to be.

After dinner, Blake seemed to get the hint it was time to leave. I told Ivy to get ready for bed, but from upstairs, she called down, "See you tomorrow, Blake! Don't be late!"

"I won't," Blake said with a laugh.

I wasn't laughing. I walked her to her car, trying to find the words to tell her this wasn't a good idea. But somehow, I couldn't say it.

"What time should I be here?" she asked.

"Uh, 7:30," I mumbled.

"Great, I'll be here at 7:15 to help," she said, kissing me on the lips before driving off.

Man, I was in trouble. Most women would run for the hills when faced with four kids, but Blake seemed to be diving in headfirst.

I considered texting Kelly a heads-up about Blake coming to drop off but decided against it. Better to ask for forgiveness later—or hope Blake miraculously came down with the stomach bug and skipped it altogether. Kelly wasn't much of a fan of Blake to begin with. After meeting her, she smirked at me with one of her trademark judgmental looks and said, "So, is this another rebound? Or just your next midlife crisis?"

That night, I sat on the edge of my bed, staring at my phone. My instinct was to text Natalie. To tell her I wasn't ready to see her this week. To tell her I thought about her all the time.

I couldn't say that. I shouldn't even be thinking it. I didn't even know if she was still married. The last time I saw Natalie was at the school mass on the last day of school, with her husband, Jason.

Natalie wasn't mine anymore. She never really was.

Chapter 3

Unfinished Business
Natalie

Walking into The City Center for my first project meeting felt like stepping onto a tightrope. Excitement and anxiety coursed through me in equal measure. This was everything I'd been working toward, a chance to showcase my designs and finally make my mark.

But as I parked my car and grabbed my portfolio, the lingering memory of last week at the school gate came rushing back. Will. And her.

I tried to shake it off. There was no room for distraction, not today. Lori would expect me to come prepared and polished, and I refused to let her—or myself—down.

The space was still a construction zone, dust swirling in the late morning sunlight. Workers buzzed around with clipboards and blueprints, and the faint sound of hammering echoed from the unfinished walls.

"Morning, Natalie!" Lori's sharp, energetic voice cut through the chaos. She strode toward me, a phone in one hand and a coffee cup in the other, effortlessly commanding attention.

"Morning," I replied, forcing a smile as I fell into step beside her.

"We'll be meeting with the leasing agent and a couple of restaurant owners today," she said, barely glancing up from her phone. "Oh, and the agent is bringing his team, so you'll want to have your initial design ideas ready to discuss."

Her words registered slowly, a sinking feeling settling in my stomach. Leasing agent. His team.

And then I heard his voice.

I turned, and there he was, standing near the entrance with a clipboard in hand, and laughing at something one of his colleagues said.

Will Parker.

He looked different—polished, confident, and entirely in his element. His blond hair was neatly combed, and he wore a tailored navy blazer that made him look every bit the successful professional.

For a moment, I froze. I guess I knew it was a possibility that he'd be involved in a project like this one, but I'd hoped to be saved from that torture.

"Natalie, are you coming?" Lori asked, already halfway across the room.

"Uh, yeah," I stammered, quickly falling into step behind her.

Will noticed me then. His eyes locked on mine, just for a second, and the air seemed to shift between us. But instead of the acknowledgment I'd expected—or feared—he turned back to his team, his expression unreadable.

Lori led me to the center of the space, gesturing between us.

"I'll leave you two to get started," she said casually, a knowing look flickering across her face. "You've worked together before, so I'm sure you'll pick this up quickly."

Will stepped forward, his expression neutral, though I caught the faintest flicker of something in his eyes.

"Natalie," he said, extending his hand. His tone was polite, professional. Too professional.

I took his hand, maintaining the same careful distance. "Will."

His handshake lingered for a second longer than it should have, and I couldn't help but notice the way his jaw tightened.

"It's good to see you again," he said evenly.

"Likewise," I replied, pretending I didn't already know the exact way his hand felt on my body or how his lips tasted.

The meeting went as smoothly as I could have hoped, though I could feel Will's presence like a gravitational pull, no matter how hard I tried to ignore it. He asked questions about the design plan, nodding thoughtfully at my responses.

When the meeting wrapped, Lori turned to me. "Natalie, can you email me the finishes we're considering for the restaurant?"

"You got it," I said, jotting a quick note in my notebook.

As the rest of the group dispersed, Lori included, Will lingered.

"Looks like we'll be working together," he said finally, his voice low enough that only I could hear.

"It seems that way," I replied, keeping my tone neutral, though my heart was pounding.

He hesitated, his gaze searching mine. "You okay with that?"

I lifted my chin slightly, refusing to let him see how much his question rattled me. "It's work, Will. I'm here to do a job."

He nodded, his expression unreadable. "Good. Me too."

That evening, I sat in my new office, trying to focus on sketches for the restaurants. But no matter how hard I tried, my mind kept drifting back to the meeting.

Seeing him again had been harder than I expected. And knowing we'd be working together—regularly, closely—felt like walking into a storm I wasn't sure I'd survive.

But this project was my chance to prove myself, to finally step into the career I'd always dreamed of. I couldn't afford to let anything, not even Will, derail me.

At least, that's what I told myself.

Chapter 4

Accent Pieces

Natalie

Seeing Will had thrown me into a little tailspin. I'd just started to feel like I was leaving him behind, stepping out of the emotional fog and back into my life. Nobody really knew what had happened between us except Camille and Meredith, my younger sister. I'd filled them in on all the messy details—how I'd ended things, how I couldn't give Will what he wanted, how I felt trapped between two lives.

And now, two run-ins with him in one week.

I couldn't believe how quickly he'd moved on. Not that he didn't have every right to. The last time we were together, I was still married. I was the one who ended things for good. Still, seeing him with someone else was a gut punch I hadn't prepared for. It wasn't jealousy exactly; it was more complicated than that.

I wondered how Kelly felt about the new woman in his life. Will and Kelly had a history, a shared life with their kids. *Did Kelly know about her?*

And this woman, she must mean something if Will was bringing her to school. His kids must know her well. That thought was harder to digest than I expected.

But I didn't want to be bitter. Will deserved to be happy. I'd made my choice, and I couldn't have it both ways. It was time to get my life back on track.

It was a fresh day, and I needed to focus on the new restaurant. In the morning, I headed to Moda, the tile store. I'd already visited the day before to pick out some initial samples and finalize the design. I wanted to be prepared. Lucas Bennett, the restaurant's investor, was meeting me there.

When I arrived, Lucas wasn't there yet. Perfect. That gave me a little time to wander the showroom and see if inspiration struck. The restaurant's kitchen would be exposed to customers, so it needed to make a statement. I'd been toying with the idea of whitewashed subway tile paired with brass accents, but I wanted to see if there were any other options that caught my eye.

I was pulling samples, laying them out, and mixing and matching when I heard a voice behind me.

"Are you Natalie?"

I turned, startled, and saw a man standing there. He had a British accent and happened to be gorgeous—green eyes and features so perfectly balanced they seemed almost unfair. His hair was hazelnut-brown and thick, parted slightly to the side, with one longer strand brushing his forehead.

"I... uh, yes, I'm Natalie," I stammered, suddenly feeling like a teenager meeting a movie star.

"Lucas Bennett," he said, extending a hand. "I believe you're the mastermind behind today's ideas?"

I smiled, trying to pull myself together. "I was just pulling some samples and putting a few concepts together. Let me show you."

As I laid out my initial vision, Lucas's eyes lit up.

"Brilliant," he said. "I love this."

"I have a few more ideas I can show you too," I offered, feeling a flush of pride.

"No need," he said, gesturing to the samples. "I think you've nailed it. And the green woodwork idea you mentioned? Absolutely inspired. Paired with the tiles and brass, it's exactly the look we're after. Lori said you were talented, but I didn't realize you'd be this good."

"Well, thank you," I said, feeling a little flustered by the compliment. "I've already triple-checked the measurements and gone over everything with the contractor. Once we finalize the selections, I'll work on putting the order together. Most of this is in stock, so it should arrive in three to four weeks."

"Perfect," Lucas said, his gaze steady. "May I ask you another question?"

"Of course," I said, smiling.

"Where's a decent place to grab an espresso and a bite to eat around here? I'm still getting my bearings in Orange County."

Before I could answer, Kathy, the store rep, chimed in. "There's a lovely little café near the pier. Great coffee and pastries."

"Thank you," Lucas said, turning back to me. "Care to join me?"

I hesitated. It wasn't like I was doing anything wrong. I wasn't having an affair. I was free to have coffee with anyone I wanted. And Lucas seemed... harmless. This could just be a friendly, professional outing.

"Sure," I said, trying to sound casual. "Let me just finish up with Kathy, and I'll meet you outside."

Kathy smiled warmly. "I'll take it from here, dear. Go Enjoy yourself."

"Are you sure?" I asked in a low voice.

"Absolutely," she said, waving me off. "Now go!"

Outside, Lucas was standing near his car, looking completely at ease.

"Ready?" he asked, straightening up when he saw me.

"Ready," I said, adjusting my bag on my shoulder.

The café Kathy had mentioned was close by. As we walked, we chatted about the restaurant project, our shared love for design, and his transition to life in Orange County.

"I wasn't certain I'd like it here," he admitted, glancing at the ocean in the distance. "But there's something about the pace of life that's beginning to grow on me."

"It's a good balance," I said. "Not too fast, not too slow. Plus, the weather doesn't hurt."

He laughed. "No, it doesn't. And the people are... surprising."

"Surprising how?"

"Let's just say I wasn't expecting to meet someone as lovely as you." His accent highlighting the word lovely in a way that immediately made my cheeks warm.

I quickly changed the subject, asking more about his vision for the restaurant. By the time we reached the café, the conversation was flowing easily, and I felt more relaxed than I had in weeks.

Over coffee, Lucas shared more about his background, his years in London, his decision to move to California, and his dream of opening a restaurant that felt like a home away from home.

"I want it to feel warm and inviting," he said, stirring his espresso. "Somewhere people linger. Not pretentious, but still beautiful."

"That's exactly what we're building," I assured him.

"I knew I was in good hands when Lori told me about you," he said, his green eyes locking with mine for a moment too long.

I broke the gaze, focusing on my coffee. "So, have you met anyone else in the area yet? Friends, neighbors?"

"Not really," he admitted. "Other than Jasper, of course. He's my best mate and a chef. It's been our dream for years to open a restaurant together. Between his culinary talent and my business background, we've always wanted to create something truly unique."

"That's good," I said. "At least you've got someone close by, to share your vision with.

"True," he said with a small smile. "Though he's so busy experimenting with recipes, I barely see him. But having him around has made the move a bit easier."

He told me he grew up in Sussex, attended Oxford University, and had one younger sister, Maura, who worked as a writer in London. His life sounded polished, fascinating—like something out of a novel.

He mentioned he'd been married once but had no children. The marriage lasted only a year. When I asked what happened, he gave me a wry smile. "She ran off with one of my closest mates. Can't say I saw that coming."

The way he said it carried the faintest edge, a shadow of bitterness beneath the humor. I debated sharing more about my own situation but decided to keep it vague. "I'm recently divorced," I said, conveniently leaving out the messy details.

Lucas mentioned his recent move to Laguna Beach. "I bought a small ranch-style house. It's cozy, but it has potential," he said.

"I love Laguna," I said. "One of my favorite restaurants there is Broadway. Have you been?"

"I haven't," he said, shaking his head.

"Well, we'll have to go," I said before I could stop myself. *What was I doing?*

I glanced at my watch, realizing I needed to wrap things up. My day wasn't slowing down anytime soon. "I'm so sorry, but I must run. You have my card with all my info—feel free to call if you have any questions. I'll also send over some wallpaper and light fixture options by tomorrow morning."

Lucas stood, smiling warmly. "Of course. Thank you, Natalie."

Then, to my surprise, he leaned in and kissed me on both cheeks.

"It was so nice to meet you," I said, gathering my things.

"The pleasure was all mine," he replied, his charming accent was a melody to my ears.

Chapter 5

Renos and Realizations

Natalie

After leaving the café, I felt a renewed sense of purpose. My next stop was Lauren's house, where I was overseeing a renovation project.

When I arrived, the transformation was incredible. The new oak floors gleamed in the sunlight streaming through the windows. The fresh coat of crisp white paint gave the whole house a modern, airy feel, and the sleek black Anderson windows tied everything together.

"Hi!" Lauren said, rounding the corner to greet me. "Look at this place! It's amazing."

"It's sensational," I said, grinning at her.

It really was coming together beautifully. The old brown wood trim and travertine floors were gone, replaced by a clean, timeless aesthetic. Even the clunky old ceiling fan in the living room had been swapped for a stunning chandelier that served as a true statement piece. Lauren had impeccable taste, especially when it came to details, and I loved helping her bring her vision to life.

We toured the house, checking on the progress of the bathrooms and the kitchen. Everything was on schedule, and the quality of the work impressed me.

"Can you believe this is the same house?" Lauren asked, marveling at the changes.

"It's gorgeous," I said. "Charlie's room is my favorite, though. She's going to flip when she sees her little gymnastics setup."

Charlie, Lauren's daughter, was a budding gymnast, and we'd carved out a space for her in the loft with tumbling mats and a balance beam. It was a small touch, but I knew it would make her so happy.

After double-checking the contractor's work and reviewing the timeline, Lauren and I stepped outside to chat.

"We're still good for Friday?" she asked.

"Absolutely," I said. "Plan on coming over after school. The kids can swim, and I'll let Camille know to bring her boys too."

"Perfect. See you at the gate," Lauren said with a smile.

Back at home, I quickly tackled some last-minute work and gathered everything I needed for the afternoon—Bebe's dance bag, snacks for the kids, and my never-ending to-do list. As I headed out the door to pick them up, I realized something: I hadn't thought about running into Will all day.

Maybe it was the buzz of my conversation with Lucas, or the satisfaction of seeing Lauren's house come together, but for the first time since seeing him a week ago, my thoughts weren't consumed by my ex-lover or the mistakes I'd made.

Lucas, with his irresistible accent and easy smile, had reminded me of something I hadn't felt in a long time, excitement.

I didn't know where this was all headed—if anywhere—but for now, it felt good to look forward to the possibility of something new and uncomplicated.

Chapter 6

The Single Reveal
Natalie

After a busy week of shuttling the kids to ballet, baseball practice, and helping with homework assignments, Friday arrived as a relief. It was my weekend with the kids, and I couldn't have been more grateful for some down time at home. Jason and I had managed to find a good rhythm with our co-parenting schedule. We were both flexible when it came to each other's work commitments, and our sitter, Emily, was a godsend. She'd been with us long enough that the kids adored her, and her new role as a student teacher meant her afternoons were free when we needed her.

Somehow, we were thriving in this new way of life.

The upcoming holidays, however, had me nervous. This would be our first time navigating them separately. Jason and I had agreed he would have the kids for Thanksgiving and New Year's, while I'd have them for Halloween and Christmas. It sounded manageable on paper, but the thought of not spending Thanksgiving with the kids made my heart ache. It also pained me that he wouldn't be with them on Christmas morning.

I extended an olive branch, inviting him to come over for both Halloween and Christmas. He seemed genuinely grateful, and to my surprise, he invited me to his Thanksgiving celebration. His parents would be visiting, and the gesture was kind, but I declined. Meredith was flying out to spend Thanksgiving with me, and I was looking forward to catching up with her.

When I arrived at school on Friday afternoon, I offered to pick up Charlie along with Bebe and James.

I spotted Camille standing near the gate and walked over to her.

"Incoming," she whispered, nodding toward the parking lot.

And there he was—Will. Of course, he looked amazing, dressed in a tailored suit that fit him perfectly. It was infuriating how attractive he always appeared. Why couldn't he have a bad day, just once?

He looked right at me. I wanted to look away, but I couldn't. For a moment, it felt like we were having a silent conversation, trying to say all the things we couldn't. The connection lingered until the bell rang, jolting us both back to reality.

The kids came pouring out of the building. Camille's twins and James ran out first, full of energy, followed by Charlie, Bebe, and Ivy. Ivy, however, was in tears.

Will immediately noticed and headed straight for her, crouching down to ask what was wrong.

"I want to go play at Bebe's house," Ivy sobbed. "She's having Charlie over."

I hated seeing her upset, and I felt terrible she felt left out. I leaned down to Bebe.

"Did something happen?" I asked gently.

"She just really wants to play with us," Bebe said, looking worried.

"Okay," I said. "Let's invite her over to swim."

"Really?" Bebe's face lit up with excitement.

"Of course," I said, already planning the logistics.

Camille overheard and stepped in to help. "I have a third booster seat in my trunk. We'll put James in it and make room for Ivy in your car," she said.

"Thank you," I told her, relieved.

With the plan settled, I walked over to Will, who was still comforting Ivy.

"Hi," I said, giving him a small smile. "We'd love to have Ivy over."

"Can I, Dad? Please?" Ivy pleaded, her tear-streaked face brightening with hope.

At this point, all the girls were chiming in, begging Will with puppy-dog eyes.

"Well, how can I say no to these faces?" he said with a laugh, his gaze softening as he looked at me. "I'll pick her up around 6:30."

I nodded and gave Will a small smile.

The girls squealed with excitement, and Will kissed Ivy on the cheek before leaving with his boys.

Back at my house, the kids changed into their swimsuits. Camille arrived with her boys just a little after we got home. I told the kids to help themselves to snacks from the pantry before heading outside. Once the kids were out of earshot, Camille turned to me.

"So, how did that go?" she asked, her eyes sparkling with curiosity.

I shook my head, laughing. "I can't let my past affair get in the way of their friendship."

Just then, Lauren walked in, catching the tail end of the conversation. "Did I hear the word 'affair?'" she asked, raising an eyebrow.

We all laughed. Camille, ever the instigator, was giddy. "Let's get her up to speed."

"Camille!" I protested, but it was too late.

Lauren had become one of my closest friends in the short time she lived here, and I trusted her not to judge me. Still, confessing my affair felt like a big step.

By the time Camille was done filling her in, Lauren looked more stunned than judgmental.

"Wait," she said, holding up her hand. "You're telling me that the hottest dad at St. Isidore's is single, you've already had an affair with him, and you're not with him now? Why not?"

"It's complicated," I said. "It wasn't the right time. I was married while we were together. He also has a daughter in high school who hates me, and if I stayed with him, it would've made things worse."

Lauren leaned back, crossing her arms. "He's picking Ivy up here later?"

I nodded.

Camille and Lauren exchanged amused looks. "This is going to be fun," Camille said, grinning.

The kids swam while the three of us sat on the patio, catching up on shows, swapping easy recipes, and laughing. It amazed me how in just a year and a half of living here, these women felt like family.

The kids inhaled the pizza I ordered for their post-swim dinner. When the last crust was discarded, Camille started gathering her boys to leave. Lauren followed suit.

"Do you guys really have to go?" I asked, suspicious of their quick exits.

"Yes, love," Camille said, laughing. "Call me tomorrow. Farmer's market. Drop the kids off at my house; I'll have our nanny there."

Lauren smirked. "Have fun," she said, following Camille out the door.

I rolled my eyes. I knew exactly what they were up to.

Right on cue the doorbell rang at 6:30, my heart was racing. I opened the door to find Will standing there, looking like trouble dressed up in perfection.

"Hi," he said, his voice upbeat. "Is Ivy ready?"

"Oh, sorry," I said quickly. "The kids started a movie about twenty minutes ago. I'll go get her. Come in."

He stepped inside, looking around as his eyes caught on the office to his left. "Did you redecorate?" he asked, slowing as he glanced into it before we continued toward the living room.

"Well, Jason moved out and then we divorced, so... ," I said, feeling the weight of the words. "I turned this into my office."

His expression shifted, his jaw dropping slightly. "I had no idea," he said, his voice filled with sincerity. "I'm so sorry. I feel responsible."

"No," I said quietly. "We had problems long before you and I."

For a moment, neither of us said anything. The silence was heavy but charged, the air between us thick with unspoken words.

"I'll go get Ivy," I said finally, breaking the moment.

Upstairs, I found the kids cuddled under blankets in the playroom. "Hi, guys," I said. "Ivy, your dad's here."

"Aww, bummer," Ivy said, pouting. "I want to sleep over!"

I laughed. "Maybe next time, okay?"

Bebe got up to walk Ivy downstairs, and the two of them immediately launched into plans for their future sleepover.

"Is that so?" Will said, grinning at them before looking at me.

The corners of my mouth lifted, a warmth stirring inside me.

While the girls said their goodbyes, I glanced back at Will, into the deep pool of his baby blues, instantly feeling like he could see straight through my soul. I looked away before he could read every thought I was trying to hide.

After they left, I got the kids ready for bed and tucked them in. When I went to my room, my heart still unsettled from the way Will's presence lingered in me. I reached for my phone and had texts from Camille and Lauren on our group thread.

Lauren: Did you get a goodnight kiss?

Camille: Tell us everything. Don't leave out any details.

I rolled my eyes, laughing.

Natalie: You guys are too much.

I set my phone down, another text came through.

Unknown Caller: I had no idea you got divorced.

It was an unknown number. But I knew who it was. *Will.* I had deleted his contact info back in the spring when our affair ended.

I stared at the screen, my heart racing again. If I replied, was I opening a door I'd already closed?

Chapter 7

The Next Best Thing

Will

After I picked up Ivy from Natalie's and found out she was divorced from Jason, my head was swarming with questions. *When did this happen? Am I the homewrecker Madison called me? Is Natalie okay? Is there a chance for us now? Shit... what about Blake?*

The moment I saw Natalie, I wanted to kiss her. My body still hadn't caught up with my brain when it came to her. I needed answers, and I needed them soon. So, I did what I'd been holding back from doing all night—I sent her a text.

Will: I had no idea you got divorced.

The wait for her response felt agonizing. Every time my phone buzzed, I hoped it was her. Finally, her name popped up.

Natalie: Don't you have a girlfriend?

Damn. She wasn't letting me off the hook easily.

Will: Not the point.

But it was the point, wasn't it? I couldn't stop thinking about why she hadn't reached out to me. She must have been going through so much, and I could have been there for her. I'd been through a divorce; I knew how isolating it could feel. But deep down, I knew that wasn't the kind of support I wanted to give her. I wanted more than to be a shoulder to cry on.

I couldn't help but wonder if she didn't tell me because she didn't want to lead me on. Maybe she thought I still wasn't what she wanted—a man with four kids and a teenage daughter who would probably hate anyone I dated. Natalie had been clear before; she didn't want the stepmom role.

But knowing she was single now made me restless. I wanted to run back to her house, knock on her door, and tell her everything I'd been holding back.

Then she texted me again.

Natalie: Can we meet Monday morning? My house this time? I'll get the bagels.

She added a wink emoji.

Bagels and mornings with us. The thought of it made my chest tighten. We never even ate the bagels. I started typing a cheeky response but got distracted by a text from Blake.

It was a picture of her out with friends. She looked stunning, as always, polished, and flawless. Under the photo, she'd written, *Miss you.*

For most guys, Blake would have been a dream come true. But with Natalie on my mind, Blake was... second. No freckles on her nose, no spark that made my skin buzz.

I snapped out of it and responded to Natalie.

Will: Okay, we can talk Monday. And we'll really eat the bagels this time.

Her reply came quickly.

Natalie: If you say so, William.

Was she mocking me? Flirting? Either way, I couldn't stop grinning at my phone.

The weekend flew by in a whirlwind of soccer tournaments. Chase and Carter had back-to-back games on Saturday, and Madison babysat Ivy while I went to watch. Sunday rolled around, and Kelly took Madison horseback riding for some quality time, leaving me with Ivy to bring to the tournament. It would make a long day with an eight-year-old girl.

Blake texted that morning, asking if she could take Ivy for a pedicure and some shopping. I hesitated, unsure how Kelly would feel about it, but after running it by her, she reluctantly agreed. "At least she seems more reliable than a babysitter," Kelly said, her tone dripping with judgment.

I had to admit, Blake was trying. If I was serious about her—and that was a big "if"—she would have to mold into the role of a stepmother. That wasn't negotiable. But even as I watched Ivy happily climb into Blake's pristine Mercedes SUV, my mind drifted to Natalie.

Why weren't we together? I knew the answer. Natalie had been honest about why it couldn't work, she didn't want to take on my baggage. Still, knowing she was single now reopened all the questions I thought I'd put to rest.

Sunday afternoon passed in a blur of games. Carter's team made it to the championship, and between matches, I texted Blake to check in.

Will: Carter's team won! Moving on to the finals. Kelly can pick up Ivy if needed.

Blake: We're good! She's having a blast. Look!

She attached a photo of Ivy grinning ear to ear, her tiny feet soaking in a pedicure tub, surrounded by shopping bags. Blake looked flawless in the photo, too, her smile confident and radiant.

On paper, Blake was everything a guy in my position could want—a twenty-nine-year-old stunner making an effort with my kids. But she wasn't Natalie.

I made a quick decision, knowing Blake needed to get Ivy home, and gave her my garage code, telling myself I could always change it later.

Will: Thanks for taking her. Here is my garage code. 0707. See you at home.

Blake: Sounds great. Can't wait to see you.

I started to feel a twinge of regret for letting her take Ivy all day. It was leading things in a direction I wasn't sure I was ready for, but for now, I had to just roll with it.

After the championship game and a pizza celebration with Carter's team, we headed home. Ivy was already there, showered and in her pajamas, practically glowing from her day out with Blake.

"Daddy!" she shouted, running into my arms. "Look at my nails!"

Her nails sparkled with pink glitter, and she couldn't wait to show off her new clothes. "Blake says I look like a princess!"

"You are a princess," I said, kissing her forehead. "You had a good day, huh?"

"The best!" she beamed.

After tucking Ivy into bed and checking on the boys, I went downstairs. Blake was still there, tidying up the kitchen.

"Wine?" she asked, looking hopeful.

I hesitated for a moment but decided it was the least I could do after her effort with Ivy. "Red or white?" I asked.

Her face lit up. "Red."

I grabbed a bottle and started opening it, but my phone buzzed on the counter. A quick glance told me it was from Natalie.

Natalie: Still on for tomorrow?

I wanted to reply, *God, yes.*

Will: Yes, still works for me.

Natalie: Should I really get bagels?

I paused. The question was loaded with memories. Every time we'd had bagels before, they ended up forgotten while we tangled ourselves in each other. My mind raced with what tomorrow might bring.

Blake's voice broke my train of thought. "Everything okay?"

Will: Nah, I'll bring coffee.

Then I turned my attention back to the wine.

"Sorry about that," I said, pulling out the cork. "I was looking for a special bottle from Spain but couldn't find it. This one's a close second."

"Sounds perfect," she said, settling onto the couch and motioning for me to join her.

I poured the wine and sat next to her, trying to focus on the moment. She leaned in and shifted closer to me on the couch, her glass of wine perched delicately in one hand as the other rested lightly on my chest. "You know," she said softly, "I could help you in the mornings with the kids if you ever need it. Make things easier."

Her fingers began tracing lazy circles over my shirt, her touch warm but not quite enough to distract me from the thoughts of Natalie swirling in my head.

"Thanks," I said, managing a small smile. "I've been managing fine for now."

Her hand lingered on my chest, then began to drift lower. "I'd love to help more," she murmured, her voice taking on a suggestive edge. Before I could respond, her fingers found the zipper of my pants and tugged it down in one smooth motion.

I froze, glancing toward the staircase instinctively.

"Relax," Blake whispered, her lips brushing against my ear. She pulled a throw blanket over our laps, her devilish smile daring me to object. "The kids are asleep."

"Ivy is, maybe," I said cautiously, my heart thumping unevenly. "But the boys—"

She cut me off with a quiet laugh. "That's why we have the blanket," she teased, slipping her hand beneath it.

Her hand wrapped around me, her touch slow and deliberate. I closed my eyes, trying to focus on the sensation, but my mind kept wandering. Her touch was skilled, her rhythm steady, but it didn't spark the reaction I knew she was hoping for.

Blake leaned closer, her lips grazing my neck as her hand moved faster. "Just relax," she murmured again, her breath warm against my skin.

I tried, but my body wasn't cooperating. My mind kept circling back to Natalie, the way her touch used to make every nerve in my body come alive. This wasn't the same.

Blake paused, sensing my hesitation. "Am I distracting you too much?" she teased, her tone light but with a hint of concern.

"No," I said quickly, shaking my head. "You're great."

I kissed her softly, wanting to end things on a positive note. "I should get to bed soon," I said, my tone apologetic. "It's been a long day."

Blake gave me a playful pout but didn't push further. "Okay," she said, releasing her hand off me, she sat up and smoothed her hair.

I zipped up feeling a little sheepish about the situation but could easily blame this on the fact that my kids were upstairs. This was not the time.

I escorted her to the door and followed to her car. Before leaving, she grabbed my face and kissed me deeply.

"I'm really falling for you, William," she said softly.

I didn't say it back. Instead, I kissed her again and promised to text her tomorrow.

That night, I lay awake, staring at the ceiling. My thoughts weren't on Blake, or the day I'd just had. They were on Natalie. Her sweet smile, the way she used to look at me, the moments we abandoned breakfast for sex.

I wanted that back.

Tomorrow couldn't come fast enough.

Chapter 8

Rinse, Repeat, Regret
Natalie

It was Monday morning, and Will was coming over to talk. I wasn't sure what more there was to say about my divorce, but a little chat wouldn't hurt. At least, that's what I told myself.

The truth was, I felt nervous. Not because I didn't want to talk, but because I couldn't stop thinking about Will. I wanted him in my bed, plain and simple. It had been months since I'd been with anyone, and my body ached with the kind of longing that was impossible to ignore. But this wasn't just physical—I craved Will. Anytime I saw him, my body went into autopilot, unable to resist the pull.

But he had a girlfriend. A serious one, apparently, if he'd brought her to school. I needed to get him out of my head.

As if on cue, I got an email from Lucas.

Subject: Project Details

Hey! Would you meet me at the restaurant later this week so I can introduce you to Jasper, the chef? We can go over more details for the project at the site.

And perhaps after, you would let me take you to dinner Friday night at Broadway? 7 PM?

Lucas

A date with the charming Brit. Maybe that's exactly what I needed to break this spell.

The clock snapped me back to reality. I was running behind and had to get the kids to school and get back in time for my meeting with Will.

He arrived right on time at 8:30. The doorbell rang, and I rushed to answer it, my pulse already racing. When I opened the door, there he was, standing on my porch with that perfect thick blond hair and those annoyingly piercing blue eyes. He held up two coffee cups.

"One vanilla latte," he said, handing me one with a perfect smile.

"Thanks," I said, smiling back. "Come in."

I led him to the kitchen, where he leaned casually against the counter. His presence filled the room, and I couldn't stop stealing glances at him.

"So, how was your weekend?" I asked, trying to keep things light.

"Great," he replied. "Carter and Chase had a soccer tournament."

"How'd they do?"

"Carter's team took the championship," he said with a proud grin. "Chase's team made it to the semifinals but fell short. How was your weekend?" He asked.

"Farmer's market, baseball, dance, the usual," I said, shrugging.

He was watching me closely, his gaze lingering. The tension between us was impossible to ignore. I could feel it simmering just below the surface, like a spark waiting for oxygen.

"So," I blurted, desperate to break the silence. "How's your girlfriend?"

Why did I ask that?

He looked momentarily confused. "She's fine," he said slowly. Then, he tilted his head. "But aren't we supposed to be talking about you?"

I felt my cheeks flush. "I guess that's why we're here," I said softly.

"I wish you'd told me," He said, his voice low. "I would have been there for you."

"I know," I said, my throat tightening. "But I needed to handle it on my own for a bit."

He stepped closer, his gaze never leaving mine. He reached out and gently touched the tip of my nose with his finger, a playful gesture that sent shivers down my spine.

I parted my lips slightly, silently begging him to kiss me. His finger traced the bridge of my nose, then my lips. I couldn't resist; I nipped at his finger lightly, eliciting a small smile from him.

His finger continued its path, moving down my chin to the top of my cardigan. Slowly, deliberately, he unbuttoned it, one button at a time, until it hung open, revealing the black lace bra I'd worn beneath it.

His fingers brushed down my stomach, tracing delicate lines that made my body quiver. His hand paused just above my waist. I should care about the mess this could make. But, all I could think was don't stop. Please don't stop.

"I shouldn't do this," he murmured, though his actions betrayed his words.

Then his hand slipped beneath my waistband, his fingers teasing me, tracing along my edges. My breath hitched as he moved lower, finally sliding one finger inside me.

I gasped, my hands instinctively reaching for him. I unzipped his pants, freeing him, and he was already hard and ready for me. Without hesitation, his hands moved to remove my leggings and panties. He lifted me onto the counter, his lips crashing into mine as I wrapped my legs around him.

In one swift motion, I guided him inside me, a sharp gasp escaping my lips as our bodies connected. The world around us blurred, every thought dissolving until only the feel of him remained. We moved together with an urgency that bordered on frantic, the rhythm between us instinctive and unrelenting.

His hands gripped my hips, fingers digging into my skin as he drove deeper, the intensity of it sending heat rippling through me. His mouth found my neck, his teeth grazing the sensitive skin before he trailed hot, open-mouthed kisses down to my collarbone. I arched beneath him, my nails raking down his back, desperate to pull him even closer.

"God, you feel incredible," he rasped, his voice thick and ragged. The praise sent a rush of pleasure through me, a heady, dizzying thrill that made my pulse race.

My legs wrapped around him, pulling him even deeper, every thrust igniting something dark and consuming within me. His movements grew rougher, our bodies colliding with a force that left me trembling, the friction between us exquisite and unbearable.

He shifted, angling his hips just right, and I shattered. My body tightened around him, pleasure tearing through me with a ferocity that left me gasping, clutching at him as if he were the only thing keeping me tethered to the earth.

But he didn't stop. He drove into me harder, his own control unraveling as he chased his release. I could feel the tension building in him, the way his breathing grew ragged, his muscles flexing beneath my touch.

I dug my nails into his shoulders, the pain mingling with pleasure as his pace grew more desperate. His name spilled from my lips, a broken plea that only seemed to drive him wilder. His mouth found mine, our kiss messy and scorching, our breaths mingling as we pushed each other past the edge of reason.

When he finally came, his release was raw and shuddering, his body pressed tightly against mine as if he could somehow fuse us together. We clung to each other, the aftermath leaving us tangled and breathless, our hearts pounding in sync.

He pulled me close, his forehead resting against mine.

"I miss you like crazy," he whispered.

"Me too," I admitted, my voice barely audible.

We stayed like that for a moment, holding each other, neither of us wanting to break the spell. Eventually, we pulled ourselves together, slowly getting dressed.

"I don't have to be at The City Center till around 12:30," I said.

"Same here," he replied.

"Want to take a shower?" I asked, a playful smile tugging at my lips.

"With you?" he said, raising an eyebrow.

"Yes," I said, laughing.

We made our way upstairs to my oversized bathroom. I started the shower, and steam began to fill the room as the water warmed. When we stepped into the stall, the heat of the water felt like a second skin. Will pulled me under the spray, his hands finding my waist as droplets cascaded over us.

His mouth found mine, the kiss deep and unrelenting. My fingers found their way into his wet hair, tugging gently as the water ran down our faces. His lips roaming from my neck to the hollow of my throat, lingering there as if he couldn't get enough. "You're so beautiful," he murmured against my skin.

I leaned back against the tile, gasping as his hands slid down my body. The slickness of the water only heightened every sensation, making me more sensitive to his touch. He knelt in front of me, his hands gripping my thighs as his mouth moved between them. The steam curled around us as I arched into him, my hands braced against the wall for support.

When he rose again, his eyes locked on mine, and he lifted me effortlessly, pressing me against the cool tiles. I wrapped my legs around him as he entered me, the contrast of the cold tile and the heat of his body almost too much to bear.

We moved together, the rhythm slow at first, then faster as the tension built. The water washed away every thought except the way he felt inside me, the way he held me like I was the only thing that mattered.

We both reached the edge, our breaths mingling in the humid air. When we finally let go, it was like the world stopped spinning, leaving only the sound of water hitting the tile and our ragged breathing.

We stayed under the spray for a moment longer, laughing softly as he helped rinse the shampoo out of my hair. It was easy, intimate, and felt like a glimpse of what could be—if only.

As we stepped out of the shower, we began to dry off, reality creeping back in.

"I just made you cheat—twice," I said, the guilt creeping into my voice.

Will turned to me, his expression serious. "Natalie, I want you. But I need you to be on board with everything I come with. I want someone who's ready for all of it, for me, my kids, everything."

The words hit me like a punch to the gut. "What about your girlfriend?" I asked quietly.

"Blake," he said, finally saying her name. "She seems willing to do it all. She wants the role."

Hearing her name made my stomach flip. It felt too real now, too raw.

"Will, I've told you before, I can't be a stepmom. I can't take that on."

He ran a hand through his hair, frustration etched across his face. "Then what the fuck, Natalie? You bring me here, seduce me, but you don't want anything more?"

Tears filled my eyes. "I don't know why I let this happen," I said, my voice cracking. "My body and soul want you, but I don't know how to make it work."

He stepped closer, his hand cupping my cheek as he wiped away a tear. "I still love you, Natalie," he said softly. "I want all of you. But if you can't deal with my children and trying to make it work, I have someone who does."

His words were a dagger to my heart. "I don't know what to say, Will."

"Call me when you figure it out," he said, his voice heavy with disappointment. And then he walked out the door, leaving me standing there, shattered.

Chapter 9

Fiction or Fate
Will

I couldn't believe it. Natalie came into my life again so fast and was gone just as quickly.

Why did I let this happen? I should have known she wasn't going to change her mind and suddenly be ready to move in, marry me, and take on the role I so desperately wanted her to have: my wife and stepmom to my kids.

I was willing to take on her children, no hesitation. I know four kids is a lot to ask, and maybe I was a fool to think she could adjust. But she's naturally great with kids. I see the way Bebe and James light up around her, the way Ivy can't stop talking about "Miss Natalie." Madison? Yeah, she's a wild card, but I know Natalie could win her over. She's too likable, too warm not to.

Still, here I am, sitting with the weight of what just happened between us. The way she felt today—her body, her warmth—it was everything I'd been craving. Being inside her felt like home, like coming back to a part of myself I'd lost.

And now I've gone and cheated on Blake. The woman who claims she wants it all—me, the kids, the messy chaos of my life. She doesn't just say it; she shows it. But none of that seems to matter when I'm with Natalie.

Every moment with Natalie makes me feel alive. Her touch wakes me up in a way no one else can. How can I make her see that?

By the time I arrived at The City Center just after noon, I was still trying not to replay the morning in my head. Lori had called earlier, asking me to meet her in one of the vacant spots. She wanted to go over leasing plans before we brought in potential tenants.

I found her inspecting one of the storefronts, already imagining its future potential. "This space could be perfect for a boutique," she said, her tone decisive. "I want Natalie to start designing concepts for it. She'll know what to do."

A few minutes later, Natalie walked in. She gave us a polite, professional hello, as if we hadn't spent the morning devouring each other.

Lori studied her for a moment. "You look lovely," she said. "Did you just get a facial?"

Natalie nervously patted her face. "Oh, thanks! No, it must be my new face cream."

Or maybe it's the multiple orgasms I just gave you.

Natalie's eyes flicked to mine, a slight flush creeping up her neck. Did she know I was thinking it?

Lori led us through the space, outlining her vision. "Will, you've got a few prospects lined up, right?"

"Yes," I said. "One of them is meeting us this afternoon."

"Perfect," Lori said. "Natalie, stick around to pitch your design ideas to the tenants. We need to wow them and make it impossible for them to say no."

"Of course," Natalie said, her voice steady despite the tension humming between us.

Lori gave us both a look that could only be described as don't screw this up, then waved goodbye.

The silence that followed felt heavy. Natalie shifted uncomfortably.

"The tenants will be here around 1:30," I said finally. "Do you have someone to pick up your kids if the meeting runs long?"

Her eyes widened. "Shoot. Thanks for reminding me. Let me make a few calls."

She stepped away, phone in hand. I could hear her apologizing to someone— probably their sitter—who couldn't help on such short notice. Then she called who I assumed was Camille, I could hear her saying into the phone, "you can't bring two more kids to the dentist. I will figure it out, love."

Sounded like that was also a no-go.

When she returned, she looked worried. "I don't know if I can stay past two," she said.

"I have an idea," I said. "I'll handle the lease pitch and the financials with the tenants. When I'm done, I'll head to the school and grab your kids. You can hang back and focus on the design."

Her brows knit together. "Won't Ivy be confused?"

"No, she has choir today, and Kelly's picking up the boys after lacrosse," I said.

"But Bebe and James..."

"Bebe knows me. I'll let her know you sent me. If there's any confusion, we'll FaceTime you. It'll be fine."

Natalie hesitated, then nodded. "Okay. I trust you."

Her words felt like a lifeline, but I didn't dare read too much into them.

The tenants arrived on time—two sisters looking to open their first retail shop. I gave them a tour of the space, explaining the square footage, leasing terms, and the vision for the center. By 2:00 pm, I handed things off to Natalie.

As they discussed color palettes and layouts, I excused myself and headed to the school to pick up Bebe and James.

When I arrived, I spotted Bebe scanning the crowd for her mom. I went over to her and crouched to her eye level.

"Hey, Bebe, your mom's still at work. She asked me to come get you. Is that okay?"

James looked to Bebe for the answer, and she tilted her head, considering.

"Are we going to our house or yours?" she asked.

"How about mine?" I said. "And we'll grab In-N-Out on the way."

That sealed the deal. Both kids jumped up and down, cheering.

By the time we got to my place, they were happily munching on fries. I took a quick photo of them and sent it to Natalie.

Will: Meet at my house whenever you're done.

Natalie: Thank you! The sisters are taking the space. Can you send over the contract?

Will: High-five, Bradford. Way to close the deal.

She sent back a smile emoji.

At my house, I had Bebe pull out her homework while James practiced his spelling words. "If you get everything done, you can play Nintendo."

The promise of screen time worked like a charm. Just as we were finishing up, the doorbell rang.

"Mommy!" Bebe and James shouted in unison when Natalie walked in.

"Hi guys!" She said and gave them each a hug.

"Hey," I said, my chest tightening at the sight of her. "Welcome to the party."

She smiled, shaking her head. "Guess what? The sisters have a friend who's a baker. She wants to see that corner space tomorrow."

"Wow," I said, genuinely impressed. "I should hire you. Two deals in one day?"

Her cheeks flushed, and she gave me a small, bashful smile.

"Mommy, can we stay and play Nintendo?" Asked James.

Natalie looked at me and said, "Only if it's okay with Mr. Parker."

"Of course," I said. "Let me set it up for you guys. Follow me."

After I got them situated, Natalie and I were alone in the kitchen.

"Want to stay for dinner?" I asked. "The kids already ate, but I was thinking of grilling some steaks."

"Fancy," she teased.

"How do you like it?"

"Bloody as hell," she said, laughing.

"Okay, Mia," I said with a wink, referencing "Pulp Fiction."

"Don't be a square," she shot back, drawing an imaginary square in the air.

God, I think I loved her even more in this moment.

While I grilled, my phone buzzed. It was Lori, and I put her on speaker so I could keep cooking.

"Natalie's really bringing my vision to life," Lori said. "I appreciate the introduction."

When I hung up, Natalie looked at me, her eyes soft. "You told Lori about me?"

"She asked who designed my place," I admitted.

Natalie stepped closer, her hands lightly brushing my arms. "Thank you," she said, her voice barely above a whisper. She cupped my face, her lips pressing softly against my cheek.

I froze, wanting to pull her closer, but then my phone buzzed again. This time, it was Blake.

Natalie noticed the name on the screen and immediately stepped back.

"I should take this," I said reluctantly.

"Hey," Blake said cheerfully. "I was thinking of coming over tonight to finish what we started last night."

I hesitated, trying to think of a quick lie, like the dickhead I was becoming. "I've got some work to catch up on, how about tomorrow?"

"Sure," she said, sounding a little disappointed. "I'll be thinking about you, Goodnight, William."

"Goodnight," I replied, hanging up.

When I turned back, Natalie was looking out the window, her features tight.

The steaks were done, and I carried them inside. "Dinner's ready," I said, setting the plates on the table.

"I think I should go," Natalie said softly.

"Stop," I said, my voice firm. "Eat with me. It's still mooing, just like you wanted."

She managed a small laugh. "Okay. I'm starving."

After dinner, Natalie helped clear the plates, then called Bebe and James down to get ready to leave. I walked them to the car, wanting so badly to kiss her, to ask her to stay forever. But instead, I said, "Good work today."

She smiled faintly. "You, too."

As I watched her drive away, I wondered—like I always did—where our paths would lead.

Chapter 10

Double Take

Natalie

I couldn't believe the day I just had. It started with an email from the hot Brit who wanted to take me on a date, followed by me having sex with Will—twice—and ended with him practically running out of my house. Then, later, we were playing house at his. All of this after landing another client and a strong possibility for another.

I had to admit, it felt nice to be around Will. But I knew this wouldn't last. It could only be like this every other week, the weeks when his kids were with their mom. Will had his children fifty percent of the time, one week on, one week off.

Not that I didn't like his kids. I did. I adored Ivy, the boys were polite and sweet. But Madison was in such a fragile state. A teenager. She was navigating the most delicate years of her life, and I couldn't ignore how easily she could be hurt.

I remembered all too well what it was like to be her age and feel replaced.

My mother had never been particularly maternal. She was distracted, more focused on her own dreams than our day-to-day lives. Even when she was physically there, it always felt like her mind was elsewhere. After the divorce, she drifted further. There was no dramatic exit—just a slow fade, like she'd quietly opted out of motherhood.

So, my dad did what he thought was best. He went looking for someone to fill the space. Someone who looked the part. And within six months, Veronica was in the picture.

They met through a colleague; they were both in insurance. They dated for six months, got engaged, and were married shortly thereafter.

Veronica came from money and carried herself like it gave her authority over everything. She was old-fashioned, emotionally distant, and always had something to say like, "When I was your age, I was at boarding school. I didn't need anyone." Her words were polished and precisely sharp enough to make you feel inadequate without ever sounding unkind.

She never raised her voice. She didn't have to. Her disapproval came through hollow smiles and glances that could shrink you without a word. Her silence changed the energy in a room. We were never enough. Never mature enough. Never truly hers.

She didn't want kids. My dad couldn't see it, but Meredith and I could. She pushed us toward independence like it was a chore on her list. Every summer, we were sent away to sleepaway camp. She took any opportunity to keep us at a distance.

To my father, she was composed and capable. But we knew the truth. Everything she did was calculated to keep us out of her world, all while making it look like she had done her part.

She never once told us she loved us.

The only thing she truly invested in was our college applications—not because she cared, but because it got us out of the house. For her, success wasn't about our future. It was about our absence. It was about our silence.

The only real warmth we had during those years came in small doses. Our grandparents lived a half hour away and would visit when they could. Our aunt would take us for weekends from time to time. Those moments were rare, but they reminded us of what it felt like to be wanted—to be loved without having to earn it.

Meredith and I clung to each other. Even though we had our own rooms, we almost always ended up in mine, whispering late into the night about how different our lives would be one day. I used to tell her about the life I wanted. Two children, a boy and a girl. We'd bake cookies together. My husband would be handsome. Our house would look like something out of *Home & Garden*, just like the vision board I'd made and taped beside Brad Pitt on my bedroom wall.

What I wanted more than anything was a life that looked whole—even if it was a little broken underneath. I thought if I could make it beautiful enough, safe enough, maybe it wouldn't fall apart the way mine had.

Meredith would smile and say she wanted to work in fashion and photography, but marriage wasn't for her. Not after what we'd seen.

Looking back now, I understand both of us better. I spent years trying to build something flawless, while Meredith built walls around her heart so no one could ever leave her the way we'd been left.

I realize now how much emphasis I put on curating perfection. The perfect husband, the perfect house, the perfect kids, myself, all lined up like proof that I was doing everything right.

Maybe that's why I'm so careful now. Why the idea of becoming a stepmom makes something inside me tighten. Because I know what it's like to grow up with one.

I know what it's like to live with a woman who doesn't love you. Who keeps you at a polite distance. Who smiles for company but never lets you in. Who sees you as someone to manage, not someone to love.

And the thing that scares me most?

No matter how much I love Will, or how hard I try, somewhere along the way, I worry I will unknowingly become her.

The next day I decided I needed to call Meredith. She always had a way of helping me see things more clearly, especially when it came to messy family dynamics.

"Hello, hello," Meredith said cheerily when she answered. I could hear faint music in the background.

"Hey, are you busy?" I asked.

"Sort of. It's lunchtime, but I'm around models, so you know the drill, no eating in front of them. Shoot, what's going on?"

"Well, a lot. I'll give you the highlights now, and we can talk more later."

"Okay, let's hear it."

"For starters, I'm working with a hot British guy named Lucas. He asked me out on a date."

"Ooh, I like it already," Meredith said.

"I also had sex with Will. Twice. Yesterday. And he still has that girlfriend."

"Shit."

"Yeah," I said with a nervous laugh.

Meredith sighed. "I'm going to call you the second I get off. I need time to digest all of this."

"Okay. But in the meantime, I think I might be a slut."

"Natalie, stop," she said. "You're just living out what you should have done in your twenties. Sex is better in your thirties anyway. I'm loving this version of you."

I laughed despite myself. "We'll talk later?"

"Absolutely. I'll call you in a couple of hours. Love you."

"Love you, too."

After we hung up, I went to my office to get some work done. I needed to focus. The bakery meeting was tomorrow, and I wanted the space to feel cohesive and inviting. I started brainstorming ideas, pulling together palettes of soft neutral tones and imagining the display shelves lined with high-end baked goods.

Halfway through the process, I decided to email Lucas back.

Hi Lucas,

Sorry for the delay in getting back to you. Are you and Jasper available tomorrow afternoon to meet at the restaurant?

Let me know what works for you.

Natalie

PS: I would love to go to dinner with you Friday.

I hit send and then spent the next twenty minutes debating whether the message sounded too casual—or worse, too eager.

Shaking off the thought, I went upstairs to take a quick Peloton ride, shower, and get ready for school pickup. As I was drying my hair, Meredith called again.

"Okay, I have time now," she said. "Give me all the details."

I filled her in, telling her about Lucas, about Will and the messy web I'd woven for myself.

"I think I need to give Lucas a shot," I said. "He doesn't have kids. No stepmother complications."

Meredith snorted. "So, you had sex with Will, had a semi-breakup, and then had a family night? Natalie, come on. You know who the obvious choice is."

"Teenage daughter. Four kids. I don't want that," I said. "I always pictured myself with two kids, not six."

"Fair. But can you really get over Will? You two seem like magnets."

"Not the point. He also has a girlfriend. And even if he didn't, he could have anyone he wants. If it's not her, there'll be someone else. Lucas, on the other hand, is single and has no strings attached. I have a chance to explore something new."

Meredith laughed. "You're greedy with your hot men. Save one for the rest of us."

We shifted to Thanksgiving plans. Meredith was coming to stay with me for nine days, and the kids would be with Jason for seven of them. It was going to be a long break from the kids, but Meredith would keep me occupied.

By the time I arrived at school, we'd wrapped up our conversation. I found a parking spot right away, a small miracle, and headed to the gate to wait.

Camille waved me over, and we chatted until Lauren joined us.

"What's everyone doing this weekend?" Lauren asked.

"Solo for me," I said. "Jason has the kids. But I have a date on Friday."

Their heads snapped toward me in unison. "Really?"

"Yes, with this British businessman I met at work. He's opening a new restaurant in The City Center."

"Well, well," Camille said, smirking. "Why don't we come over to your house Saturday and have a girls' night?"

"That could work," Lauren said. "Jake's out of town for a game in Denver, so I'd need a sitter."

"I'll see if Emily's free," I offered.

"That would be great," said Lauren.

Camille nodded. "My nanny's watching my boys. Tate is out of town too. Or maybe we need a night out instead. Let's take Lauren to Bourbon House."

The mention of Bourbon House made my stomach flip. Last time I was there, I ended up having sex with Will in the ballroom.

The children started coming out, cutting our conversation short. I spotted James and Bebe, and we said our goodbyes.

The evening was a blur of homework, dinner, and the usual bedtime routine. After the kids were asleep, I went over the design inspiration for the retail store. I wanted everything to be perfect for my meeting tomorrow.

Satisfied, I closed my laptop and climbed into bed. My fingers hovered over my phone, tempted to text Will and tell him how he'd been on my mind all day. But I stopped myself.

It was better this way.

Still, he crept into my dreams all night.

Chapter 11

The New Ingredient
Natalie

The next morning, I got up earlier than usual so I could squeeze in a quick Peloton ride and shower before everyone woke up. It wasn't my typical routine, but I needed the movement to clear my head after the emotional roller coaster of the day before.

After dropping the kids off at school, I returned home and started getting ready for my meeting. I blow-dried my hair, applied just enough makeup to look polished but not overdone, and slipped into a casual yet sophisticated pantsuit. It was the perfect balance of professionalism and creativity for the day ahead.

I spent a little time reviewing my notes for the bakery and finalizing details for the restaurant I was working on with Jasper and Lucas. My sketches and samples were ready, but I wanted to make sure I could confidently sell the vision to everyone involved.

By 9:30, I was pulling into The City Center's parking lot. I spotted that both Will's and Lori's cars were already there. Great. I hated when they were there ahead of me, it made me feel like I was late, even when I wasn't.

I hurried to the space for the bakery and found them already inside.

"Good morning," Lori said, her tone brisk, but friendly.

"Morning," I replied cheerfully, nodding at both Lori and Will.

"I brought some samples for the bakery," I added, pulling a few boards from my bag and placing them on the wall.

Lori stepped closer, tilting her head to get a better look. "I like it," she said. "Very French and chic. Hopefully, this fits the style of the woman we're meeting today."

Will nodded in agreement, his eyes scanning the samples. "It's good. It has integrity and feels authentic, which is important for this center."

I smiled, pleased by their reactions. "Glad you both like it. Hopefully, it helps sell the vision."

As if on cue, the two sisters we'd met earlier arrived with another woman. She was stunning—long, curly blonde hair, a natural glow to her skin, and a casual style that looked like she'd just rolled out of bed and started her day with yoga and meditation. She wore leggings and a white long-sleeve shirt but looked like she belonged on the cover of a fit magazine.

"This is Lisa Simmons, the baker," one of the sisters said as they introduced her to us.

Lisa smiled warmly, and as her gaze landed on Will, I noticed their eye contact linger just a little too long. My stomach twisted. Of course, she found him attractive. Everyone did. But did he find her attractive too?

I forced myself to focus, stepping forward to shake Lisa's hand. "It's so nice to meet you. I'm Natalie Bradford. I would love to show you what I've been working on."

I walked her through the samples and opened my laptop to display the sketches I'd prepared. She leaned in, genuinely interested, and her praise was effusive.

"You're so talented," she said, her voice sincere. "I can tell you've put a lot of thought into this. It's beautiful."

"Thank you," I said, feeling a small surge of pride.

As we talked more, Lisa shared that she had spent time in France learning how to bake with natural ingredients. She was passionate and knowledgeable, and it was clear she'd poured her heart into her craft.

We discussed appliances and a few details about the space before Will stepped in to go over the lease terms and monthly costs. I didn't have much more to contribute, so I excused myself to give them room to talk.

But instead of feeling relief, I felt a knot of jealousy tighten in my chest. Watching Lisa and Will interact made me feel uneasy, like I was witnessing the beginning of something I didn't want to see.

I stepped outside to clear my head, and that's when I saw Lucas walking toward me with another man.

"Hello," Lucas said, his British accent cutting through my jealousy like a gust of fresh air.

He introduced me to Jasper, who looked put together, with jet-black hair, neatly trimmed facial hair, and framed glasses.

"Do you want to see the progress of the restaurant?" I asked, eager to redirect my attention.

"Absolutely," Jasper said with a smile.

As we walked toward the restaurant space, I glanced back and noticed Will and Lisa exchanging phone numbers. A handshake sealed their interaction, but my imagination filled in the blanks with possibilities.

I refocused on Lucas and Jasper as I showed them the updates on the restaurant. They were both impressed, marveling at the woodwork and light fixtures.

"We're making headway," I said, gesturing around the space. "If everything stays on schedule, we're looking at opening in a couple months."

Lucas brushed his hand over the countertop as I spoke, and his fingers lightly grazed mine. The touch was fleeting but enough to make my cheeks flush. I quickly busied myself explaining the cabinetry and layout, hoping he wouldn't notice.

Jasper, meanwhile, was opening and closing the cabinet doors, clearly enjoying himself.

A few moments later, Will walked in.

"Hi, Will," I said, snapping out of my moment with Lucas. "This is Jasper and Lucas."

"Yes, I've met Lucas," Will said, his voice even. "How are you?" he asked the Brit in a flat mannered tone.

"Very well, mate," Lucas said.

We stood around for a little longer, and I couldn't help but notice that Will was watching Lucas more intently than necessary.

As we wrapped up, Lucas turned to us. "Jasper and I were thinking of grabbing lunch. Would you like to join us?"

"Sure," Will said before I could answer.

I hesitated. This could get awkward fast, my affair and my potential future date in the same room. But I nodded. "Sounds good."

Jasper and Lucas walked ahead, and Will offered to drive me.

As soon as we got into his car and the doors closed, Will spoke. "I don't know about that Lucas guy."

I laughed. "What's that supposed to mean?"

"He seems too chummy."

"Chummy?" I repeated, raising an eyebrow.

Will glanced at me. "He was eye-fucking you."

"You're delusional," I said, laughing.

He didn't respond right away. Instead, I asked, "How was Lisa?"

"She signed," he said. "She loves your vision."

"That's great," I said. "She was eye-fucking you too."

Will smirked. "Natalie, the ball is in your court. For now."

His words hit harder than I expected, the weight of them settling in my chest.

We pulled into the parking lot of the restaurant and joined Lucas and Jasper for what I knew would be an awkward lunch.

Chapter 12

Jealousy on the Rocks

Will

After we settled in for lunch at a seafood place, Jasper and Lucas already had drinks, laughing loudly over oysters.

"Oh boy. I don't know if I should be drinking in the middle of the day," Natalie said with a soft laugh.

"One won't kill you," Lucas replied in that infuriating British accent of his.

Everything he said made Natalie chuckle. I couldn't tell if she found him funny or if she was just charmed by his accent. Either way, it grated on me. I didn't know what was going on with this guy, but he seemed into her. If I wasn't mistaken, she seemed into him, too.

It was ironic, really. She had accused me of hitting it off with the baker, yet here she was, practically glowing under Lucas's attention.

Sometime between Jasper and Lucas's second and third drinks, Lucas casually placed his hand on Natalie's arm while making some joke. It was subtle, but it set me off. My jaw clenched so hard I thought I might crack a tooth.

Natalie noticed and brushed his hand off lightly, laughing, but I couldn't tell if she was uncomfortable or if she liked it.

Eventually, Natalie glanced at her phone and announced, "I have to pick up my kids soon."

That was my cue. "I should head back to work," I said, standing abruptly.

Jasper smiled warmly and shook Natalie's hand. "It was so nice to meet you," he said politely, his tone friendly. He didn't bother me as much as his friend did.

Then Lucas asked, "Can I walk you to your car?"

Natalie shook her head. "Actually, Will drove me here. My car's back at The City Center."

Lucas kissed her cheeks and smiled, his gaze lingering a little too long. "Looking forward to Friday," he said.

Friday? What the hell was happening on Friday?

I stayed quiet as we walked back to my car. My thoughts raced as I replayed the interaction. By the time we got to her car at The City Center, I couldn't hold it in anymore.

Natalie was about to open the door when I snapped, "Are you going out with that guy?"

She froze, turning to face me. "Well... sort of," she admitted. "He asked me to dinner in Laguna."

"When did he ask you? Before or after I fucked you the other day?"

Her face reddened. "Will, you're dating someone. I'm sorry for our... slip-up the other day."

"It won't happen again," I said coldly, even though the words stung me as much as they hurt her.

I saw tears start to roll down her face, and my heart twisted. All I wanted to do was pull her close, kiss her, and tell her to be with me. That I'd choose her over anyone.

But instead, I kept my face blank. She got out of my car and into hers without another word. I drove off, feeling like an absolute asshole.

That evening, Blake was coming over. I wasn't in the mood, but I'd already canceled on her too many times this week.

She showed up looking flawless, as always, her hair smooth and glossy, her makeup perfectly done. She carried a bag of groceries in one hand and a small duffel bag in the other.

Blake insisted on making dinner, chicken piccata, a recipe passed down from her great-grandmother. It smelled amazing, and I couldn't deny that she had a talent for making everything look perfectly curated.

We ate at the dining table, chatting about her day and her plans for the weekend. I nodded and made polite conversation, but my mind was elsewhere. I kept glancing at my phone, half-hoping Natalie would text me even though I knew she wouldn't.

Blake noticed. "Is everything okay?" she asked.

"Yeah, just work stuff," I lied, offering a small smile.

After dinner, we moved to the couch to watch a movie. Blake stretched out, draping her long legs over mine. She started tracing slow circles on my chest with her fingers before kissing my neck. Her hand trailed lower, brushing over the top of my pants.

I decided I wasn't going to stop her. I needed to let this woman in, to give her the chance she deserved.

I turned toward her and kissed her back, hard. Her skin was smooth under my hands, her perfume was making me a little dazed. I wanted to feel that spark, that magnetic pull I felt with Natalie, but it wasn't her. Still, it felt nice.

Blake's breathing grew heavier as I slid my hand between her legs. She was more than ready. Her hands were all over me, pulling me closer, her mouth hot against my neck.

I pressed her back against the couch, my lips finding hers again. She tasted like wine and something desperate, something that matched my own need to forget. To feel anything but the hollow ache Natalie had left behind.

Blake's fingers tugged at my shirt, dragging it over my head before her hands skimmed down my chest. Her eyes gleamed, her mouth curving into a smile that looked more like triumph than desire. I decided to lead Blake upstairs to my room.

When we got to my bed, she sat down, and she pulled my pant loop toward her. She started to unbuckle my belt and tug down the zipper, her impatience matching my own need to shut my mind off. I kicked off my jeans. She slid her hands along my hips, urging me closer, her breath hitching as I settled between her legs. I yanked her dress higher, fingers tracing the curve of her thighs before slipping beneath the fabric to find her already bare. She hadn't bothered with anything but the tight black dress she'd shown up in.

"Will," she whispered, her voice a plea. Her nails scraped down my back, leaving faint lines that stung.

I pulled her dress over her head, letting it fall to the floor in a careless heap. Blake's skin warm, her eyes fixed on mine like she was waiting for me to admit something I wasn't ready to.

This was just sex. Something to fill the space Natalie had left. Something to make me forget how much I wanted her.

I put on a condom and pressed into Blake, burying the guilt, the frustration, the longing, with each rough, desperate thrust. Blake's head fell back, her lips parted, eyes glazed with pleasure. She called my name, her voice thick and ragged.

But it wasn't enough. Not even close.

"Oh, Will," she whispered, her voice trembling. "I love you."

The words startled me. I wasn't ready for that. I hesitated for a fraction of a second before continuing, deciding to just finish.

When it was over, she curled up beside me, her hand resting on my chest.

"Will, I'm sorry I said that." She murmured.

"It's okay," I said, keeping my tone light. "You were caught up in the moment." She didn't say anything else and I fell asleep.

I woke up early the next morning in a cold sweat. I'd been dreaming about Natalie, her laugh, the way her eyes fluttered when she was caught off guard. In the dream, she disappeared, and I couldn't find her no matter how hard I searched.

Blake stirred beside me, rolling over and kissing my shoulder. "Are you okay?" she asked sleepily.

"I'm fine," I said.

I got up, needing to take a run to and clear my head. "Stay as long as you'd like," I told her before heading downstairs.

Blake stretched, the sheets falling slightly, exposing her smooth skin. She caught me looking and smiled. "Maybe I'll stay for a little while longer."

After my workout, I found Blake in my button down, sipping coffee at the kitchen table.

"So, Mr. Parker," she said playfully. "No kids this weekend. Would you like to take me on a date?"

I nodded. "I'd love to. How about tomorrow night?"

"That sounds perfect," she said, her smile lighting up her face. "You know, I could stay the whole weekend."

Her words felt invasive, even though she meant well. "I'd love that," I lied, "but I have plans with my best friend, Evan on Saturday."

As soon as she left, I texted Evan.

Will: Want to grab drinks at Bourbon House on Saturday night?

Evan: Sure, as long as you're paying.

I shook my head. Typical Evan.

Still, my thoughts drifted back to Natalie. Where was she going tomorrow night? They both had mentioned Laguna, and I had a strong suspicion about which restaurant they'd choose.

Broadway. It had to be.

I called the restaurant, but they were fully booked. "We'll take the bar," I told the hostess over the phone.

"Sir, bar seating is first come, first serve," she replied.

"No problem," I said, already forming a plan.

Chapter 13

The Top, The Bar, and The Brit

Natalie

By Friday afternoon, my weekend without the kids had officially begun. For the first time in a while, I was looking forward to it. At first, these weekends felt daunting; quiet hours stretching endlessly, but tonight, I had a date. A real date. With a Brit, no less.

Lucas seemed charming, confident, and refreshingly uncomplicated. No ties, no ex-wife, no teenagers. Just a man with a great accent and an easy smile.

Before getting ready, I FaceTimed Meredith for wardrobe approval. She was my go-to for fashion advice, given her proximity to high-end designers. She never hesitated to send me pieces to elevate my closet, often with unsolicited commentary.

"I think I've nailed it," I said, holding the phone up to show her my outfit: black, boot-cut jeans that made me feel tall, paired with sleek black booties, a sheer lace top that revealed just enough of my black bra, and a leather jacket to tone down the daring vibe.

Meredith grinned. "Your rack looks great in that top."

I rolled my eyes. "It's not too much?"

"Not at all. Trust me, everyone will be wearing something like that. You look amazing."

By the time my Uber pulled up outside the restaurant, I was starting to feel the thrill of possibility. This was my chance to experience something new, to focus on a man without baggage.

Lucas was waiting outside when I arrived. His crisp button-up shirt and easy posture immediately put me at ease.

"Hello," he said, his accent practically melting me on the spot.

"Hi," I replied, smiling as he held the door open for me.

We stood in the small hallway by the hostess, and as Lucas gave her his last name, something caught my eye. For a brief second, I thought I saw Will standing at the bar behind a blonde woman.

It couldn't be.

I shook the thought away as the hostess led us to our table, and I made a point not to look back. It couldn't be him. There was no way he'd show up here, tonight, of all nights.

As Lucas and I ordered drinks, I reminded myself to stay present. Will didn't matter right now. This was my time to enjoy a date with a man who was straightforward, unattached, and interested in me.

We talked easily about work. Lucas was insightful and curious, and his genuine interest in my life was refreshing. I told him about my kids, even showing him a picture.

"They're adorable," he said, smiling. "They look like their mother."

I laughed softly, brushing off the compliment. "Thank you. It's been a process, figuring out co-parenting, but we're making it work. Honestly, I've gotten used to being on my own with them. Prior to the divorce, my ex traveled so much."

Lucas shared that his ex-wife didn't want children. "That ship's sailed for me now," he added. "I'm forty-two, and I've made peace with it."

"You don't think you'll change your mind?" I asked, curiosity getting the better of me.

He shook his head. "No. It's just not in the cards for me. And I'm okay with that, I'm happy with my cat, Pete." He studied me for a moment, his gaze thoughtful. "What about you? How old are you, if you don't mind me asking?"

"I'm thirty-seven," I said. "Do you have a photo of Pete the cat?" I laughed.

He smiled. "You're still young. Plenty of time to figure out what you want. And of course I have a photo."

"Not that young," I said, laughing. "But I feel like I'm at the right age for where I'm supposed to be and I'm more than happy with two children. Now let's see this, Pete."

He pulled out his phone to show me his orange cat, Pete.

The conversation flowed, and for a moment, I let myself relax. But then, out of the corner of my eye, I saw the blonde woman from earlier walking past our table toward the bathroom.

Blake.

My gut twisted. If Blake was here, that man with her must be Will.

Before I could turn around to confirm, Lucas leaned in. "I think that's Will over there at the bar," he said casually. "Perhaps we should go say hello."

Panic bubbled in my chest. "Nonsense," I said quickly. "There's no need to bother them."

Lucas didn't seem to notice my hesitation. "He just made eye contact with me. Let's go say a quick hello."

Before I could stop him, Lucas was already leading the way. I followed reluctantly, dreading whatever interaction awaited.

"Hello, mate," Lucas said cheerfully. "Let's have a drink."

Will's gaze flicked to mine, and a smirk tugged at the corner of his mouth. "Sure. What are you having, Natalie? White wine tonight, or something stronger?"

"Something stronger," I said flatly, my tone betraying my nerves.

Blake appeared, her towering frame commanding attention. "Hi," she said brightly.

Will introduced us. "This is Blake," he said. "Blake, this is Natalie. She's working on a project with me, and our daughters are in the same class at St. Isidore's."

"Nice to meet you," I said, forcing a polite smile.

Blake smiled back; her tone syrupy sweet. "Cute top. I have one just like it."

I bit the inside of my cheek, swallowing the sharp retort that threatened to slip out. "Thanks," I said stiffly.

Lucas stepped in, introducing himself to Blake. "How do you do?" he asked, his British accent on full display.

"Oh my gosh, I love your accent," Blake gushed, her enthusiasm grating on me.

When our drinks arrived, I barely took a sip before suggesting we head back to our table.

"Well, join us for another drink after," Will said, his smirk deepening.

"We'll see," I replied coolly.

"We'd love to," Lucas added, oblivious to the tension simmering beneath the surface.

As we walked back to our table, I heard Blake's voice behind us. "They seem nice," she said to Will.

I could barely focus for the rest of dinner. My mind kept drifting back to the bar, replaying every detail of Will and Blake together. Was it a coincidence they were here, or had Will figured out my plans and decided to crash my date?

After we finished eating, Lucas suggested grabbing a nightcap.

"Sure," I said, though my heart wasn't in it. All I wanted to do was go home and cry.

As we walked past the bar, I saw Blake leaning into Will, her leg brushing against his. She was looking at him with an intensity that made my pulse spike.

We stepped outside of the cramped restaurant, the open air breathing life back into me. I stopped abruptly at the end of the street. "You know what, Lucas? I'm so sorry, but I think I'm going to call it a night. I have a headache."

"Oh," he said, surprised. "Can I take you home? I'll ride in the Uber with you."

I laughed lightly. "I'll be okay but thank you."

Lucas waited with me on the corner until my car arrived. As the Uber pulled up, he spun me gently toward him and kissed me. It was a good kiss—soft, tender and sweet.

But he wasn't Will.

"Thank you for a nice evening," I said, stepping into the car.

On the ride home, I texted Meredith.

Natalie: Need to talk ASAP.

She called me the second I walked through the door. "What's going on?"

I told her everything.

"What if I can't get over Will?" I asked, my voice cracking. "Seeing him with Blake was maddening."

Meredith was calm, as always. "Take a breath. Remember, he'd take you back if you were all in. But you have to decide, Natalie."

"I think I should stick it out with the Brit," I said half-heartedly.

"I think you need therapy," she teased, laughing softly. "I'll be there in two weeks. We'll figure this out together."

I laughed, despite the lump in my throat. "I love you. Thanks for letting me vent."

After we hung up, I saw a text from Lucas.

Lucas: Listening to a record with Pete. He was hoping to meet you.

He was sweet. Perfect, really.

But with Will crashing in on every step I took, I didn't know where my heart was anymore.

Chapter 14

Behind the Eight Ball
Will

T he evening went exactly how I thought it would, I crashed Natalie's date with the British guy. But I didn't expect to catch them at the worst possible moment. She was getting into an uber, and he kissed her.

I wanted to die.

Blake didn't seem to notice. She was busy chatting about another bar she wanted to go to. I nodded along, but my mind was miles away. As if the universe was playing a cruel joke on me, she took me to the same bar I'd gone to with Natalie, her sister, and Camille—the night Natalie and I had sex in the ballroom at Bourbon House.

God, that was so hot.

It was the same place I was planning on meeting Evan tomorrow night. I wanted to be somewhere I could remember Natalie. I know I was just torturing myself but being here with Blake was a different kind of torture. I needed to get out of my own head.

I needed to let Natalie go. She was dating someone else. I had a girlfriend who wanted to be part of my life. Blake was great on paper, and I was the one holding back.

At the bar, I grabbed us a couple of beers. Blake suggested we play pool, and I agreed, hoping it would distract me from my spiraling thoughts. She was surprisingly good—flirty and confident, talking smack the entire game while nearly kicking my ass.

She was gorgeous, no doubt about it. She had a lot going for her. I needed to stick with this.

After the game, she leaned into me, brushing her hand lightly over my chest.

"Want to come back to my place?" she asked, her voice low and inviting.

I hesitated. "I'm not sure," I said. "I don't really have anything with me."

"You don't need anything," she said with a playful smile.

Her hand lingered on my arm, and I couldn't come up with a good excuse fast enough.

"Alright," I said, giving in.

Blake's place was a sleek, one-story flat in Laguna with a killer view of the ocean. Being in the real estate industry had its perks.

"Great place," I said, genuinely impressed.

"Thanks," she replied, handing me a scotch on the rocks. "I got this off market in 2020 when the market and rates were great."

"Good timing," I said.

We sat on her couch, sipping our drinks and admiring the view.

"I'll be right back," she said, disappearing into the bedroom.

When she returned, she was wearing red lingerie that clung to her body like it was made for her. She looked like a holiday Barbie.

She tapped something on her phone, and soft music filled the room.

"I've been having such a great time with you," she said, her voice low and sultry.

She straddled me, taking my drink and setting it on the coffee table.

Her hands roamed over my chest, but my body wasn't responding. My mind drifted back to Natalie, her laugh, her eyes, the way she felt wrapped in my arms.

Blake leaned closer, her lips brushing against my neck. "You like that?" she murmured.

I nodded, but the words felt hollow. "Uh, yeah," I muttered, my hands resting lightly on her hips.

Blake's movements became more insistent, but the harder she tried, the more distant I felt. I couldn't do this.

"Blake," I said, gently gripping her wrists to still her.

She pulled back, confusion flickering across her face. "What's wrong?"

"I'm so sorry," I said, running a hand through my hair. "I have a headache. I shouldn't have come back with you tonight."

Her expression softened. "Do you want some Tylenol or water?"

"No, I'll be okay," I said quickly. "I just...I'm not in the right headspace right now. It's not you. You've been amazing."

Blake sighed, clearly disappointed, but she managed a small smile. "It's okay, Will. I get it."

"I'd love to see you again," I said, trying to salvage the moment. "Maybe dinner on Sunday? At my place?"

Her smile grew a little. "That sounds great."

I kissed her on the cheek, grateful she wasn't angry, and called myself an Uber.

As soon as I got in the car, I pulled out my phone.

I had to text Natalie.

Will: Natalie...

Chapter 15

Back To You
Natalie

After I climbed into bed, I decided I would give Lucas another chance. I told myself it was time to move forward, even if my heart wasn't entirely ready to let go of the past.

My phone buzzed on the nightstand.

I reached for it, expecting it to be Lucas again.

Will: Natalie...

What the hell? Every time I even *thought* about moving on, he found a way to reappear, crashing into my carefully constructed plans and scattering them like leaves in the wind.

I stared at the screen, debating whether to ignore it, to be strong and finally put my phone away.

But I wasn't strong when it came to Will.

Natalie: Yes...

Will: Can I come over?

My heart and body screamed *YES!* My head whispered *no.*

I closed my eyes, took a deep breath, and let my heart win.

Natalie: Okay.

Twenty minutes later, Will was at my door.

I opened it, expecting...well, I wasn't sure what I was expecting. But it wasn't this.

Will looked furious and frustrated, his jaw tight, his hands running repeatedly through his hair as he paced in the entryway.

"Why don't you come sit down?" I offered softly, unsure of his mood.

"I don't want to sit," he snapped, still pacing. "I don't even know why I'm here. I left a gorgeous woman in red lingerie because all I can think about is *you.*"

My stomach dropped at his words. I didn't know what to focus on, his confession or the image of Blake getting ready to seduce him.

"I don't know what you want me to say, Will."

"You drive me crazy," he said, his voice rising. "I have this amazing woman who wants all of it with me."

"Then be with her!" I shouted, the frustration bubbling up inside me.

"She isn't you," he said, his tone softening, as if the weight of those words alone was enough to undo him.

Before I could respond, he crossed the space between us. His hand reached out, brushing my hair away from my face, his thumb lightly grazing my cheekbone. He tilted my chin up and touched the tip of my nose, almost reverently.

Then he pulled me into a kiss.

It was deep, consuming, and filled with the kind of passion that made the world blur around us. I may have blacked out for a moment, lost in the sheer intensity of it.

When I pulled back, breathless, I didn't say anything. Instead, I took his hand and led him upstairs to my room.

I tugged Will toward the bed and eased him down, stepping between his legs so we were eye to eye. The air was thick, charged, heavy with unspoken emotions and raw desire.

He leaned back slightly, he rested his hands on my hips steadying me as I reached out, lightly brushing my fingers along his jawline. His stubble was rough under my fingertips, a stark contrast to the tenderness in his gaze.

I leaned in, pressing a featherlight kiss to his cheek, then his ear, and finally his lips.

For a moment, his kiss was unhurried, savoring, each brush of his mouth deliberate, as though he wanted to memorize the taste of me. Then the tempo shifted, his hands slid around my waist, firm and insistent, tugging me closer until I was on his lap straddling him.

A low sound rumbled in his chest as his hands clamped tighter on my hips, rocking me against him. The friction stole my breath, a jolt of heat sparking low in my body. I pressed down harder, needing more, and the groan that escaped him only spurred me on. Our rhythm built, frantic and unsteady, until I was dizzy with wanting.

His mouth tore from mine, trailing fire along my jaw, down my neck. My head fell back as his lips and tongue claimed every inch of skin they found. Fingers tugged at my top, slipping beneath, he yanked it over my head in one swift motion. He undid my bra exposing my chest to him. He put a nipple into his mouth, I let out a small cry.

I fumbled with the buttons of his shirt, desperate to feel him, my hands trembling as I pushed the fabric aside and flattened my palms against the hard planes of his chest. He was all heat and muscle under my touch.

Before I could catch my breath, his hands slid lower gripping my thighs. In one swift surge, he shifted, rolling me beneath him. A gasp tore from my lips as my back hit the mattress, his weight pressing me down, surrounding me.

His mouth found mine again, hungrier now, his knee between my legs. My hands clawed at his belt, frantic, tugging it free until the leather slipped loose. I pushed at his pants, shoving them down over his hips, desperate to feel him. He broke the kiss long enough to strip them away, kicking free of his pants and dragging his briefs with them. His hands returned to me, urgent and rough, peeling my pants from my body in one swift pull, taking my underwear with them. Cool air hit my skin, but before I could shiver, his heat was there, his body pressing into mine, bare against bare.

His lips trailed along my neck, leaving a path of warmth that sent goosebumps down my spine. He moved lower, capturing my nipple in his mouth, his tongue drawing slow, deliberate circles that made me gasp.

His kisses continued down my torso, each one igniting a fire in its wake. When he reached the curve of my hip, I arched into him, my hands tangling in his hair.

Then he was there, his lips and tongue coaxing me into a state of pure bliss. My body trembled as waves of pleasure washed over me, and I cried out his name as I came undone.

I reached for him, pulling him up to meet my gaze. I wrapped my hand around him, his breath caught. He let out a low, guttural sound that sent a thrill through me.

I pulled him toward me, guiding him inside.

The moment he entered me, we both exhaled, a long, shared breath that felt like relief and release all at once.

We moved together, a rhythm that felt instinctive, like we'd been made for this. Every touch, every kiss, every whispered word was electric.

I lost count of how many times I fell apart in his arms, each climax pulling me deeper into him. Finally, he let go, his body tensing as he buried his face in my neck, his breaths coming fast and ragged.

He collapsed onto me, his weight comforting and grounding as we both came down from the high.

We lay there in the quiet, the only sound the soft hum of our breathing.

Will shifted, propping himself up on one elbow to look at me. His hand brushed a strand of hair from my face.

"Do you want to stay?" I asked softly.

His answer came without hesitation. "I do."

I curled my naked body into his, and his arm wrapped around me, holding me close.

Within moments, we both drifted off, intertwined like we were the only two people in the world.

Chapter 16

When The World Stays Outside

Will

The morning light slipped softly through Natalie's curtains, casting a warm glow across the room. She was tucked against me, her body fitting perfectly like she belonged there. I'd always wondered what it would be like to wake up next to her, to have her in my arms all night.

That one night last year when she stayed with the kids on my couch due to Madison being drunk and me needing to care for her didn't count. Not when she left before sunrise, sneaking out like a secret. Not when Madison had caught us, standing there in her judgmental teenage glare. That wasn't a moment to cherish.

But this? This was perfect.

Natalie stirred slightly, her lips curving into the faintest smile. Her tiny freckle on her nose, looking cute as ever. Like she could sense my thoughts. She stretched her arms over her head, her hair a mess of waves spilling over her pillow. When her eyes fluttered open, she looked like a damn fairy tale came to life.

"Hi," she said softly.

"Hi," I replied, leaning in for a kiss.

She pulled the sheet up, laughing. "I need to brush my teeth first."

"Then I guess I should, too. Got a spare?"

"Indeed, I do," she said, still grinning.

She sat up, clutching the sheet against her chest as she searched for her clothes. I couldn't resist. I pulled her back down, my lips finding hers again.

She let out a soft laugh, but there was no hesitation in her kiss this time. She melted into me, and my hands moved instinctively, tracing the curves of her body. Her hips arched toward me, and I could feel her wanting me as much as I wanted her.

Within moments, I was inside her, no words needed, no hesitation between us. Our bodies found a rhythm as if they'd always known it, moving together with a quiet urgency that made the world fall away. Her soft moans met my breathless murmurs, each one spurring me closer to the edge, but I held back, wanting to remember every second.

Her hands slid over my back, her nails digging in just enough to leave a trace, anchoring me to her. I kissed her neck, her shoulder, the corner of her mouth as she arched beneath me, her legs tightening around my waist. Watching her come undone in my arms, eyes fluttering shut, lips parted in surrender, was more intoxicating than anything I'd ever known.

When I felt the tension building beyond control, I paused just long enough to whisper, "Is this okay?"

Her breath hitched, and she nodded. "Please," she whispered, her voice shaky but sure.

That single word undid me.

We gave in together, the moment crashing over us in waves raw, and real. I collapsed onto her, her skin warm and damp against mine, our heartbeats slowly syncing.

As we lay there, catching our breath, I teased, "Now we can brush our teeth."

She laughed; her cheeks flushed. "Oh my gosh, I hope my breath wasn't gross."

"It wasn't," I assured her. "You smell like flowers."

"Liar," she said, but her smile told me she didn't believe it.

I slipped on my pants as she found a tee shirt and panties. We stood side by side at the bathroom sink, brushing our teeth together. It felt...normal. Like this was something we'd done a hundred times before.

I stayed on her side of the double vanity, instinctively avoiding what must have been Jason's side. It wasn't my place.

When we finished, Natalie turned on the shower and looked over her shoulder. "Shall we move into here?"

"Why yes, I love showering with you," I said, my voice playful.

The shower was steamy and slippery, and I couldn't keep my hands off her. I kissed her neck, her shoulders, her back. When I turned her around, water running over her skin, I dropped to my knees, letting the spray fall across us both.

She gasped as I pressed my mouth to her, her body arching back against the tiles. My hands held her hips steady, guiding her as she raked her fingers through my hair. Her moans echoed off the walls, louder than the rush of water.

"Don't stop," she murmured.

I moved harder, slower giving her all the permission she'd given me. Her thighs trembled as she clung to me for balance. She pressed herself forward when she came.

We didn't speak. We didn't need to. She sagged against the wall, spent and glowing, while I rose and pulled her into my arms, her head resting against my chest.

Eventually she looked up at me with that blissful, satisfied smile and reached for a towel.

"I'm going to make us some breakfast," she said, pressing a kiss to my lips before slipping out of the bathroom, barefoot, dripping, and completely mine.

I took a moment to glance around her room while getting dressed. It was neat but lived-in, a reflection of her personality. A picture of her kids sat on the dresser, and a white jewelry box painted with sparkles and pink streaks—Bebe's handiwork, no doubt—rested beside it.

These small, personal touches made me feel closer to her, like I was seeing a side of Natalie that had been forbidden before.

The smell of coffee and bacon greeted me as I walked downstairs.

"Hello," she said, turning to smile at me as she flipped the bacon.

I stepped behind her, kissing her cheek. She giggled, the sound lighting up the room.

"How can I help?" I asked.

"Grab plates from that cabinet," she said, nodding toward the kitchen island.

I followed her instructions, then poured coffee for us, remembering how she liked it.

"I know you have a sweet tooth," I teased as I placed her mug on the counter.

She smiled, a little shy. "Bad addiction."

"I like it," I said, watching her as she plated our breakfast.

We sat at the counter, eating like we did this every morning. It felt easy, natural, like a life we could have together.

My phone buzzed on the counter, pulling me out of the moment. It was a text from Blake.

Blake: Hey baby, just thinking about you. Hope your headache is better.

I wanted to ignore it, to stay in this bubble with Natalie, but she noticed my hesitation.

"You can respond," she said softly.

"It's okay," I replied, setting the phone down. She didn't push, but I could tell she knew exactly who it was.

After breakfast, we cleaned up, and Natalie suggested a trip to the farmer's market.

"I thought we'd spend all day in bed, naked," I said with a smirk, picking her up and carrying her back to her room.

She laughed, and we tumbled onto the bed. The rest of the day blurred into naps, a movie, and more moments of lovemaking and laughter.

We must have fallen asleep. By the time I checked my phone again, the sun was hanging lower, and it was almost 5:30. Blake had texted three more times:

Blake: Just checking to see if you're okay.

Blake: I'm starting to get worried.

Blake: Are you alive?

Will: Sorry, I lost my phone in the Uber. Just got it back.

I was turning into a lying asshole.

Her response was immediate, followed by a photo of her in lingerie:

Blake: Thank goodness. Call me later if you want to come over.

I knew I wouldn't.

Natalie stirred beside me, stretching her arms over her head. "

"What time is it?" She asked sleepily.

"A little after 5:30."

"Oh no, I need to get up. I have a girls' night to get ready for."

I smiled. "Sounds hot."

She rolled her eyes, checking her phone. "My Uber's coming at seven. I have to do something about this hair."

"It looks perfect to me," I said.

She started rummaging through her closet while I gathered my clothes.

"What are you doing tonight?"

"Meeting Evan for dinner at eight. I better head home."

I walked over to her, tilting her chin up to kiss her. "I loved today."

"Me too," she said, her eyes soft.

"Come over after your girls' night?" I asked.

"Isn't that too much time together?" she teased.

"Not for me," I said. "Pack a bag. I'll take it with me, so you'll have what you need."

She hesitated for a moment before nodding, grabbing a small bag and tossing in a few things.

I kissed her one last time before heading out, knowing I'd spent the rest of the night thinking about her.

Chapter 17

Another Round

Natalie

I was running late, frantically brushing on mascara, then scanning my jewelry box to find something that matched my outfit. My cream sweater dress clung perfectly, paired with tan booties and a YSL clutch. Meredith would've been proud, but I hadn't even had time to check in with her for approval.

My mind wasn't on my outfit, though, it was on Will.

The day we'd spent together had been blissful, like a stolen piece of heaven. I couldn't remember the last time I'd felt that carefree or loved. But as wonderful as it was, the weight of reality had already started creeping in. *Could I keep doing this?* Getting lost in him for a day, only to face the endless complications of his life—and mine?

I shook my head, forcing the thoughts away. The clock was ticking, and my Uber had just pulled into the driveway.

The car door opened to Camille, already lounging in the back seat.

"Hello, love," she said with a knowing grin. "You're glowing!"

"Am I?" I asked, a little self-conscious.

"Absolutely. What have you been doing all day? Was it with that hot British lad?"

I laughed, shaking my head. "Not exactly."

Camille arched a brow. "Not exactly, huh? Spill it as soon as Lauren gets in."

We pulled into Lauren's driveway, and she emerged looking elegant. Her newly renovated house stood behind her like something out of Architectural Digest.

"Hi, ladies! You all look gorgeous!" Lauren said, sliding into the car.

"You too, darling," Camille replied.

"I love your blouse," I added, admiring her chic outfit.

"And the house—it looks absolutely beau-tiful," Camille said, the word rolling off her tongue with that unmistakably French lilt.

"Well, thanks to Natalie's design magic," Lauren replied with a grin.

I smiled, a little flustered. "It's easy when you're working with someone who has exquisite taste."

Camille leaned in, her voice conspiratorial. "Okay, stop stalling, Natalie. Why do you look like you've just stepped out of a spa?"

Lauren laughed. "No kids this weekend?"

I rolled my eyes. "You're both ridiculous."

Camille smirked. "What happened with the Brit? Did he pluck your feathers?"

I burst into laughter. "You're unbelievable," I said, dodging the question as the Uber pulled up to Bourbon House.

The hostess led us to a cozy table in the back, the same spot where I'd sat with Will for our "business meeting". The memory gave me chills as I tried to focus on the present.

As we settled in, Lennox, the manager, appeared with his usual charm.

"Hello, ladies," he greeted us. "You all look stunning tonight."

We placed our cocktail orders and began scanning the menus. I was half-listening to the specials when I saw Will.

He walked in with a man I presumed was Evan. They were laughing as they made their way to the bar, but his eyes found mine almost instantly.

No way.

He said something to his friend, then headed straight for our table, wearing that infuriating smirk I couldn't help but love.

"Hello, ladies," he said smoothly. "Funny seeing you here."

"Likewise," I replied, trying to keep my tone neutral.

"I'll let you get back to it," he said. "Unless, of course, you'd like to join us?"

Before I could decline, Camille jumped in. "I think we'd love to, and who's that with you?"

"Yes, that's my good friend, Evan," Will replied. "I'll see if Lennox can combine our tables. Natalie, is that okay with you?" He smirked again, clearly enjoying the situation.

When he walked away, Camille turned to me with wide eyes. "*Mon dieu,* That's why you're glowing!"

"Shh!" I hissed. "It's complicated. He's still involved with that blonde, and it's messy."

Lauren leaned in, whispering, "Did you sleep with him?"

"Maybe a few times," I admitted. "Last night. This morning. All day today. Who's keeping count?"

They both burst into laughter, earning a few curious looks from nearby tables.

Lennox worked his magic, and soon enough, our tables were pushed together. Evan was introduced, and it didn't take long for him to charm everyone with his quick wit and infectious laugh. Evan was hilarious, and Will's perfectly timed remarks had us all in tears. It felt easy, natural, like we'd all known each other forever.

At one point, I leaned over to Will and whispered, "Are you stalking me?"

He laughed softly. "Fair about last night, I tried to figure out where you were. Not tonight, though. This was fate. Besides, you know I come here all the time. Maybe you're the stalker."

"Camille picked the place," I said, arching a brow.

"Sure," he said, winking at me. Somehow, he made it look smooth instead of cheesy.

Will insisted on paying the bill, waving off our protests. As Lauren pulled out her phone to order an Uber, she leaned over to me.

"You need to give him a shot," she said quietly.

I nodded, though doubt still lingered. I wanted to, but I couldn't ignore the hurdles: his kids, Blake, the chaos of it all.

"I'm going home with him tonight," I whispered to Camille and Lauren.

Camille grinned. "You should. Honestly, I'd go home with his friend, *il est canon.*"

We all laughed as we hugged goodbye. Will waited with me while the Uber came for Camille and Lauren, slipping some cash to the driver and giving him a few instructions.

Evan took an Uber home as well, giving me a quick hug before he left. "It was nice to finally meet you, Natalie," he said, his tone warm and genuine.

I felt a strange pang of emotion at his words. *Will had mentioned me to his best friend.*

As the valet brought Will's car around, I noticed him glance at his phone. His face tightened briefly before he slipped it back into his pocket.

"Everything okay?" I asked.

"Fine," he said quickly, but I could tell he was lying.

I pushed aside the thoughts lingering in the back of my mind—Blake, our exes, the kids.

Tonight was ours.

Chapter 18

Side by Side Sinks

Will

When we pulled into the garage, I killed the engine and turned to Natalie. Her hand rested lightly in her lap, her eyes lingering on the dashboard. I reached over, threading her fingers through mine.

"I know you're scared of this life together, but I think it could be a good one," I said softly.

Her eyes flicked to mine, and for a moment, I thought I saw the walls she'd built up around herself begin to crack. "I know," she whispered.

Before I could say more, my phone buzzed in my pocket, breaking the moment. I glanced at the screen. Blake.

Natalie's gaze dropped to our joined hands. She gave me a small smile, pulling her hand free. "Answer it," she said.

"I'll see you inside," she added, slipping out of the car as I let her know the garage door was unlocked.

I sighed as I watched her walk away, her back straight, her steps measured. Reluctantly, I picked up the call.

"Hey," I said, trying to keep my tone neutral.

"Hiiiii, you're alive," Blake said, her voice overly chipper. The noise of music and chatter in the background confirmed she was out with her friends.

"What's up?" I asked, keeping it short.

"I want to come over," she said. "I feel like we need to talk."

She wasn't wrong. We did need to talk. If I were being honest with myself, I'd been a terrible boyfriend to Blake. Even if Natalie weren't in the picture, I had no business being with her. Blake deserved better, someone who was all in, someone who didn't constantly compare her to another woman.

"Listen, I think we do need to talk," I said. "But not tonight. Let's do it tomorrow when we're both clear-headed."

She sighed. "Fine. But just so you know, I've been hit on by a very hot bartender all night."

I resisted the urge to roll my eyes. "Please be safe, Blake. Call me tomorrow."

"Fine," she said, her tone softening. "I really care about you, Will."

"Goodnight, Blake," I said, hanging up before the guilt could take root.

For a moment, I sat there in the quiet of the garage, staring at the dashboard. Tomorrow, I'd set her free. But tonight, all I wanted was Natalie.

When I stepped inside, Natalie was curled up on the couch, her knees tucked against her chest.

"Everything okay?" she asked as I walked over to her.

"It will be," I said, sitting beside her. "I need to talk to Blake tomorrow. End things. Even if you decide you don't want this, I can't keep stringing her along. I'm cheating on her, and I'm not in love with her."

Natalie's lips pressed together, and she looked away briefly before meeting my eyes. "I'm sorry I came between you two."

I studied her, trying to read her expression. "I don't think you are," I said with a small smile.

She laughed softly, shaking her head. "Maybe I'm not. But I do feel bad. You are hard to get over."

I leaned closer to her, drawn to her in a way I couldn't explain. "You don't have to get over me, Natalie."

Her lips parted, and for a second, I thought she might argue. Instead, she tilted her head up and lightly grabbed my face and kissed me. Soft at first, then deeper, letting the rest of the world fall away.

"Let's go to bed," I murmured.

Upstairs, I handed her the overnight bag she'd brought earlier. She rummaged through it, pulling out some cozy clothes before disappearing into the bathroom. When she returned, her hair was piled on top of her head in a messy bun, and she was wearing an oversized sweatshirt that made her look beautiful.

"You look hot," I said, leaning against the doorframe. Blake had dressed herself in silk and lace to be desired. Natalie, standing there with her hair piled up and an old sweatshirt hanging off her frame, made me want her in a way that was far more consuming, because it wasn't about show. *It was her.*

We brushed our teeth side by side at the double vanity. Her movements were calm and deliberate, each action thoughtful and precise. I watched her out of the corner of my eye, so composed, so aware of every little detail. It's one of the things I admired most about her. But even in her quiet confidence, I could still sense her hesitation.

"You're so neat," she said, glancing around the bathroom. "It still barely looks like anyone lives here."

I smiled. "Think you could get used to it?"

She didn't answer.

"Maybe you could mess it up a little," I added, watching her in the mirror.

Her cheeks flushed as she turned away, pretending not to hear.

I didn't push, I just finished getting ready and climbed into bed.

When she joined me, she hesitated for just a moment before curling up beside me, her head resting on my chest. I wrapped my arm around her, holding her close.

"You, okay?" I asked, brushing a strand of hair from her face.

"Yeah. Just thinking," she said softly.

"About?"

She let out a small laugh. "Everything. You. Me. How this could all work."

"It will work," I said, my voice steady. "I'll make sure it does."

She didn't reply right away. When she spoke, her voice was quiet. "We'll see."

Her words hung in the air as I pressed a kiss to her forehead. She fit so perfectly in my arms, like she was meant to be there.

But I couldn't ignore the nagging thought in the back of my mind—what if it wasn't enough for her? Were we back where we started? And am I willing to wait while she decides? All the power in her hands.

Chapter 19

Lust, Love and Lemon Muffins

Natalie

It was sometime in the middle of the night when I woke, my body curled instinctively against Will's warmth. The room was completely dark, the heavy blackout curtains shrouding any hint of time, but the quiet stillness told me it was far from morning.

I blinked a few times, adjusting to the silence. My cheek rested against his chest, and I could feel the slow rise and fall of his breathing. The steady rhythm calmed me, grounding me in the moment. I shifted slightly, and that was all it took.

Will stirred beneath me, his hands finding their way to my waist as if he'd been waiting for me to move. His touch was gentle at first, a soft graze of his fingers over the fabric of my shorts. Then, with a quiet exhale, he tugged at the waistband, his intentions clear but unhurried.

"Come here," he murmured, his voice rough from sleep.

I let him guide me as he rolled me on top of him, his hands firm yet tender as they settled on my hips. For a moment, we just stayed there, my knees bracketing his sides, my hands pressed against his chest. His eyes, though barely visible in the darkness, held a quiet intensity that made my breath catch.

Neither of us spoke. There was no need for words. The quiet hum of the night wrapped around us, amplifying every small sound, the soft rustle of sheets, the hitch in my breath, the low hum that escaped his lips when I leaned forward.

His hands slid up my thighs, slow and deliberate, as though he wanted to memorize every inch of me. I moved against him, matching his pace, each motion a wordless conversation between us. His grip tightened slightly, grounding me, pulling me closer.

It wasn't hurried or frantic, but deliberate and deep, like neither of us wanted to let the moment slip away too quickly. The world outside his room felt impossibly far, as if nothing else existed but this—us.

We came undone at the same moment, I collapsed against him, my head tucked beneath his chin, my heart pounding in time with his. His arms wrapped around me tightly, anchoring me in place as though he couldn't bear to let go.

I stayed on top of him, my fingers lazily tracing patterns on his chest. His hand ran up and down my back in slow, soothing strokes, his breathing evening out.

"Don't move," he whispered after a while, his voice soft but resolute.

"I wasn't planning on it," I murmured back, letting my eyes close as the warmth of his body pulled me under again.

He kissed my cheek softly, and we both drifted back to sleep.

When I woke again, the room was still dark, though the clock on the nightstand read almost 10 a.m. I couldn't remember the last time I'd slept this late.

I reached for my phone and saw a missed FaceTime call from the kids. Guilt bubbled up in my chest, though I reminded myself that they were fine with Jason. Quietly, I slipped out of bed, searching for the clothes that had been discarded during the night. Finding them, I pulled on my shorts and sweatshirt and padded downstairs to call them back.

The kitchen was warm and inviting, with sunlight streaming through the windows. I started making coffee as I dialed Jason's number. After a few rings, Bebe's cheerful voice answered.

"Hi, Mommy! I miss you," she said.

"Hi, Bebe. I miss you too," I replied. "I'll see you after school tomorrow. Are you having fun with Daddy?"

"We are!" she said matter-of-factly. "We went to dinner last night and got pizza."

"That sounds like fun," I said. "Can I talk to James for a second?"

I heard her call for her brother, and as she did, Will appeared in the doorway. He was shirtless, wearing just a pair of fitted sweatpants, his hair messy from sleep. God, he was sexy.

"Hi, Mommy," James's voice came through the phone, sounding confused. "I can't see you. Why aren't we on FaceTime?"

"I'm about to drive to the farmer's market," I lied. "It's not safe to FaceTime and drive."

"Oh," he said, accepting my answer. "Don't forget to get strawberries."

"I won't," I said, laughing softly. "I love you, sweetheart."

"Daddy wants to talk to you," James said before handing the phone off.

"Hi," Jason's voice came through, calm and measured. "I just wanted to confirm, I'm bringing in Bebe's science project tomorrow for school, right?"

"Yes, that's right," I said. "Thanks for handling that."

"No problem," he said. "Everything's been going well I was wondering if we could meet up for coffee or lunch next week?"

"Um, sure," I said, caught off guard. "Let's touch base tomorrow and find a time."

"Sounds good. Take care," he said before hanging up.

When I turned around, Will was at the counter, putting bread in the toaster and setting out jams and butter. He walked over to me, placing a cup of coffee in front of me before kissing my cheek.

"Good morning," he said, his voice warm and soft.

"Good morning," I replied.

I took a sip of coffee, letting the moment sink in.

"So," I began, "I really need to get to the farmer's market today. And I have some work I need to finish. But I was thinking that I could come back later."

Will's eyebrows lifted in surprise. "You don't have the kids tonight?"

"Nope," I said. "Jason's keeping them until tomorrow morning and dropping them off at school. It's his first solo drop-off. I have faith he'll manage."

"I'm surprised you want to spend another night with me," he said teasingly.

"I think I want to try this but, slowly," I said, meeting his gaze.

"I can slow down with you, Natalie," he said, his tone sincere.

I decided, for now, to believe him.

When I got home, I felt a strange mix of emotions. My body was sore from days of passion, but my mind buzzed with thoughts of work, the kids, and what exactly this was with Will. It felt like stepping into another world when I was with him, but eventually, I'd have to reconcile it with the real one.

After a quick shower, I dressed and grabbed my basket for the farmer's market. The beauty of Southern California was there's always a fresh market nearby, no matter the day.

When I arrived, I headed to the fruit stand, taking in the vibrant colors of the produce.

"Hi, Natalie!"

I turned to see Lisa, the baker, waving at me.

"Hi, Lisa," I said, smiling. "Great to see you. Are you gathering ingredients for something delicious?"

"Yes! I'm working on some lemon muffins this week," she said brightly.

"That sounds amazing," I replied.

"I'd love to drop off some samples for you and your family sometime soon," she offered.

"That's so thoughtful," I said. "Why don't you come over later this week? We can go over more of your vision for the bakery." I handed her my phone. "Can I get your number?"

"Of course," she said, typing her information into my contacts.

As I watched her walk away, I couldn't help but feel conflicted. Lisa had such a warm energy, and I wanted to hate her for that moment with Will, but I knew better. Will was all in with me, I just needed to decide if I was all in with him.

After finishing at the market, I stopped at Costco for a few more items, then headed home to organize everything for the week ahead. By the time I was done, it was mid-afternoon, and my thoughts drifted back to Will.

Natalie: Should I head over soon? What should I bring?

Will: Bring something sexy that I can rip off you.

I laughed.

Natalie: If by sexy you mean a big T-shirt and shorts, I've got those packed.

Natalie: I grabbed us some dinner at the market. I'm planning to make lemon fish tonight.

Will: It all sounds delicious. Especially the big tee shirt.

Natalie: See you soon. XO

Will said he was willing to take it slow with me but was I ready to travel this journey with him? Or was the high from our time together fueling me to move forward before I could really think it through?

Chapter 20

Too Many Cooks

Will

I'd been lazy all day, watching football and dozing on and off. It had been a long weekend filled with drinks, heavy meals, and endless sex with Natalie. My body was worn out, but in the best way.

The doorbell chimed, pulling me from the couch. When I opened the door, there she was— in lounge wear, her hair piled on top of her head. She didn't wear makeup, and I loved that about her. She didn't seem to try and was still the most beautiful woman I'd ever seen.

"Hi there," she said with a soft smile as I grabbed her bag of groceries and let her inside.

"I missed you all day," I said, pulling her close and giving her a playful squeeze on her ass.

She laughed, swatting my hand. "I see you're still in the same sweats from earlier."

"Guilty," I admitted. "What can I say? I needed a lazy Sunday after you had your way with me all weekend.

She shook her head, but her cheeks flushed. I loved seeing her like this, completely comfortable with me. I hadn't felt this way with anyone in a long time.

I escorted her into the kitchen, where she started unloading the groceries. "Make yourself at home," I said. "I'll take your bag upstairs and be right back to help."

"Okay," she replied, already pulling out ingredients to prepare dinner.

I jogged up the stairs, carrying her overnight bag, but just as I started back down, the doorbell rang again.

I froze.

Pulling out my phone, I saw a missed call and text from Blake. The message read:

Blake: On my way. Be there soon.

Shit, shit, shit.

How had I missed this? I'd been ignoring her all weekend, completely caught up in Natalie, and now Blake was standing at my doorstep.

I glanced toward the kitchen, where Natalie was humming to herself as she prepped the food. My jaw tightened. There was no way this would end well.

I opened the door, stepping outside and closing it behind me.

Blake stood there, her hair sleek, makeup flawless, and a sweater and jeans that screamed "perfect girlfriend." She was holding a bottle of wine and a bag of groceries, looking ready for the dinner I'd completely forgotten about.

"Hey," she said, her smile fading as she noticed my tense expression. "I'm officially starting to worry about you. You've been MIA all weekend."

I opened my mouth to respond, but her gaze shifted to the driveway.

"Whose Range Rover is that?" she asked, her voice sharp.

My throat went dry. "Blake... I'm a real asshole, and you're about to find out just how much."

Her eyes widened, and I could see the pieces clicking into place.

"What's going on, Will?" she demanded, her voice trembling.

"I owe you an apology," I said, running a hand through my hair. "There's someone inside. Someone I've been... seeing."

Blake's face twisted in disbelief. "Seeing? You mean cheating? Like, right now?"

I nodded, shame washing over me. "It's complicated—"

"No, it's not!" she snapped. "Who is it?"

I hesitated, but before I could respond, she pushed past me, shoving the bag of groceries into my chest.

"Blake, wait—"

But it was too late.

Natalie froze the moment Blake walked into the kitchen. Her face went pale as she realized what was happening.

Blake's eyes locked on Natalie like a predator sizing up its prey. "Maybe you don't remember me," she said with a cold smile, "but we met Friday night at the bar. I'm Blake. Will's girlfriend."

Natalie's mouth opened, then closed again. "I... I'm sorry about being here," she stammered. "I was just leaving."

She grabbed her purse, leaving the groceries she'd brought on the counter. As she walked past me, she avoided my eyes completely.

"Natalie, wait—"

But she was already out the door.

Blake turned back to me; her arms crossed. "You're such a piece of shit," she said, her voice low and shaking.

"I know," I said quietly.

"You've been acting strange all week. I knew something was going on," she said, tears brimming in her eyes.

I didn't know what to say. She was right, I'd been stringing her along, avoiding her because I was too much of a coward to end things.

"How am I supposed to feel right now, Will?" she asked, her voice rising. "You bring me here, make me think we're building something, and the whole time you're screwing her? Does she even want to be a stepmom to your kids?"

The question hit me hard, but I stayed silent.

Blake let out a bitter laugh. "Of course not. She gets you all to herself for the weekend, and I'm the one dealing with your baggage. I bet she doesn't even know what she's signing up for."

I took a deep breath. "You're right. I've been a terrible boyfriend, and you don't deserve this."

Her voice cracked as she said, "You were willing to throw this away? I was prepared to take on everything—your kids, your messy life. I cared about you, Will. I was falling in love with you."

"Blake," I said, stepping closer. "You're an amazing woman, and you deserve someone who can give you everything you want. But I'm not that guy."

She stared at me, her tears spilling over. "I thought you were."

"I thought it could be a possibility," I admitted. "But I've been lying to myself, and to you."

Blake grabbed her bag and walked toward the door. "You know what, Will? I hope she's worth it."

And then she was gone.

The silence in the house was deafening.

I sat on the couch, my head in my hands. Everything had blown up in my face, and I had no one to blame but myself.

Natalie was gone, and I didn't know if she'd ever come back. Blake was gone, and she had every right to hate me.

I'd spent so much time trying to keep everything together, but in the process, I'd ruined it all.

I didn't have a plan.

But one thing was clear: if I wanted any chance with Natalie, I had to make things right. No more excuses. No more avoiding the truth.

This time, I'd have to fight for her.

Chapter 21

Balancing Acts
Natalie

What I thought was going to be an evening of dinner, laughs, and love-making with Will turned into an absolute nightmare.

As I was prepping dinner, the doorbell rang. I heard Will making his way to the door, the muffled sound of a woman's voice becoming louder as he opened it.

Oh no, it's probably Blake. Before I knew it, she was inside, walking straight into the kitchen. My stomach dropped. I couldn't stand there and pretend everything was fine.

On the drive home, my heart pounded. The adrenaline from the encounter wasn't wearing off, and guilt was starting to set in. I hadn't been prepared to see Blake, let alone be in the middle of their unresolved relationship. Selfishly, I hadn't thought much about her or her role in Will's life. I'd only considered how it made me feel when I saw them together.

What am I doing? I thought, gripping the steering wheel. Will and I had kids. Complicated lives. A past we couldn't undo. So many things could go wrong.

When I got home, I hurried inside and called Meredith.

"I'm the other woman," I said the second she picked up, collapsing onto the couch.

"Well, hello to you, too," she replied, unfazed. "Should I be grabbing a glass of wine or calling a lawyer?"

"I'm serious."

"I know you are," she said, her tone gentler now. "But let's not rewrite the story. Will wasn't exactly head over heels for this girl if he's out here falling for you. He loves you, Nat. He wants you."

"I can't be a stepmom," I said, the words tumbling out.

"So, you've said," she replied, a touch of sarcasm in her tone.

"I know, I know," I sighed. "But it's a lot to consider."

"It is," Meredith agreed, her voice softening. "But take some space. Let Will figure his shit out. And remember, you're newly single. You'd have a lot of obstacles to overcome, but maybe love is all you need."

"I wish it were that easy," I said, glancing at my phone. "Will's calling. I'll talk to you later?"

"Of course," Meredith said. "I'll be there soon enough."

"You're the best," I said before clicking over.

"Natalie," Will's voice came through the line, soft but full of tension.

"Hey," I said.

"I'm so sorry. I forgot she was coming. I should have ended things with her before starting anything with you."

"Will," I said, hesitating, "do we need time to figure things out? Tonight just felt... messy."

"I was afraid you'd say that," he admitted.

"Every time we get close, the reality sets in," I said, my voice cracking.

"You knew about Blake," he countered. "This wasn't out of left field. I'm just an idiot for not ending it sooner."

"Okay, fair," I said, exhaling. "But let's make sure we're being safe about this, for our kids' sake."

"I can live with that," he said, his tone lightening. "So... is dinner and our sleepover off for tonight?"

I laughed despite myself. "I think I need a rain check."

"I'll miss you in your big tee shirt and shorts," he teased. "I'll keep them safe for you."

"Thanks," I said with a soft laugh. "Goodnight, Will."

"Goodnight, Natalie."

After we hung up, I felt a little better, but also completely drained. I wandered into the kitchen and grabbed a bowl of yogurt, eating mindlessly as I replayed the night in my head.

Just as I finished, my phone buzzed. A text from Lucas.

Lucas: Hey, Natalie, I wanted to see if I could take you to lunch one day this week.

Shit. I'd completely forgotten about him.

Another text came in, this one from Jason, asking if we could meet for coffee on Friday. I quickly checked my calendar and replied to Jason.

Natalie: Sure, 10 a.m.?

Jason: Works for me.

He attached a picture of Bebe holding her science project.

Natalie: Wow, I'm impressed.

I wrote back, feeling a pang of longing for the kids. He hearted the message, and that was that.

Even though the break this weekend had been nice, I missed James and Bebe. It had been such a roller coaster, more emotions and drama with men than I ever imagined I'd be dealing with at my age.

The next morning, I woke to my alarm at 7:30, feeling slightly more rested but still worn out. I went through my morning routine, grateful not to have to drop the kids off at school.

After a quick Peloton ride and some emails, I headed to The City Center to check on the bakery. Lori was waiting for me, clipboard in hand and a familiar look of exasperation on her face.

"Natalie," she started, "we've got a problem. The flooring samples need approval by Thursday, and the timeline for the custom counters just got pushed. Also, we need to decide whether to pivot to the alternate light fixtures, or the electricians will be sitting on their hands by next week."

I nodded, my brain scrambling to keep up. "Okay, I'll look into all of this right away," I said, forcing a smile.

As I left, I spotted Will leaning against the side of the building, his phone in hand. He looked up as I approached, his face lighting up with a smile that used to make my stomach flip. Now, it just made me feel... complicated.

"Hey," he said, slipping his phone into his pocket and walking toward me.

"Hey," I replied, my voice quieter than I meant it to be.

"You, okay?" he asked, his brow furrowing in concern.

"Just a lot on my plate," I said with a weak smile, gesturing toward the bakery behind us. "Lori's got me juggling a million decisions, and it feels like nothing is going according to plan."

"I can help with some of that," he offered quickly. "I mean, between the real estate side of things and—"

"No," I interrupted, shaking my head. "You're already doing enough. Besides, it's not just the restaurant. It's... everything."

His face softened, and for a moment, I wanted to let it all spill out, to tell him how overwhelmed I was by Blake showing up, by the kids, by my ex-husband suddenly wanting to meet for coffee. Lucas wanting to have lunch. But I held back.

"Natalie," he said, his voice low, "I don't want to make things harder for you. If you need me to step back..."

"No," I said quickly, surprising both of us. "I don't want that." I sighed, my gaze dropping to the pavement. "I just need time to figure all of this out. It's a lot."

He nodded slowly, his expression unreadable. "Okay. I'll give you time. But I'm here if you need me. For anything."

The sincerity in his voice made my chest ache. I nodded, stepping back toward my car. "Thanks, Will."

"Anytime," he said softly, watching me as I turned to go.

I could feel his eyes on me as I opened the car door, but I didn't look back. If I did, I wasn't sure I'd be able to leave.

Paralyzed with emotions and the chaos of every relationship around me I sat in the parking lot with the tile samples scattered across the seat; mimicking my thoughts about Will, Jason, Lucas, my kids, Will's kids; the list went on. I exhaled slowly, unclenching my hands. "Just one day at a time, Natalie," I whispered to myself. "One choice at a time."

Chapter 22

Parenting in Progress

Will

I'm used to being the guy who has it all figured out. I close deals, solve problems, and move on. But with Natalie? Nothing about her fits into neat little boxes.

She wasn't supposed to leave last night. I'd pictured us having dinner, talking, maybe falling asleep with her head on my chest. Instead, she walked out the door with barely a goodbye. And now, I was the idiot standing here, watching her leave work flustered by everything and wondering if I'd already screwed this up.

Blake's unexpected arrival was my fault, no question. I should have handled it. I should have ended things weeks ago. But Natalie's reaction was something else, like she'd been waiting for an excuse to pull away.

Madison's voice snapped me out of my thoughts.

"Dad, are we eating or what?"

I looked up from the grill. Madison stood at the open doorway to the living room, arms crossed, her expression a perfect mix of exasperation and teenage indifference. Behind her, Chase and Carter were watching Monday Night Football, while Ivy had her crayons spread across the kitchen table.

"Five minutes," I said, flipping the burgers.

"Sure," she muttered, turning back into the house.

Dinner with all four kids was precious to me. Between Madison's packed schedule, the boys' sports, and Ivy's earlier bedtime routine, getting everyone together felt like a small miracle. Tonight, it was my first night of the week with them, and I loved having them home with me.

Dinner went as usual. Chase and Carter were cracking fart jokes, which sent Ivy into hysterical laughter. Madison sat quietly, picking at her salad with a look that screamed I'd rather be anywhere but here.

Once the chaos subsided, I sent the boys to finish homework and Ivy to get ready for bed. That left Madison and me alone at the table, the silence between us louder than the earlier noise.

"You've been weird all night," Madison said finally, breaking the quiet. "What's going on?"

"Nothing's going on, Sweetheart." I said, trying to sound casual.

She rolled her eyes. "Right. Because you're so good at hiding things."

I leaned back in my chair, studying her. Madison had Kelly's sharp eyes, the kind that could cut through any excuse. She'd always been able to read me better than the rest of the kids, and right now, she wasn't buying my attempt at deflection.

"It's complicated," I admitted.

"Is it about that child you're dating?" she snarled.

"Madison, she's twenty-nine," I said, keeping my tone calm.

"Almost half your age," she shot back.

"I'm not even forty-four yet," I reminded her, though it felt weak.

"Still, it's gross. And Mom says she tries too hard."

Kelly wasn't wrong. Blake did try too hard, in ways that eventually turned me off. But that didn't excuse what I'd done, or why it had been so easy to let things with Blake fizzle out.

"Madison, this is grown-up stuff."

She leaned forward, her eyes sharp. "I think you're forgetting how this kind of thing affects everyone else. It's not just your life, Dad. You don't get to drag us into something you're not even sure about."

I sighed. "You don't have to worry. It ended."

"Oh," she said, leaning back. "I think that's for the best."

She has a point.

Before I could respond, she pushed her chair back and stood. "I have homework," she said, turning toward the stairs.

"Madison."

She paused but didn't look back.

"I love you," I said quietly.

"You too, dad."

Later, I cleaned up the kitchen, wiping down the counters and loading the dishwasher. It wasn't much, but it gave me a moment to think without interruptions. Once the kitchen was done, I headed upstairs to check on the kids.

Ivy was tucked into bed with a book in her hands, waiting for me to read with her. I smiled as I sat down beside her.

"Daddy," she said after we finished the story.

"Yes, Ivy?"

"Can we have Bebe over this weekend?"

"We could maybe arrange that," I said carefully.

Her smile widened as she snuggled under the covers. "Promise?"

"I'll try," I said, kissing her forehead. "Goodnight, Ivy."

"Goodnight, Daddy."

I left her room and made my way to the boys.

Chase was at his computer, deep into a game. I gave him a quick warning. "Are you done with your homework?"

"Yes, Dad."

"Lights out by ten."

"Okay, Dad," he said, barely looking up.

Carter was next, sitting cross-legged on his bed, engrossed in a Nintendo game. I leaned against the doorframe. "Did you finish your homework?"

"Yep. Barely had any tonight."

"This goes off in thirty, okay?"

"Got it," he replied, his fingers still flying across the buttons.

Madison's door was cracked open, and I peeked inside. She was sitting at her desk, headphones on, focused on what looked like homework.

"Hey, Maddie," I said, tapping lightly on the doorframe.

She sighed and pulled her headphones down. "Yes, Dad?"

"Just wanted to say goodnight. Don't stay up too late."

"Okay," she said, her tone clipped.

I hesitated for a second, hoping she might say something more. When she didn't, I nodded and quietly closed her door.

Back downstairs, I sat in the living room, the house silent except for the light sound of the dishwasher. My phone sat on the coffee table in front of me, and I stared at it like it held the answer to everything.

Part of me wanted to call Natalie, to tell her everything, about Madison, about how I felt, about how badly I wanted this to work. I wanted to ask if she was okay, if she'd made it through the day without feeling as overwhelmed as she had earlier. But I couldn't. Not yet.

Instead, I picked up the phone and typed out a message.

Will: Can we talk?

My finger hovered over the send button for a long moment. Then, with a sigh, I hit delete.

Some things couldn't be fixed with a text message.

Chapter 23

A Taste of Distance
Natalie

This week was already slipping through my fingers, and it was only Tuesday, I had a lot to get in. With Thanksgiving looming. I was hyper-aware of how little time I had left with James and Bebe before they went with Jason for a full week.

That night, after dinner, James was sprawled out on the floor, his trucks scattered around him in a precise line only he understood. Bebe was at the table, her head bowed over her coloring book, tongue poking out in concentration as she carefully filled the lines with bright yellows and greens.

"Mom, do you think this needs glitter?" Bebe asked, holding up her page, a smiling unicorn surrounded by a rainbow.

I laughed, leaning against the counter as I watched them. "Sure, why not? Let's get the glitter," I replied, even though I'd regret saying yes, the moment I found pieces of it stuck to my light hardwood floors for months, maybe even decades.

But I was in that mode where I said yes to everything, knowing I'd miss them next week when the house would be too quiet again.

Thank goodness Meredith is coming.

Thinking about them being gone shook me up more than I wanted to admit. I was the one who ended things with Jason. The one who decided to split up our family and walk away. And while I kept telling myself it was for the best, there were still moments—like now—when I questioned everything.

They were going to spend Thanksgiving with Jason, not me. And even though I knew that was fair, part of me couldn't help but feel like it was my penance for stepping outside our marriage and for breaking what we had, even if it had already started to crack.

Later that night, I tucked the kids into bed, clinging to the routine more than I wanted to admit.

James was first, already yawning as I pulled the blanket up to his chin.

"Mom," he said sleepily, "do we have to go to Dad's for Thanksgiving?"

I brushed a hand through his hair. "You'll have so much fun on Thanksgiving with Daddy, Bebe, Nona and Papa."

"Yeah, but I'll miss you."

I swallowed the lump in my throat. "I'll miss you too. But we'll have a celebration with Aunt Meredith when you get back. Deal?"

"Deal," he murmured, his eyes fluttering closed.

Bebe was next. I kissed her goodnight as she clutched her favorite stuffed animal.

"Mom, do you think Dad will let me paint my wall with pink and glitter?"

I laughed softly. "Probably not, but maybe you can get a piece of pink glittery artwork for your wall."

She smiled; her eyes already heavy with sleep.

I kissed her goodnight and headed to my bedroom.

I wanted to text Will, just to check in. I knew his kids were back with him. I decided to give him space. We both needed it.

The next morning, I went to The City Center to check on some final details for the bakery, boutique, and restaurant. I was going over the layout for the display cases with a contractor when I spotted Lucas across the space, deep in conversation with another worker.

I froze, suddenly realizing I'd never responded to his lunch invitation.

"Excuse me for a minute," I said to the contractor, handing him my notes.

Lucas looked up as I approached, his easy smile breaking across his face. "Natalie," he said, stepping toward me. "I was beginning to think you'd forgotten all about me."

"I wasn't—well, not on purpose," I said, feeling a little sheepish. "I meant to text you back, but things have been... busy."

"Let me guess," he said, leaning casually against the counter. "The children, work, and the never-ending to-do list?"

"Exactly," I said, relaxing a little. "What brings you here?"

"I've been finalizing the arrangements for the opening week," he said. "Lori suggested I stop by to ensure everything was in order. I suspect she thinks I'm a bit of a perfectionist."

We spent the next few minutes discussing details, schedules, events, and some marketing ideas Lucas had. His calm energy and polished tone made the conversation flow casually, and I found myself smiling more than I had all week.

As we wrapped up, Lucas leaned in slightly, lowering his voice. "So, what are your plans for Thanksgiving? Spending it with the children?"

"Not this year," I said, feeling a pang of sadness. "They'll be with their father this year. It'll just be my sister and I."

His face lit up. "Then you must come to mine. Jasper's cooking, and he's been positively itching to show off his Thanksgiving menu. Though between us, it does feel rather absurd for two Brits to be presiding over an American holiday. You and your sister are most welcome to come to tell us if we pass inspection."

I hesitated. "I wouldn't want to impose—"

"Nonsense," he interrupted. "You'd be doing us a favor. Jasper thrives on an audience, and I dare say he's already planned far too much food. It'll be quite relaxed, I promise."

The idea of spending Thanksgiving alone with Meredith seemed dull in comparison. "All right," I said finally. "That does sound lovely. Let me confirm with her, but I think we'd love to join."

"Splendid," Lucas said, his smile widening. Then, leaning in, he kissed me on the cheek.

I was a little caught off guard but played it off as a cultural thing.

As I walked back to the contractor, a flicker of guilt settled in my chest. Thanksgiving with Lucas and Jasper sounded easy and enjoyable, something I should have been looking forward to. But my mind wandered to Will.

We hadn't talked all week, and even though we said we'd take things slow, everything still felt messy. Agreeing to Lucas's invitation felt like another layer of complication, one I wasn't sure I had the energy to unpack. What were Will and I even doing?

My phone buzzed in my pocket, snapping me out of my thoughts. I pulled it out, my heart jumping slightly when I saw Will's name on the screen.

Will: Hope the week is going well. Let me know if you need anything.

What did I need? That was the question I didn't have an answer for. I slipped my phone back into my pocket, unsure of what to say.

Later that evening, after James and Bebe were in bed and the house had settled into its usual quiet, I picked up my phone. Will's message still sat unread at the top of my screen. I opened it, staring at his words for longer than I should have before typing out a reply.

Natalie: Sorry, it's been busy with the kids leading up to Thanksgiving. Hope you're having a good week.

I hit send and set the phone aside, expecting to feel lighter. But when no response came before I turned in for the night, a strange unease settled in my chest.

The next morning, I woke up and instinctively reached for my phone. Still no message from Will. My stomach twisted slightly, but I forced myself to push the thought aside. There wasn't time to dwell on it.

James was tearing through the house, looking for his missing shoe, while Bebe stood in front of the mirror, twisting a strand of her hair.

"It's fine, Bebe," I said, trying to coax her out of her perfectionist spiral.

"It's not fine!" she protested, stamping her foot. "It's not perfect enough!"

Meanwhile, James raced into the kitchen, triumphantly holding up the offending shoe. "Found it!"

"Great. Now both of you, backpacks and shoes—now," I said, glancing at the clock. "We're going to be late."

By the time we made it out the door and through the school drop-off line, I felt like I'd already run a marathon.

When I got back home, the quiet was almost jarring. For a moment, I stood in the entryway, letting the stillness settle over me. Then I headed to the kitchen to prepare for Lisa's visit.

I set a vase of hydrangeas on the table, carefully fluffing the blooms to make sure each one sat just right. With a potential client coming over, I wanted to look like I had my act together. As I adjusted the final stem, my phone buzzed on the counter.

I glanced at the screen. Will's name lit up.

Will: All good here. I get it.

I stared at the message for a moment, the tension in my chest easing slightly. His tone was casual, polite, nothing more. Was it a little too casual? I set the phone back down and focused on the flowers, deciding not to dwell on it.

The doorbell rang. I went to answer it, pushing Will's message to the back of my mind.

Lisa greeted me with a cheerful smile and her arms loaded with a tray of muffins and an assortment of pastries. "I figured you'd want to try a little bit of everything," she said as I held the door open for her.

"You're so thoughtful. This is too much, you didn't have to go through all this trouble," I said, guiding her into the kitchen.

"Of, course I did. These are my best sellers," she said, setting the tray down on the counter.

I poured coffee, and we started going over color pallets and ingredient sourcing for the bakery. Lisa's passion for her craft was compelling, and for a while, I forgot about the weight of the week.

But then she glanced at me, a curious smile playing on her lips. "So... I was at The City Center the other day meeting with Lori, and I ran into Will Parker."

My stomach tightened. "Oh?"

She nodded. "Nice guy. Very... composed."

"Yeah, he is," I said, keeping my voice even.

Lisa leaned forward, lowering her voice like she was about to share a secret. "What's his deal? I didn't see a ring on his finger. He seems... interesting."

"Interesting?" I repeated, trying to play it off.

"You know. Quiet, but you can tell there's something going on under the surface. He's the kind of guy who makes you curious."

I forced a smile, my mind racing. "He's definitely good at what he does."

Lisa tilted her head, studying me. "You work with him a lot, right?"

"Here and there," I said quickly, reaching for my coffee.

She nodded, mercifully dropping the subject as she turned back to the tray of muffins. But her words lingered. The casual way she'd spoken about Will only stirred my insecurities.

We discussed a few more design options for the bakery. Trying to stay focused and present, I spent an awfully long time talking about lemons and the merits of yellow and navy. By the time I had nothing more to give, and our meeting was winding down, Lisa gathered her purse and keys from the counter. I walked her to the door.

"Your home is lovely. I can already tell you will do an amazing job on the bakery."

"Thank you," I said. Even though my mind was searching for excuses to get out of this whole arrangement.

I couldn't shake her interest in Will. And her questions about him.

What was his deal? And why did I feel like I was further from knowing the answer than ever?

Chapter 24

The Space We Keep
Natalie

I couldn't shake the weird feeling creeping over me about Will. Maybe we were taking things too slow. Maybe too much space had grown, and he was tired of waiting for me to figure out what I wanted.

I tried focusing on work, wrapping up the last-minute details for the bakery, the boutique, and the restaurant. Lori had sent over information about another café moving in, asking Will and me to review the plans with the new tenants next week. As if I wasn't overwhelmed enough, Lucas's restaurant grand opening was set for a week after Thanksgiving. I'd need to arrange for our sitter to watch the kids that evening since it would be my week with them.

Between the deadlines and my swirling thoughts about Will, especially the possibility of him forming a connection with Lisa—I felt like I was sinking. Time got away from me, and when I checked the clock, I realized I had to rush to school pickup.

Driving there, my frustration bubbled up. It was like this unspoken stand-off, and now, Lisa's comments about him were adding fuel to the fire. I must be on the verge of getting my period. That, or I was just a walking disaster. A brownie suddenly felt like it might fix at least one of those problems.

When I pulled into the school parking lot, Will was already there, leaning casually against his car and typing something into his phone. He looked annoyingly perfect in a fitted black Vuori shirt and light gray denim. How could someone look that good just standing around?

Determined not to acknowledge him, I headed straight for the gate. Of course, he noticed me.

"Hey, Natalie! Wait up!" His voice trailed behind me.

I kept walking. Childish? Absolutely. But I was in no mood to talk to him.

He caught up anyway. "Whoa, what's going on? Are you okay?"

I stopped and turned to face him. "I don't know," I said sharply. "I had an interesting meeting with Lisa."

"Oh. Is everything still on target with the design plans?" He seemed genuinely puzzled.

"Yes, Will. She loves the design. Almost as much as she seems to like you."

"What?" His brows furrowed. "What are you talking about?"

"She mentioned your conversation," I snapped. "How you seem interesting and how something about you makes her curious."

"I have only talked business with her," he said, clearly taken aback. "Are you pissed at me?"

"I've barely heard from you all week, and then she shows up at my house with a mountain of pastries and a story about how you caught her attention."

"I was just giving you space. I thought you were busy with the kids and work."

"I am busy," I shot back.

I spotted Camille standing at the gate, chatting with Lauren. "If you'll excuse me, I'm going to talk to my friends."

Without waiting for a response, I walked away, leaving him standing there.

Camille didn't miss a beat when I approached. "What's up, love? You look like you're ready to bite someone's head off."

"Just a bad day," I muttered.

"Come over after school," she said. "Lauren, you too. We can vent and drink wine."

"I guess we could do that," I replied. "Thanks, Camille."

The children soon poured out of the gate. Bebe came running, hand in hand with Ivy. "Mommy, I'm going to Ivy's this weekend!" she declared excitedly. "Charlie can't come, though. Her dad is playing football."

This was news to me. "We'll see, girls," I said, not wanting to commit to plans I didn't know about.

Will walked over to us. "Hey, kiddo," he said to Ivy. "We've got to get going."

Ivy turned to him. "Daddy, please tell Miss Natalie about our playdate."

Will rubbed the back of his neck. "Ivy wants Bebe to come over," he said. "I don't know what your plans for break are."

"Sorry, Ivy," I said gently. "Bebe will be with her dad all week. I can give your dad his information if you want to set something up."

Ivy pouted but nodded. "I'm going to my mom's tomorrow," she said. "But Bebe can come to either house. Please, Miss Natalie?"

I gave Will a glance, trying to act like we were just two parents coordinating schedules. "I'll share Bebe's dad's info," I said. "But we have to go. Say goodbye, Bebe."

The girls hugged tightly before we left, Ivy waving as we walked away.

As I drove home, frustration settled back in. Now I was mad at myself for how I'd acted. I also wondered what Will would do over break if his children were with Kelly. The only time we seemed to thrive was when we were alone.

I grabbed Lisa's pastries to bring to Camille's. Lauren and Charlie were already there when I arrived, and I set the treats out for the kids, knowing full well Camille and Lauren wouldn't touch them.

I told them everything, about Lisa, about Will, and about my own emotional mess.

"What a bitch," Camille said, referring to Lisa. "Who brings over muffins and starts talking about their crush?"

"She's trying to make you fat," Lauren added with a smirk, and we all burst out laughing.

Eventually, we moved on to other topics. Lauren invited Meredith and me to a Chargers game on Sunday. "We have great seats," she said. "You should come."

"That's so nice," I said. "I'll check with Meredith."

"Also, girls' night on Saturday?" Camille suggested. "Should we go out or stay in?"

"Anything but Bourbon House," I said, referring to the trouble-inducing restaurant.

The laughter that followed eased some of my tension.

Later, when I checked my phone, I noticed a text from Will.

Will: Call me when you can.

Embarrassment bubbled up. I'd been unnecessarily harsh earlier, and now I didn't know how to respond. After getting the kids home, feeding them dinner, and surviving the bedtime routine, I debated whether to call him. Instead, I opted for a text:

Natalie: Hey, are you around?

Will: Give me a few. Wrapping up with the kids.

An hour later, just as I was dozing off, my phone buzzed.

"Hey," I answered groggily.

"Did I wake you?" Will's voice was soft.

"No. I'm sorry about today."

"I'm sorry, too," he said. "I let too much time go by. Things have been hectic here, too. We just need to be patient with each other, okay? And for the record, I'm not interested in Lisa. I'm only interested in you, Natalie. I told you I was willing to give you space and wait for you to figure this out and I will. I want you."

His words melted my frustration. "Okay," I said quietly.

"As Ivy told you today, the kids will be with Kelly for Thanksgiving, Friday to Friday," he added.

"We're almost on the same schedule," I said with a soft laugh. "My kids are with Jason Saturday to Saturday."

"Your first Thanksgiving without the kids," he noted. "Are you okay?"

"I don't know," I admitted. "Meredith is coming, so I'm grateful for that."

"Well, if you can sneak away for a night, let me know. Or I'll come there."

"I would like that."

"We will figure this out...us." Will said with a calm tone that reassured me.

"Okay. Goodnight, Will."

"Goodnight, Natalie."

Relief washed over me, and I drifted into a peaceful sleep.

Chapter 25

When Someone Else Steps In

Natalie

Friday morning arrived too quickly, and my to-do list was already mocking me before I even got out of bed. Thanksgiving break was looming, I needed to pack lunches, make breakfast, pack their clothes and special items they would want to bring, and my head was spinning with all the tasks waiting for me at work. On top of everything, I had agreed to meet Jason today.

I shuffled into the kitchen, tossing apples into lunchboxes while mentally running through my checklist. I needed to squeeze in a workout to clear my head— and to work off Lisa's muffins. I hated how good they were, and they had come in handy to serve the kids this morning. Small victories, I thought grimly.

After school drop-off, I hurried home, threw on workout clothes, and hopped on the Peloton for a quick session. It helped, a little. By the time I'd showered and changed, I felt marginally more prepared to face whatever Jason had planned for this meeting.

The coffeehouse Jason picked was on the corner of a busy street, making parking a challenge. I finally found a spot. He was already seated when I arrived, a latte waiting for me.

"Hi," I said, a little out of breath.

"I took the liberty of ordering for you," Jason said, gesturing to the cup in front of him.

"Thanks." I took a sip, the warm foam settling some of my nerves.

"So, what's going on? I know we haven't gotten past the New Year for the kids' schedules," I began, pulling out my planner. "I thought we could get a few months mapped out. Of course, we can adjust if needed."

"That's not why I asked you to meet," Jason said, his tone unusually serious.

"Oh?" I looked up from my planner, taken aback. "What's on your mind?"

"I met someone."

The words hit me like a punch. I blinked, unsure of how to respond. Jason was tall, dark, and handsome—of course, someone would want to snatch him up. But I hadn't expected it to happen so soon.

"It's getting serious," he continued. "I want the kids to meet her on Thanksgiving."

I swallowed hard, trying to keep my composure. Meeting Bebe and James felt monumental, an explosion I hadn't been prepared for. When Jason and I were coming to the end, I remember the paralyzing fear of picturing a stepmother to my children. That fear had almost kept me in a lifeless marriage.

"Nat?" Jason's hand brushed mine, and I instinctively pulled back.

"I don't know what to say. I'm... surprised," I admitted.

"I know it's a big ask, but I think the kids will like her. I think you'll approve, too. She wants to meet you, as well."

I let out a bitter laugh. "When did you meet her?"

"In July. We work out at the same gym."

Of course. How cliché.

"Her name is Brooke," he added. "She works in marketing."

"Does she have kids?"

"No, she doesn't. She's never been married, either. She just turned thirty-one in September."

Young, I thought. *She'll probably want children of her own, and Bebe and James will no longer be Jason's shining stars.*

A lump formed in my throat. This is my fault, I thought bitterly. If only I could have gotten past the kiss he shared with his colleague, Shannon, while we were married. If I hadn't been so wrapped up in my own needs to see how far we had drifted.

Jason must have sensed my emotions spiraling. "Natalie, I didn't mean to hurt you. Honestly, I figured by now we'd both have found happiness with other people."

I was jolted by Jason's comment. He'd already found someone new, serious enough to call happiness? The thought left me raw. I wiped at my eyes, embarrassed by the tears forming.

"If she makes you happy and is a good person, then... okay. The kids can meet her," I said, my voice thin with reluctance.

Jason put his hand on mine. "I didn't think I'd ever find someone after you. You're one of a kind and I took you for granted. You deserve the world."

It was probably the sincerest thing Jason had ever said to me. This Brooke woman had clearly unlocked a version of him I'd never seen before.

"I should go," I said, standing abruptly.

"I'll be by around ten tomorrow to pick up Bebe and James. Thanks for meeting me today—and for being cool about all this."

I nodded, forcing a smile as I walked out. But when I got to my car, the tears came in waves. My children could possibly have a stepmother. The thought terrified me. I had been so afraid of becoming one myself, and now it was happening on the other side.

I spent the rest of the afternoon trying to snap out of my funk. There was too much to do, work deadlines, packing the kids' bags for the week, and getting ready for Meredith's arrival that evening.

By the time I arrived at school pickup, I felt a little more composed. I parked early, hoping to find a moment to call Will. I dialed his number, but it went straight to voicemail.

Bebe and James burst out of the school gate, racing toward me with their usual energy. As we drove home, my phone buzzed with an incoming call. It was Will. I glanced at the screen, hesitating.

Bebe caught sight of his name on my screen in the car. "Mommy, why didn't you answer? That's Ivy's dad, right? He probably wants to plan our playdate!"

"I'll call him later, sweetie. We'll set something up soon."

"Promise?"

"Yes, Bebe."

When we got home, I saw a text from Meredith.

Meredith: Just landed. Be there soon!

Forty-five minutes later, the door swung open, and the kids raced to greet her.

"Aunt Meredith!" they shouted in unison.

"How are my favorite people?" Meredith said, scooping them into a hug.

After settling her things in the guest room, she unveiled a collection of small gifts for Bebe and James to squeals of delight. Their joy was infectious, giving me a brief reprieve from the weight on my chest.

I threw together an easy pasta dish for dinner, comfort food for the soul. Afterward, Meredith offered to do the dishes while I went upstairs to start baths and the bedtime routine for the kiddos.

Bebe clung to me as I kissed her goodnight. "I'm going to miss you so much, Mommy."

"I'll miss you too, sweetheart," I said, my heart aching.

I left Bebe's room, and went into James's. He looked at me curiously as I tucked him in. "Why aren't you coming to Thanksgiving, Mommy? I can ask Dad to save you and Aunt Meredith a seat."

Bile rose in my throat. He had no idea about Brooke, no idea that his dad was introducing someone new to their world. The thought of how it might all play out left me nauseous.

"That's sweet of you, James," I said softly. "But Thanksgiving is Daddy's special day with you and Bebe this year."

"Okay," he said, though his face fell. "I think Daddy still thinks you're really pretty. You could come if you want."

If only it were that simple. "Goodnight, James," I whispered, kissing his forehead before retreating to the bathroom, where I promptly threw up. My body was rebelling against the weight of the day, Jason's news, the idea of Brooke, and the thought of my babies meeting her.

Meredith was waiting in the kitchen with a glass of wine and a neatly rolled joint. "Rough day?" she asked, gesturing to the seat across from her.

I sat down, grateful for her presence. "I met Jason this morning."

"And?" Meredith raised a brow. "Please don't tell me he wants to get back together with you."

"No," I said, letting out a hollow laugh. "He met someone. It's serious. He wants Bebe and James to meet her—on Thanksgiving."

Meredith's mouth dropped open. "Shut the front door. Are you serious?"

I nodded, my eyes welling up again. "I'm having a hard time wrapping my head around it. I haven't even had time to process it."

"Of course, you're emotional, Nat. Anyone would be."

"This person could be their stepmother," I said, my voice cracking. "She's going to be their Veronica."

"I think Jason has better taste than Dad did," Meredith said dryly. "Have you told Will?"

"We've been playing phone tag. I was going to tell him, which feels big for me, to share something like this with him. But I know he's been through this with Kelly."

Meredith leaned forward, her tone firm. "You should call him, Nat. Let him in. Let him be there for you."

I hesitated, then let out a deep breath. "Let's smoke first. I need to relax."

"Deal," Meredith said, grabbing the joint and leading me to the patio.

Later that night, after the haze of the evening had cleared and Meredith had gone to bed, I sat with my phone in hand. The events of the day were still swirling in my mind: Jason's unexpected sincerity, Brooke's looming introduction, James's sweet innocence, and the undeniable truth that this was the new normal.

Taking a deep breath, I dialed Will's number. This time, he answered.

"Hey," he said, his voice warm but a little hesitant. He sounded like he was asleep.

"Hey," I replied, my voice shaking slightly. "Did I wake you?"

"What's going on?" he asked.

"I met Jason today," I said, pausing for a moment. "He's... met someone. It's serious. The kids are meeting her on Thanksgiving."

Will was silent for a beat. "How are you feeling about that?"

"It's tearing me up inside," I admitted. "I know it's irrational, but the thought of someone else being in their lives, being part of their milestones—it's hard."

"It's not irrational," Will said gently. "It's normal to feel that way. I've been there. When Kelly introduced Jeff to the kids, it felt like the ground shifted beneath me."

His words were comforting in a way I hadn't expected. He understood. He wasn't just saying the right thing, *he knew.*

"What if they like her more than me?" I whispered.

"You're kidding," Will said. "You're their mom. No one can take your place."

I nodded, even though he couldn't see me, and let his words sink in. "Thank you," I said softly.

"For what?"

"For picking up when I called. For understanding."

"Always," he said. "If you need me tomorrow, call. Anytime. I miss you."

"I miss you, too."

I hung up feeling a little lighter. Jason's world might be changing, but mine didn't have to collapse. I still had my kids. And maybe, just maybe, I had someone who truly cared about me too.

Chapter 26

Start Me Up

Will

After Natalie's emotional week, I felt like she was finally opening up to me. Seeing her mad at me for the first time, with her little fury bubbling at school, was strangely adorable. She looked so damn cute; she didn't even realize it—but I did. And I was falling for her even harder.

When she shared about Jason meeting someone new I felt grateful. It was a big step for her, and selfishly, I couldn't help but wonder if this would nudge her toward letting herself move on.

The past few years taught me a lot about marriages—what works, what doesn't, and what I could have done differently. I wasn't an expert, but I knew one thing: with Natalie, I had to be patient. She was going through it.

By Saturday, I wrapped up work to clear my plate before the holiday mayhem. Lori had been hounding me about paperwork, and I made sure every detail was finished so she couldn't breathe down my neck next week.

That evening, I had dinner plans with my sister Sarah, her boyfriend Todd, and Evan at a classic Newport spot, A's Restaurant. Tomorrow, Evan and I would settle in for a full day of football and beers, but tonight, I was cutting loose. No kids. No responsibilities. I decided to Uber so I could let go properly and nurse the hangover guilt-free in the morning.

Dinner was filled with laughter. Evan kept us roaring all night, and Todd fit in like he'd been a part of the family for years. Toward the end of the meal, Sarah excused herself to the restroom, and Todd cleared his throat.

"Since we have a moment here," he began nervously, "I wanted to ask for your permission to propose to Sarah."

For a moment, I was stunned. Then I stood, hugged him, and said, "Todd, I didn't think anyone would ever come close to being good enough for Sarah, but turns out you are."

Todd's eyes welled up, and Evan, for once, didn't make a joke. He slapped Todd on the back and said, "Sarah is like a sister to me. I know you will take good care of her."

"You have our approval," I added. "But have you talked to the big guy yet?"

"I did," Todd said, looking relieved.

Sarah returned just as we were regaining our composure. "Was someone crying here?" she asked, eyeing us suspiciously.

We laughed it off. I suggested a nightcap at Lido House, a bar nearby.

We played shuffleboard and kept the drinks flowing until Sarah finally announced, "Nothing good happens after midnight. We're calling it."

We waved them off and stayed a little longer, but Evan, unsurprisingly, was soon surrounded by a group of twenty-something women. While he worked the crowd, I decided to send Natalie a text.

Will: Hey babe, when can I see that big tee shirt again?

I half-hoped she'd had a few drinks and would invite me over. I knew her sister and friends were over.

Natalie: She'd love to wear her big tee shirt for you. Come over and bring your hot friend.

I laughed, shaking my head, knowing this was Meredith. I nudged Evan. "We're heading to Natalie's."

"All those women are married," Evan said, narrowing his eyes. "I'm not messing with Derek Hartman's wife. That guy's huge." Lauren's husband was, indeed, a huge guy.

"Natalie's sister is single," I replied casually.

Evan's interest piqued. "Does she look like Natalie?"

I shot Evan a warning look.

"She's definitely your type," I said with a grin.

"You owe me," Evan muttered.

"I don't think you will think that when you see her, she blows all these women out of the water. Just saying."

I texted Natalie's number back, (knowing it was Meredith on the other end) confirming we were on our way, and ushered Evan out as soon as our Uber arrived.

On the ride down PCH, I connected my phone to the car's Bluetooth and blasted The Rolling Stones. Evan and I sang along to "You make a grown man cry."

When we arrived, we could hear music and laughter from the driveway. Meredith greeted us at the door, grinning. "Will and his hot friend are here!" she announced, earning cheers from Camille and Lauren.

Natalie appeared, slightly flushed from the wine, and gave me a warm smile. "Hi! Come in, come in!"

"This is Meredith, my sister," she said, gesturing to Evan. "And you remember Lauren and Camille."

"Hello, ladies," Evan said with a grin.

Stopping for a beat, he locked eyes with Meredith and shook her hand for a second too long.

The house was alive with energy. Liquor bottles and snacks covered the table, and the smell of something distinctly herbal wafted from the back patio. I spotted Evan making a beeline with Meredith, who handed him a drink and led him outside, presumably to light a joint.

"Wow, you've got quite the party going," I said to Natalie, leaning closer.

"It's been a long week," she admitted, her cheeks rosy.

Lauren announced her Uber's arrival, lamenting, "Gameday tomorrow. I need to be functional." Camille followed, laughing. "Can I get a lift, neighbour?"

I walked them to the car and talked to the driver. "Can you drop this lovely young lady a couple doors down first—and please, get them home safe." I slipped the driver a fifty.

"Thanks, man," he said with a nod. "You're racking up some good karma tonight."

I said goodbye to Natalie's friends and waved as they pulled away, giving the top of the car a quick tap before it rolled off.

When I returned, Natalie and Meredith were belting out "Dancing Queen" at full volume. Evan handed me another drink and whispered, "Meredith's cool as hell and very cute."

I gave a half shrug, I didn't need to say more. I knew his type. Pretty. Complicated. Confident. The kind that gets under your skin before you even realize it.

We ended up sitting around the living room, swapping childhood stories and laughing until we cried. At some point, I checked my watch, it was nearly 3 a.m.

"I'm pooped," Meredith announced. "It's 6 a.m. my time. I need one more hit to knock me into a slumber."

"I'll come with you," Evan said, trailing after her with a mischievous grin.

Natalie turned to me, her eyes soft. "Let's go to bed," she said quietly.

I followed her upstairs, where her room felt warm and inviting, just like her. She disappeared into the bathroom, and when she returned, she was in a big tee shirt and shorts, looking naturally radiant.

She climbed onto my lap, her movements slow and deliberate, her lips finding mine in a soft, teasing kiss. It started gently, but the heat between us quickly grew, her mouth moving to my jawline and trailing down to my neck. I felt her breath against my ear as her teeth grazed the sensitive skin there, sending a shiver down my spine.

My hands slid under her shirt, fingertips skimming the soft curve of her back as I pulled her closer to me. The way she moved against me had me gripping her tighter, my self-control already slipping.

The tee shirt was the first thing to go, her skin warm and smooth beneath my hands. I kissed along her collarbone, taking my time, but she tugged at the hem of my shirt in frustration, pulling it over my head and tossing it aside.

When her hands moved to unbuckle my pants, freeing me completely, as she continued to remove them fully. She was a vision, straddling me in nothing but her shorts, her hair falling in soft waves around her face. I couldn't hold back the low groan that escaped my lips.

I slid my hands down her sides, hooking my thumbs into the waistband of her shorts and easing them down, revealing more of her skin, inch by inch. She didn't hesitate, leaning into me and grinding against me with a deliberate intensity that made me grip her hips tightly, anchoring her to me.

When she positioned herself and moved onto me, I couldn't stop the guttural sound that escaped my throat. The fullness and heat of her wrapped around me was almost overwhelming. She gasped, her hands bracing on my shoulders as we found a rhythm, every movement perfectly in sync.

Her body moved fluidly against mine, her breaths quick and shallow as I guided her hips. I tilted my head back, savoring the way her body felt pressed so tightly to mine, the way she was utterly lost in the moment with me.

She leaned forward, her lips capturing mine again, her kisses wild and hungry now, her nails raking lightly across my chest. I held her closer, our movements quickening as the pressure built, spiraling higher and higher until it became impossible to hold on.

When we finally came, it was together. Her body tensed, and a soft cry escaped her lips as she collapsed against me, her head resting on my shoulder. I tightened my arms around her, pressing a kiss to her temple as we both struggled to catch our breath.

I kissed her tenderly, running my fingers through her hair, and gently shifted, laying her down on the bed. She gazed up at me with a soft smile, and I couldn't help but brush a stray strand of hair from her face. For a moment, we stayed like that, entwined in each other, savoring the afterglow of the moment.

As we drifted off, curled up in each other, I felt at home.

Chapter 27

Tumbling Dice

Natalie

I woke up to the soft glow of morning light filtering through the curtains and the comforting warmth of Will's body next to mine. His arm was draped over my waist, and I could feel his slow, steady breathing against my shoulder. For a moment, everything felt easy, like this was exactly where we were meant to be.

"You awake?" he murmured, his voice still heavy with sleep.

"Barely," I whispered, turning my head to meet his eyes.

He smiled lazily, brushing a strand of hair from my face. "You look beautiful in the morning."

"Liar," I teased, laughing softly.

Will leaned in, pressing a kiss to my temple. "Not lying," he said.

"I shouldn't have had that much alcohol before going to this football game." I said reluctantly. "Meredith's probably already making coffee and judging me."

"Fair assessment," Will joked, pulling me closer for one more kiss.

By the time Meredith barged into my room, Will was already dressed and sitting on the edge of the bed, tying his shoes.

"Good morning, lovebirds," she said, her tone teasing. "Natalie, you're late for our hangover recovery session. And Will, thanks for keeping my sister company."

Will chuckled and glanced at me. "I think she is trying to kick me out."

When I came downstairs, I noticed Evan already out on the front porch, waiting for Will.

After a quick kiss goodbye, I made my way to the kitchen, where Meredith was pouring coffee, glowing and trying not to smile too hard.

"Why do you look so smug this morning?" I asked, eyeing her suspiciously.

"Oh, no reason," she said with an innocent grin. "Just had a great night, that's all."

I raised an eyebrow. "This doesn't have anything to do with Evan, does it?"

Her grin widened, and she took a long sip of coffee. "No comment."

"Meredith!" I groaned. "Did you two—?"

"We just talked. It was fun."

"Oh, my God. I don't believe you. You just talked?"

"Maybe there was some cuddling," she shrugged.

"Wow," I said. "You must like him. You don't cuddle."

"It's nothing serious. But..." she gave me a wink, "It was a good spoon session."

She grabbed her Chargers jersey and said, "Now, hurry up, we have a game to catch."

The pretzel and soda that Meredith plied me with at the stadium – "Carbs and caffeine are my cure all" – did make me feel a bit more human. On our way to the game I'd longed for my couch. Although I was exhausted the energy of the crowd was contagious and I was so glad we'd taken Lauren up on the tickets.

The following day, we gave into the laziness we felt and treated ourselves to a day at the Montage. The ocean view was breathtaking, and the spa treatment Meredith insisted on booking felt like the peace and serenity I needed.

"You know," Meredith said, stretching out on the lounge chair, "I can see why Evan's such a hit. He's funny, charming, and way too cute for his own good. Kind of annoying, actually."

She never talked about guys since she dated Marcus, a colleague of Jason's. She swore off men forever after him.

"I thought he was just for fun," I said, laughing.

"He is..."

I bit back a grin.

Meredith adjusted her sunglasses and let out a contented sigh. "This place is heavenly," she said, taking a slow sip of her iced tea.

"It is," I agreed, though my thoughts drifted far from the view.

She caught my expression and raised an eyebrow. "Okay, spill. You've been zoning out since we got here."

I hesitated, swirling the straw in my drink. "I've been thinking about Thanksgiving."

"What about it?"

"Lucas's invitation," I said carefully. "I don't know if we should go."

Meredith sat up, sliding her sunglasses onto her head. "Why not? You said it'd be a good networking opportunity."

"It is," I admitted, "but it feels... wrong. Will and I are finally in a good place, and this feels like I'm throwing a wrench into everything."

"Nat, you're overthinking," Meredith said, leaning back again. "Will isn't going to hold it against you. And if he does, that's on him."

"I just don't want to ruin things," I murmured.

Meredith reached over to squeeze my hand. "You're not ruining anything. Besides, it's not like you're going to Lucas's to profess your undying love. You're going for work, and for me, because I want to eat whatever amazing food that chef Jasper is making."

I smiled reluctantly. "You've got a point."

Meredith grinned. "Of course I do. And who knows? Maybe this chef will be cute enough to distract me for the evening."

"He is very cute and has an accent," I said.

Meredith's eyes lit up. "I forgot he's from Europe. Now you must go to this Thanksgiving for me."

"Wait, what about Evan?" I teased.

"I can shop around," Meredith said, while looking at her manicure.

We both laughed, and I felt more relaxed, letting the bliss of the day take us away.

That evening after we were home and watching an episode of, "Friends," on the couch having the most relaxing day ever.

I heard my phone buzz near me, it was Will, I loved seeing his name.

Will: Hi babe, how was The Montage? Do you and your sister want to come over for dinner tomorrow? Evan will be here as well.

I loved that he was referring to me as babe. It felt like girlfriend material. I forgot how to date but, this sure felt like it.

"Mer, want to go to Will's tomorrow night? Evan will be there," I said teasingly.

"We can make time for that, "she said with a sly smile.

The next evening, we headed over to Will's for dinner and were greeted at the door by Evan, and a sleek brown lab.

"Who is this?" I asked, kneeling to pet him.

"This is Bear. He loves the ladies," Evan said with a grin.

"I bet he does! And I love him," I cooed, switching to a baby voice as I scratched behind Bear's ears.

Inside, the house smelled incredible. Will was in the kitchen, working on steaks, roasted potatoes, and a fresh salad.

"I didn't know you were so domesticated, William," Meredith teased, leaning on the counter.

"When I became a bachelor, I had to learn a few things," he replied, smirking. "Cereal and takeout every night gets old fast. Now, what can I get you ladies to drink?"

I loved how thoughtful he was—not just with me, but with my sister and friends too. He had this way of making everyone feel comfortable and taken care of.

"I'll take a glass of whatever you've already opened," I said.

Meredith grinned mischievously. "I'm going to need something stronger."

Evan jumped in, clearly eager to impress. "I can make an old fashioned, a dirty martini, margarita—whatever you like."

"I'll take a dirty martini. Extra dirty," Meredith said with a playful tone that made Evan stand a little straighter.

She had an effect on men—gorgeous and confident, she radiated charisma. It was impossible not to notice.

Dinner was lovely, filled with laughter and stories, the kind of evening where everything felt easy. Will seemed relaxed, smiling at me across the table, and I felt that same pull I always did when he looked at me like that.

By the time we moved to the couch for a nightcap, the Rolling Stones were playing softly in the background, and Bear had claimed a spot between Meredith and Evan.

"So," Will said casually, "what are you two doing for Thanksgiving?"

The question hit like a jolt, but before I could answer, Meredith jumped in. "Something with one of Natalie's clients. It's just a casual thing—nothing fancy."

Will's gaze shifted to me, his smile fading slightly. "Which client?"

"Lucas and Jasper," I admitted, feeling the weight of the words.

Meredith jumped back in, trying to soften the blow. "We didn't have any other offers, so we're really just going for the food." She grinned. "Chefs' tables are hard to pass up, you know?"

Will's jaw tightened, and the easy energy of the evening vanished.

"That's...nice," he said, his tone neutral but clipped.

Meredith, sensing the tension, quickly turned to Evan. "So, what about you guys? Any exciting plans?"

Evan shrugged. "We go to Will's parents' place."

"Should we crash?" Meredith joked, trying to lighten the mood.

Evan chuckled, but Will stayed silent, his gaze fixed on the drink in his hand.

I felt the knot in my stomach tighten. I knew exactly what was the problem.

Will's phone buzzed, cutting through the silence. He glanced at the screen and sighed. "Excuse me," he said, standing and walking into the next room.

Evan stood up, breaking the silence. "Can I freshen anyone's drinks?"

"Yes, I would love another," Meredith said.

"Sure, thanks Evan," I said.

I turned to Meredith, who raised an eyebrow. "That was tense," she whispered.

"It's my fault," I admitted quietly.

When Will returned, his expression was hard. "It's Madison," he said tightly. "She got caught drinking at a party. The police were called."

"Oh no," I said, standing instinctively. "Is she okay?"

"She's fine, but I need to deal with this," he said, already reaching for his keys.

"Thanks for dinner," Meredith said quickly, sensing his urgency.

I followed Will to the mudroom, my heart sinking. "Will, I'm so sorry," I said softly. "About Madison, and about... everything. Please let me know if there's anything I can do."

He turned to me, his gaze sharp. "You can't fix this, Natalie. You don't want this part of my life, and it feels like you don't even know what part you *do* want."

His words cut deeply, and before I could respond, he was gone.

Back in the living room, Meredith gave me a look. "That didn't go well."

Evan stood and walked us to the door. "Sorry about the buzzkill," he said.

Before we stepped outside, Evan turned to me, his expression serious. "Natalie, Will really cares about you. Please don't hurt him."

The words stung, and I couldn't bring myself to reply.

As we drove away, the weight of the evening settled over me like a heavy cloud. I felt like I had no idea how to fix what felt so close to being right.

Why did it keep going wrong?

Chapter 28

A Slice Of Truth

Natalie

It was Thanksgiving morning, and I woke up in knots, guilt tangling itself around me like the sheets I couldn't escape. The way Will and I left things made my heart hurt, like an open wound I couldn't tend to. On top of that, today was the day my children were meeting Brooke—the possible "other woman" in their lives who might someday have the word mom attached to her name.

The thought of it made my stomach twist painfully. I barely managed to sit on the edge of the bed, breathing deeply to keep from spiraling. My chest felt tight, my emotions threatening to overflow.

After rinsing my mouth and splashing cold water on my face, I stepped into the shower, letting the hot water pound against my shoulders. The steam wrapped around me, and for a moment, I let myself believe it might loosen the tightness in my chest. But no matter how long I stood there, the heaviness remained, weighing me down like the water pooling at my feet.

I toweled off slowly, dragging myself back to my bedroom. As I sat on the edge of the bed, I grabbed my phone from the nightstand, unable to resist checking for a message from Will. Still nothing. We hadn't spoken since I left his house, and the silence stung more than I wanted to admit.

When I finally opened my bedroom door, the smell of coffee and eggs greeted me, along with Meredith's upbeat voice from downstairs.

"Morning, sunshine," she said as I stepped into the kitchen. "I made you a very strong coffee and a protein breakfast. You're welcome."

"Thanks, Mer." My gratitude was genuine, even if my voice came out tinged with sorrow. "I think we should cancel today," I said quietly, sitting at the counter. "I feel guilty."

Meredith turned to me, her expression both stern and soft. "We will not. You promised me British accents and a chef-prepared meal. Will is being a jealous baby, and that's on him."

"It's not just Will," I admitted, rubbing my temples. "It's the fact that today my children are meeting *her*."

Meredith reached out and squeezed my hand. "I know, sweetie, but you need a distraction. Will is going to come around, and no one can take your place—not even if Jason marries this Brooke girl."

"Please don't say the word 'marriage,'" I groaned. "I can only handle so much in one day."

"All right, fine. But first, we need to tackle the pie," Meredith said, planting her hands on her hips with a determined smile.

I raised an eyebrow. "You do realize that 'we' includes you, right? And I've seen your attempts at baking."

"Rude," she shot back, already rummaging through the pantry. "I've watched 'The Great British Bake Off'. How hard can it be?"

We spent the next hour proving just how hard it could be. Normally, I could follow a recipe well enough to produce something decent, but my head wasn't in it today. Meredith, for all her confidence, wasn't much of a chef either. Flour dusted the counters, sticky filling splattered onto the floor, and at one point, she managed to crack an egg directly onto the stovetop burner.

"Why is it so... gooey?" she asked, holding up her egg-covered hand like it was evidence in a crime scene.

"It's an egg," I said, biting back a laugh.

"Well, I don't like it," she declared, grabbing a paper towel.

"Maybe we should just forget the pie," I said, dropping the spoon into the sticky dough with a sigh. "We'll grab something from the store on the way."

Meredith gasped dramatically, clutching her chest like I'd insulted her entire persona. "Natalie Bradford, you take that back right now."

"I'm serious," I said, waving at the mess on the counter. "This isn't a pie—it's a crime scene."

She shook her head, picking up the dough like it wasn't falling apart in her hands. "Nope. We're too far in to back out now. Look at this masterpiece."

"Masterpiece?" I raised an eyebrow. "It's barely dough. And is that... eggshell in there?"

Meredith shrugged. "Protein."

I couldn't help but laugh. "You're ridiculous."

"That's why you love me," she said, tossing a pinch of flour in my direction. "Now stop being a quitter and roll this thing out like the domestic goddess I know you are deep down."

"I hate you a little bit right now," I muttered, picking up the rolling pin.

"No, you don't," she said cheerfully. "You just hate making pies. But don't worry—I'll take all the credit if it turns out amazing."

"And if it doesn't?"

"Oh, that's easy. I'll blame you."

We burst into laughter, clutching our sides as tears pricked at the corners of my eyes. For a moment, the tension lifted, and I could breathe again.

When the pie was finally in the oven, we stood back to admire our questionable creation.

"Do you think it's edible?" she asked.

"I think we should bring wine, just in case," I said.

"Always a good plan," Meredith agreed, grabbing a rag to wipe the counters. "Now, go upstairs and find something fabulous to wear. You can't mope in sweatpants, Nat. Not today."

"Fabulous is asking a lot," I said, dragging myself toward the stairs.

"Fine," she called after me. "Wear something mediocre, but make it work!"

I stood in my closet, staring at rows of clothes that didn't feel right. All I wanted to wear were sweats. Finally, I settled on a black sweater, a plaid skort, and thigh-high black boots. I added some makeup, hoping it would mask the exhaustion etched into my face.

When I came back downstairs, Meredith was already waiting, dressed in a silky blouse and vegan leather leggings that made her legs look miles long. She'd paired the outfit with black Valentino booties, effortlessly chic as always.

"You look great," she said, giving me an approving once-over.

"I'm not wearing my fat pants today, so I guess that's an upgrade. You look incredible," I said, smirking. "That chef's going to want to eat you up."

She gave a casual shrug, getting dressed to impress was second nature to Meredith.

The soft ping-ping sound of a Facetime call came through, with Jason's name lighting up the screen. It had to be James and Bebe.

I slid *Accept* and brought the phone up, angling it toward my face.

"Mommy! Happy Thanksgiving!" James's face filled the screen, his grin wide and bright. "We're making food with Nona!"

"That sounds wonderful," I said, smiling despite the ache in my chest. "I miss you so much."

"I miss you more," James replied, his little voice sounding so sweet.

Bebe appeared next, bounding into the frame in the sweater and skirt I'd picked out for her. "Hi, Mommy! Look at my earrings!" she said, showing off tiny Mickey Mouse studs. "We went to Disneyland yesterday, and Nona let us pick out something special!"

"They're beautiful," I said, my voice catching.

From somewhere off-screen, I heard my ex-mother-in-law's muffled voice, likely making a snide remark under her breath. I had ruined her perfect boy's picture-perfect life.

Before I could dwell on it, the doorbell buzzed on their end.

"Oh, Mommy! That's Daddy's special friend Brooke," Bebe announced excitedly.

My stomach dropped. Meredith, sensing my reaction, snatched the phone from my hand. "Hi, Bebe! We love you so much. Call us tomorrow, okay? Happy Thanksgiving!" she said brightly before ending the call.

I stared at her, stunned. "Mer—"

"That was too close," she said firmly. "I can't have you spiraling today."

"Thanks for looking out," I mumbled, still processing what had just happened.

"Come on," she said, grabbing the pie and handing me the wine. "We've got a Thanksgiving to attend."

Meredith drove us up into the hills, the road winding steeply as we approached Lucas' house. It was a refurbished 1970s home, modernized with sleek lines and large windows. When we walked up, Lucas greeted us at the door, looking nice in a charcoal gray sweater and light pants, his glasses adding a polished touch.

"Ah, here you are," he said in his smooth British accent, holding the door open. "Do come in to our very first American Thanksgiving."

The house smelled amazing, the aroma of rosemary, thyme, and roasted vegetables wafted from the kitchen. The dining room was beautifully set, with candles flickering and a centerpiece of fresh greenery.

"Would you like a drink?" Lucas asked, his voice smooth and welcoming. "Wine? Or perhaps something stronger?"

"I'll take wine," I said, offering a polite smile.

"What have you got that can handle that steep drive I just drove?" Meredith chimed in, grinning.

He handed me a glass and turned to Meredith. "You must be Meredith. I've heard quite a bit about you. Jasper's been in the kitchen all morning—do you cook?"

Meredith laughed. "Not too much, I'm here to eat and pretend I helped."

"Brilliant," Lucas replied with a grin. "That's the spirit."

Jasper soon appeared; his quiet demeanor paired with charm that made him seem naturally composed. He greeted us briefly, but his attention quickly shifted to Meredith. They exchanged smiles, and before I knew it, the two of them had disappeared into the kitchen.

Lucas stayed close by, engaging me in light conversation, but I found myself distracted. No matter how kind he was, I couldn't shake the sense that I didn't belong here.

"Lovely view, isn't it?" Lucas said, gesturing toward the massive windows overlooking Laguna Beach. "It's what sold me on the place, really. Quite something, don't you think?"

"It's beautiful," I said, my voice distant.

He turned to me, his expression softening. "You're beautiful," he said quietly.

The words hung in the air, but they didn't land the way he intended. Instead of flattery, they felt heavy, like a weight pressing against the ache already in my chest.

"Dinner's ready," Jasper called from the kitchen, his voice breaking the moment.

We sat down at the beautifully set table. The food smelled incredible—roasted turkey, a variety of colorful vegetables, and our half-assed attempt at apple pie. It was perfect, but all I could think about was how much I wished I weren't here.

Lucas sat across from me, raising his glass for a toast. "To good company and good food," he said, his gaze lingering on me for a moment longer than I was comfortable with.

I clinked my glass halfheartedly, plastering on a polite smile.

The conversation flowed easily between Meredith, Jasper and Lucas, while I chimed in now and then with a quiet *uh-huh* or *mm-hmm*. The wine was good, the food even better. But none of it touched that part of me I wanted to feel stirred.

And I couldn't help but notice who always managed to stir it.

I missed James and Bebe, too. Maybe that was part of it. I felt unanchored, like I'd drifted too far from myself.

Lucas was lovely, thoughtful, attentive, everything he was supposed to be. But I still felt like an observer at this dinner. Like I was smiling on cue, nodding along, and still waiting for it to feel real.

Across the table, Meredith had everyone laughing. I was glad she was having fun, but I couldn't stop my gut from feeling complete guilt for being here.

Lucas tried to draw me into the conversation a few times, but I barely noticed. By the time the plates were cleared, I was ready to disappear.

I excused myself from the table and wandered back into the living room, drawn once again to the massive windows overlooking the city. My thoughts churned relentlessly, circling back to Will, to the silence between us, to the way my heart tugged painfully in his direction even when he wasn't here.

Lucas joined me moments later, holding two glasses of wine. "For the lady," he said, handing me one with a small smile.

"Thanks," I said, accepting it but not drinking.

"You've been quiet tonight," he said, leaning casually against the window frame. "I hope it's not the company."

I forced a small laugh, trying to keep the mood light. "No, of course not. It's just been a long week. I'm not used to being apart from my children."

He studied me for a moment, his expression softening. "Well, I hope tonight helped distract you, even a little."

Before I could respond, Meredith came out to the living room. "Nat, can I talk to you for a second?"

Grateful for the escape, Lucas excused himself and slipped into the kitchen.

"What's going on?" she asked quietly.

"I think I need to leave," I said, keeping my voice low.

She raised an eyebrow. "Leave? Natalie, are you okay?"

"I'm fine," I said quickly. "I just... I need to go."

Her expression shifted from surprise to understanding. "To Will's?"

I nodded, my throat tightening. "I can't stay here pretending I don't know exactly where I need to be. I've made so many mistakes, and I need to fix this."

Meredith studied me for a long moment, then smiled. "Then go. What are you waiting for?"

"I don't want to leave you here alone," I said, glancing toward Jasper.

She waved me off. "I'm fine. Seriously. Jasper seems great."

Jasper was just walking over to the bar cart when he heard his name. He turned with a warm smile. "What can I do for you?"

"Would you be able to give me a ride home later? Natalie isn't feeling great. She is going to head out."

"Happy to," Jasper said, looking to me. "Don't worry about her."

"See?" Meredith said, nudging me toward the door. "Go. And Nat?"

"Yeah?"

"Don't overthink it. Just tell him how you feel."

I hugged her tightly. "Thank you."

"Always," she whispered. "Now go."

I walked over to Lucas. "I'm so sorry, but I'm having an off night. I need to go. And I'm sorry if I led you on—I'm just not in a place where I can... you know."

"I see," he said with a small nod. "I understand."

"Thank you for understanding. And thank you for inviting me. Sorry for ditching you with those two," I added, nodding toward the kitchen.

"I'm used to being the third wheel," he said with a self-depricating smile.

We hugged, and I slipped out the door into the cool night air, the breeze cutting through my sweater.

Sitting in the car, I stared down at my phone, my thumb hovering over the keyboard. Then I typed:

Natalie: Will, I was wrong. About so many things.

I hit send, my heart pounding as I started the car. I didn't know how this would go. But I knew I'd regret it if I didn't show up and say what I should've said a long time ago.

Chapter 29

A Seat at the Table
Will

After a long night dealing with Madison's drinking shenanigans, I was running on fumes. She hadn't been arrested, thank God, but the call from the homeowner's parents about the situation left me humiliated and angry. Madison's attitude afterward didn't help. She didn't seem to get that the fallout wasn't just about her. I didn't have the energy to dive into why her choices were chipping away at my ability to be patient. She was grounded—again. That much was clear. I drove her back to Kelly's house that night. Kelly was angry with her as well. At least we were on the same page, for once.

Two days later it was Thanksgiving morning, and I was still stewing over more than just Madison. Natalie had left things raw between us. She knew I wasn't okay with her Thanksgiving plans—going to his house.

Lucas.

I hated even saying his name. It was bad enough that she was spending the day with him, but she was also bringing her sister along. like it was some double date. Meanwhile, I'd be sitting at my parents' house trying not to think about her, about them.

I rolled out of bed, grumpy and restless. My house was too quiet without the kids. Holidays without them always felt like a void I couldn't fill.

I knew today would be hard for Natalie. She'd been upfront about how much she dreaded her kids meeting Jason's girlfriend. But with things weird between us, and with me still pissed about her spending Thanksgiving with Lucas—it felt impossible to reach out.

I decided to focus on surviving Thanksgiving at my parents' place. I picked up Evan on the way.

Evan slid into the passenger seat and buckled in, shooting me one of those side looks he was famous for. The kind that said he knew more than I wanted him to,

"You were pretty wound up the other night," he said casually.

I kept my eyes on the road. "Was I?"

"Yeah," His mouth curved, just a little. "Don't worry, I'm not going to press. Just saying, I know when something gets under your skin."

I didn't bother answering. Silence was safer than admitting he was right.

"How's Madison?" he asked, shifting the conversation.

"Grounded."

"Of course, she is," he said, smirking. "That one's a spitfire. Reminds me of me at her age."

I shot him a look. "Please don't say that. I'm trying to keep her from becoming you."

Evan laughed, unfazed. "Good luck with that."

By the time we arrived, my mother had the house set up like a photoshoot for "Martha Stewart Living." The dining table was arranged with an obscene amount of food, cheese platters, caviar, shrimp, the works. Naturally, she'd brought out the fine China.

Sarah was glowing. It took me a second to notice the massive rock on her left hand as she poured herself a glass of champagne. Todd hovered close to her, looking smug but trying not to seem smug.

"You didn't even wait for dinner to announce it?" Evan teased, pointing to the ring.

Sarah beamed. "He proposed this morning!"

"Oh, perfect timing," Evan said, winking at Todd.

"Todd, you picked a beautiful ring," my mother said, clasping her hands together. She turned to Sarah. "It's just perfect for you, sweetheart."

Todd nodded. "It's a family heirloom. I wanted it to be special."

The conversation spiraled into wedding talk—venues, dates, colors. I zoned out, sipping my whiskey as they gushed. It wasn't that I wasn't happy for Sarah. She deserved this. Todd was a good guy, steady and reliable, the exact kind of person she needed. But watching her happiness only reminded me of how far I was from it. A failed marriage, an affair. A girlfriend I just cheated on with the woman I can't seem to get out of my mind.

At dinner, my mom was in her element, assigning seats and orchestrating the meal like it was a royal banquet. I ended up next to Evan and my dad, who looked about as thrilled as I felt to be there.

"Will, don't you think Ivy would make the perfect flower girl for Sarah's wedding?" my mom asked midway through the meal.

It stung that the kids weren't here to celebrate Sarah's big news.

"She'd love that," I said, keeping my tone neutral.

Sarah lit up. "That would be so sweet. She'd look adorable."

"She'd steal the show," Todd added with a grin.

"I'll ask her when I see her next," Sarah said.

My mother sighed, as if on cue. "I just wish Kelly and the kids were here. Holidays aren't the same without them."

I clenched my jaw, setting my glass down carefully. "Mom, let's not make this about me for once," I said, forcing a smile. "Sarah just got engaged. Let's focus on that."

After dinner, we moved to the living room. Evan slipped into storyteller mode, tossing out quick jokes that had Sarah laughing so hard she had to wipe tears from her eyes. Todd sat beside her, holding her hand like he still couldn't believe his luck.

My dad chuckled, shaking his head at Evan. "You always know how to work a crowd."

Evan grinned, raising his glass. "Hey, somebody's got to keep the Parker family entertained."

My mom leaned forward, still smiling. "One of these days, you're going to meet a girl who keeps *you* entertained."

"Don't count on it," Evan replied, lifting his wine glass in mock celebration. "Being single is an art form."

Todd chuckled. "I thought the same thing until I met Sarah."

Evan gave him a pointed look. "Careful, Todd. You're about to lose all your freedoms. Say goodbye to last-minute trips and hello to wedding Pinterest boards."

"Don't listen to him," Sarah said, grinning. "He's just bitter."

"Bitter?" Evan put a hand on his chest, feigning offense. "I'm living my best life."

I laughed despite myself. Evan had a way of lightening the mood, even when my mind was miles away.

Eventually, the conversation shifted to old family stories. My mom brought up the time Sarah had tried to bake a cake for dad's birthday and ended up breaking her easy bake oven. Dad added the cake details, earning groans from Sarah but keeping everyone laughing.

The night dragged on, and I was nursing my third glass of whiskey when my phone buzzed in my pocket. I pulled it out, glancing at the screen.

Natalie: Will, I was wrong. About so many things.

My heart stopped. I reread the message, my pulse racing.

I wasn't expecting this. Not today. Not while she was supposed to be with him.

I excused myself, heading to the kitchen for some air. The words swirled in my mind. *I was wrong.* Did this mean what I thought it did?

I wanted to see her. Needed to see her. But first, I had to figure out what to say.

Chapter 30

Begin Again
Natalie

I drummed my fingers on the steering wheel, staring at the dim glow of the porch lights in front of Will's house. Taylor Swift's "You Belong with Me" blasted through the speakers, and before I knew it, I was singing along, off-key and way too loud.

I caught a glimpse of myself in the rearview mirror and cringed. "Oh my God, Natalie. Pull it together."

I turned the music down a notch, but not enough to stop myself from singing the next verse. There was something oddly freeing about belting out heartbreak anthems at night, sitting in a parked car like I didn't have better things to do.

Or maybe it was just that Taylor got it. She got me.

I sighed, leaning my head back against the seat as the song faded into a softer ballad. "What am I doing?" I muttered.

Showing up at Will's house unannounced was borderline insane. Okay, not borderline. Full-on. Who did this? Normal people waited for a response. Or maybe didn't park outside someone's house at all.

Usually, I'm very composed. But not when it came to him.

My phone buzzed in the cupholder, and I glanced at the screen. Meredith.

Meredith: Are you at Will's?

Natalie: Yes. He's still not home, and I'm sitting in his driveway like a stalker.

Meredith: Give it 10-15 more minutes, then leave. He'll just see you were a stalker on his Ring camera.

Just then, headlights cut through the quiet, their beam bouncing off my side mirror. My heart jumped into my throat as Will's car rolled into the driveway. He parked in the garage, the engine cutting off, and for a second, I debated throwing mine into reverse and peeling out.

But before I could move, his driver's side door opened, and he stepped out, his expression shifting from surprise to curiosity, and then to something softer.

Will walked toward my car, his steps slow and cautious. He tapped lightly on the driver's side window.

I swallowed hard, my heart thundering as I rolled down the window. I tried to look composed, hoping I somehow came off looking cool.

Will leaned down, his expression shifting into something closer to amusement. "So... is this some new kind of greeting I don't know about? Sitting in my driveway in the dark?"

I let out a nervous laugh, gripping the steering wheel. "I was aiming for casual, but apparently, I overshot straight into awkward."

His lips twitched into a smirk. "And here I thought you might just be here to TP the place. Should I check for eggs in your trunk?"

"Would you believe me if I said this was an incredibly well-thought-out plan?"

"Not even a little bit."

He straightened up, tapping the roof of my car lightly before gesturing toward the house. "Well, come on, then. If you're going to stalk me, you might as well do it from inside where it's warm."

Will opened my door and gestured me inside. I hesitated for a moment, still gripping my keys like a lifeline, before stepping out of the car. I followed him to his garage.

Inside the warm glow of the lights spilled out, a stark contrast to the chilly night air.

The door clicked shut behind us, and I immediately noticed how quiet it was in the mudroom. The stillness of the house felt amplified. Will shrugged off his jacket and hung it in one of the hooks glancing at me.

"Want some water? Or something stronger?" he asked, his tone light, but there was a question in his eyes I couldn't quite place.

"Water's fine," I said softly, following him into the kitchen.

As he poured two glasses, I took a breath and leaned against the counter, watching him. "I wasn't sure you'd even want to talk to me," I admitted.

He turned, leaning against the opposite counter, his arms crossed over his chest. "Why wouldn't I?"

I raised an eyebrow. "Maybe because I spent Thanksgiving at another man's house?"

His jaw tightened for a split second, and I braced myself for whatever he was about to say.

"I was pissed," he admitted. "But I figured... I don't know. Maybe you needed space. I didn't want to push. You needed to sort through everything on your own even if I didn't like where you were doing it."

I blinked, surprised by his honesty. "You weren't pushing. I just—" I sighed, shaking my head. "I should have never agreed to go to Lucas'. It was stupid, and I knew it even before I showed up."

There was still a flicker of something guarded in his eyes. "Why'd you go, then?"

"I guess I thought it would be easier. Safer. I didn't have to explain anything or risk feeling...whatever it is I feel when I'm with you," I said, the words tumbling out before I could stop them. "All I could think about was how much I didn't want to be there. How much I wanted to be with you."

He looked at me for a long moment, like he was trying to decide whether to believe me. Finally, he exhaled and set his glass down on the counter.

"I wanted to call you," he said, his voice low. "After dinner with my parents. I didn't text back because I figured I'd just call when I got home."

I stared at him, the weight of his words settling over me. "You were going to call?"

"Yeah." He ran a hand through his hair. "But then I started overthinking it. Figured you were busy with him, and maybe I was just reading everything wrong."

I stepped closer, my heart twisting. "You weren't reading it wrong, Will. I was. *I've* been reading everything wrong, and I'm sorry. I'm sorry I went, and I'm sorry I hurt you."

He looked down at me, something soft and tentative replacing the guarded expression. "I didn't want space, Natalie. I wanted...want...you."

The space between us felt charged with everything unsaid. For a moment, neither of us moved, and then I took a step closer, reaching for his hand.

"I want that, too," I whispered.

Will's hand lingered in mine, his grip steady as he looked down at me. There was a seriousness in his eyes that made my chest tighten.

"I want all of you, Nat," he said, his voice low but firm. "Not just pieces, not just stolen moments. All of you. Are you willing to try that?"

My breath caught. His words hung in the air between us, heavy with meaning. "You mean... like a real relationship?"

He nodded, his thumb brushing against the back of my hand. "We can still take it slow. I know this isn't easy, but I'm not going to pretend anymore. I want to tell my kids about us eventually. Kelly, my parents... I want them to know what you mean to me."

I swallowed hard, the weight of his words sinking in. "You've really thought about this."

"Of course, I have," he said, his voice softening. "I wanted you to come to my Thanksgiving. I wanted you there with me. But... we were in a funk, and I didn't know if I'd lost you completely."

"You didn't lose me," I said quickly, shaking my head. "I was just scared, Will. Scared of what this could mean for my kids, for your kids... for us. But I don't want to run anymore. I want this too. I want us."

Relief flickered across his face, but he didn't let go of my hand. "We'll figure it out. I'm not saying it's going to be easy, but if you're willing to try, so am I."

I nodded, my heart swelling. "I'm in. All the way."

His lips curved into the smallest smile, and he reached up, tucking a strand of hair behind my ear. "Good," he murmured, his voice rough with emotion.

Then, slowly, he leaned down and kissed me. It wasn't rushed or frantic, it was deliberate, like he wanted me to feel every ounce of what he couldn't say with words.

Chapter 31

In A Heartbeat

Natalie

The kiss started slow, soft, and searching. But then it deepened, heat building between us like an unraveling of everything we'd held back. Will's hands cradled my face, his thumbs brushing my cheeks, and I felt myself sinking into him, into this moment, into the warmth of his lips moving against mine. My fingers tangled in his hair, pulling him closer, and for a brief second, I forgot everything. The world outside ceased to exist.

When we broke apart, I pressed my forehead to his, trying to catch my breath. My heart was racing for all the right reasons for once, and I felt like I was standing on the edge of something big, something terrifying, but something I desperately wanted.

My phone started buzzing on the counter, insistent and loud enough to cut through the haze. I ignored it at first, but when it buzzed again—and again—I stepped back, my stomach twisting.

"Sorry," I muttered, my hand reaching for it. "I should check this."

I glanced at the screen and froze. Two missed calls from Jason. Two missed calls from Meredith. My throat tightened as I swiped to see the messages.

Jason: Call me now. Emergency. It's Bebe.

Meredith: Natalie, please pick up. Jason called me. It is about Bebe.

My stomach dropped. I felt the blood drain from my face as I dialed Jason's number. He picked up on the first ring.

"Natalie," he said, his voice tense, the background noise chaotic. "We're at the hospital. It's Bebe. She's been complaining of stomach pain, and it's bad. They think it might be her appendix."

Before I could respond, I heard it—Bebe crying in the background, her voice high and trembling. "I want Mommy! Mommy, please!" The sound tore through me, raw and desperate.

I pressed a hand to my chest, my knees threatening to give out. "Oh my God," I whispered, gripping the phone tighter. "Jason, I'm coming. Put her on the phone."

There was a shuffle on the other end, and then her voice, broken and small, came through the line. "Mommy?"

"I'm here, baby," I said, trying to keep my voice steady though I could feel it cracking.

"It hurts," she whimpered, her sobs hitching. "I want you, Mommy. Please come."

Tears burned in my eyes, spilling over before I could stop them. "I'm coming, sweetheart. I'll be there soon. Be brave for me, okay? Just a little longer."

The phone shuffled again as Jason came back on the line. "She's calming down a little, but she's scared. I just... I thought you should know. We're at the pediatric unit at Hoag."

"I'm on my way," I said quickly, hanging up.

I pressed the phone to my chest and closed my eyes, trying to breathe, but the sound of her voice—small, scared, and crying—echoed in my head.

"I've got to go," I said abruptly, grabbing my bag. My movements were frantic, my mind already at the hospital with Bebe. "I'm so sorry, I just—I need to get to her."

Will was already reaching for his keys. "I'll drive."

I froze, my bag clutched tightly in my hands. "You don't have to—"

"I've got you," he said simply, his voice steady, already moving toward the door.

I stared at him for a moment, the weight of his words settling over me, grounding me. I didn't want to argue, didn't want to do this alone.

"Okay," I said softly.

He opened the door, holding it for me as I stepped into his garage, and he held the door of the passenger side to let me in.

The drive to the hospital felt endless. I sat rigid in the passenger seat, clutching my phone so tightly my fingers ached. Every bump in the road seemed to stretch the distance farther, the silence pressing down on me like a weight.

Will glanced over at me, his hand reaching out to rest lightly on mine. The warmth of his touch was steady, grounding.

"You'll be there soon," he said softly, his voice calm and reassuring. "She's going to see you and know everything's okay."

I nodded, though my throat was tight, and my chest felt like it was caving in. I didn't say anything, couldn't find the words, but his hand stayed on mine the rest of the way, an anchor against the storm inside me.

The fluorescent lights of the ER waiting room buzzed faintly, making the stark white walls feel colder and sharper. My eyes darted over the rows of plastic chairs until I spotted Jason near the corner. He was sitting forward, his elbows on his knees, his hands clasped tightly, the tension etched in every line of his body.

Next to him was a woman. She sat close to him, her posture straight and calm, her short dark hair framing round brown eyes that flicked to Jason with quiet concern. One of her hands rested lightly on his, brushing his knuckles in what looked like an attempt to comfort him.

Jason looked up as I approached, his gaze meeting mine. His expression shifted. Confusion flickered briefly as his eyes flicked to Will behind me, but he quickly masked it. Jason stood, his movements tight and deliberate.

"How is she?" I asked, my words coming out sharper than I intended, my chest tightening with every second I didn't have an answer.

"They just took her back for surgery about five minutes ago," Jason said. His voice softened slightly, but the strain was still there. "The tests confirmed it's her appendix. The doctor said the surgery is routine, but..." His words trailed off, and he glanced toward the double doors.

I nodded quickly, trying to keep my breathing steady as I pictured Bebe on an operating table, scared and without me.

Jason gestured toward the woman beside him. "This is Brooke."

Brooke stood, smoothing her trousers as she stepped forward. "Hi," she said, her voice even, offering her hand. "I've heard a lot about you."

I hesitated for a split second before shaking her hand briefly. "Hi, nice to meet you," I said, my voice flat and distracted. I turned and gestured beside me. "And this is Will."

Before anyone could say more, Meredith walked in through the hospital doors. She had brought coffee with her. She handed me one and hugged me. "It's all going to be okay." I felt so vulnerable and didn't want to lose it in front of this Brooke woman, my ex-husband or even Will. I was feeling so guilty for not being here earlier. I just missed Bebe. I wanted to just tell her it's okay.

Meredith could sense I was getting a bit overwhelmed.

The double doors leading to the treatment rooms swung open, and a nurse stepped into the waiting room. Her calm demeanor helped, though the clipboard in her hands made me brace myself.

"Bebe Bradford's parents?" she asked, glancing at Jason and Brooke.

Jason and I both stepped forward.

"The surgeon asked me to let you know that everything is going well," she said. "The surgery is underway, and Bebe is doing great so far. We'll come back with more updates when the procedure is finished."

"Thank you," I uttered.

Jason nodded, exhaling deeply as he sat back down.

Meredith was suddenly at my side, gripping my arm tightly. "See? She's in good hands, Nat," she said, her voice steady.

I nodded, blinking quickly to hold back the tears that burned at the corners of my eyes. "I know," I said, though my voice wavered.

Jason leaned forward again; his hands clasped tightly as he stared at the floor. Brooke shifted closer to him, her hand resting lightly on his back, and I had to look away.

I couldn't sit. I couldn't move. I stood frozen in place, staring at the doors the nurse had disappeared through, willing them to open again with more good news.

Will stayed close behind me, steady and quiet. He didn't say anything, but I felt his presence like a safety net, holding me up when I felt like I might collapse.

What felt like an eternity was finally lifted when the doors to the surgical wing swung open once more, and my heart lodged itself in my throat. A doctor stepped into the waiting room, still in scrubs, his face calm and unreadable. I shot up from my chair so quickly I nearly tripped over the strap of my bag.

"Bradford family?"

Jason stood at the same time I did, our movements jerky, synchronized by the same shared panic. His hand dropped from Brooke's knee as I took a hesitant step forward, my voice too stuck to speak. Jason beat me to it.

"Yes, that's us. How's Bebe?"

The doctor glanced between us, offering a small, practiced smile.

"The surgery went very well. Her appendix was inflamed, but we were able to remove it without any complications. It hadn't ruptured, so her recuperation should be smooth. She's already in recovery and will start waking up soon."

The tight knot in my chest loosened, just enough to let air in. My hands, clenched into fists, started to shake as the adrenaline drained out of me. She was okay. She was going to be okay.

"When can we see her?" I managed to ask.

"It will take about 30 to 45 minutes for her to wake up fully in recovery," the doctor said. "One parent can go back to see her then. Once she's stable and moved to her room, both of you will be able to visit."

"Only one?" I couldn't keep the frustration from my tone, even as I knew it was irrational. I just needed to see her. Needed to hold her hand and know for myself that she was fine.

The doctor nodded, unbothered by my reaction.

"We want to minimize stimulation while she wakes up, but the nurses will let you know as soon as she's ready for a visitor."

Jason stepped forward, his hands shoved deep in his pockets. "Thank you, Doctor. And... she's really, okay?"

"She's doing great. We'll go over her post-op care instructions soon, but for now, just be here when she wakes up. She'll be asking for you before long."

The doctor disappeared back through the doors, leaving the five of us in the too-bright waiting room.

As soon as the doctor disappeared, the tension in the room melted away, replaced by collective relief. Jason let out a breath, his shoulders finally relaxing. Brooke offered a small smile, glancing nervously between us, but I didn't have it in me to care how she felt right now. Meredith reached over and squeezed my hand.

"See? She's a tough kid," Meredith said, her voice light, trying to keep things upbeat. I nodded, swallowing hard.

My legs felt unsteady, but I stayed upright, perched on the edge of my chair. Meredith was on one side, Will on the other, like bookends keeping me from falling apart.

She was okay. I repeated it over and over in my head like a mantra: She's okay. She's okay.

The minutes felt endless until the nurse stepped through the doors again, clipboard in hand. Her eyes scanned the room before landing on me.

"Mrs. Bradford?"

I stood, my legs moving before my brain caught up. "Yes?"

The nurse smiled warmly. "She's asking for you."

My breath caught. I glanced over at Jason. His eyes met mine, and he gave me a quick nod.

"Go," he said quietly.

I turned to Will. He was standing just a few feet away, his expression unreadable, but his eyes met mine, steady and reassuring. He gave me a single, firm nod.

That was all I needed. My feet moved before I could even think, following the nurse toward the doors. I pushed them open and stepped into the hallway, the beeping of monitors and the sterile smell of antiseptic filling my senses. All I cared about was seeing her—my baby girl.

Chapter 32

Healing Together

Natalie

The door to the recovery room creaked open as the nurse led me inside, and there she was, my baby, looking impossibly small in the hospital bed. Her dark lashes rested against pale cheeks, and the soft beep of the monitors filled the room. Her hair was tucked back, a stark white bandage peeking out from under her hospital gown.

"Hey, sweetheart," I whispered, my voice catching as I moved to her side.

Her eyes fluttered open, slow and heavy, and for a second, she just blinked at me. Then, a faint, sleepy smile tugged at her lips.

"Mommy," she croaked, her voice scratchy.

I sank into the chair beside her bed, taking her hand carefully in mine, like she might break if I wasn't gentle enough. Tears burned at the edges of my eyes, but I blinked them back. She was okay. My baby was okay.

"I'm here, Bebe. Everything went great. The doctors said you'll be back to running circles around me in no time."

She tried to smile again but winced slightly. Her other hand crept up to her stomach.

"It hurts a little."

"I know, sweetheart. That's normal, but they've got medicine for the pain. Just rest for now, okay?"

Her head barely moved in a nod before her eyelids drooped shut again, her tiny hand still resting in mine.

The nurse reappeared, her smile soft. "She'll drift in and out for a bit. She can have another visitor soon. Do you want me to let her father come back?"

I hesitated, brushing a stray strand of hair off Bebe's forehead. Part of me wanted to keep this moment to myself a little longer, but I nodded.

"Sure."

Jason stepped into the room, his usual composed expression softened. He glanced at me, and for once, there wasn't any tension between us. We were just parents, sharing a moment of gratitude that our daughter was safe.

"She's still groggy," I said quietly, stepping aside to let him approach the bed.

Jason moved to her side, his large hand dwarfing hers as he gently stroked the back of it.

"Hey, princess," he murmured, leaning down so his voice didn't carry. "You gave us a little scare there, but you're so brave."

A nurse brought Meredith in not long after, her arms full of bags and looking slightly breathless.

"I ran home and grabbed a few things," she said, dropping the bags on the chair. "Some pajamas, toothbrush, snacks, and your phone charger. Oh, and I grabbed a few things for Bebe too—a cozy blanket and her stuffed unicorn."

I blinked at her, overwhelmed. "Mer, you didn't have to do all that."

"Yes, I did," she said firmly, waving me off. "I wasn't going to let you sit here all night with nothing but hospital coffee and fluorescent lighting."

The lump in my throat that I'd been holding back all night started to rise again. I wrapped my arms around her, squeezing tight.

"Thank you," I said, my voice breaking. "I don't know what I'd do without you."

"You won't have to find out," she said, pulling back and giving me a knowing smile. "Now go through the bag and tell me if I forgot anything. I can always run out again."

Jason glanced at the bags, his lips twitching into a small smile.

"That was quick. I didn't even notice you were gone," he said to Meredith.

"Will let me use his car and I slipped out while Natalie went in to see her," she replied. "Didn't want to make a big deal of it."

Jason's attention was on Bebe. He leaned down, brushing a kiss on her forehead, and straightened up.

I sat down, still holding Bebe's hand in mine, and opened the bag, my chest heavy with gratitude. I felt like everything might just be okay.

The nurse reappeared, holding a clipboard and glancing between us.

"We've set Bebe up in a private room for the night," she said. "There's enough space for both parents to stay if you'd like, though it's a bit tight. There's a recliner and a sofa bed."

Jason looked at me and raised a brow. "Do you want to stay?"

"Of course." Then I turned to him. "I mean, if you want to stay too, that's fine. I'm sure she'd feel better having us both here."

Jason nodded, his expression unreadable. "I'll stay."

Meredith smiled and gave me a squeeze on the arm. "See? Everything's handled. I'll be back first thing in the morning with coffee and breakfast for you guys."

"Thank you for everything, Meredith," I said, my voice catching.

"Thanks for taking care of everything, Mer," Jason said.

"Oh, and I'll let the others know what's going on," she said. "Call if you need anything. I'll see you both tomorrow."

Once we settled into the private room, Jason pulled the recliner closer to Bebe's bed while I stretched out on the small sofa bed, the bags Meredith brought tucked under the table. The room felt peaceful, even if we were in a hospital room, as the events of the day finally started to settle. It reminded me of when Bebe was born and the three of us crammed in a small room.

Jason glanced at me over his shoulder, his voice quiet. "She's lucky to have you."

I looked back at Bebe, her small chest rising and falling steadily. "She's lucky to have us both."

It wasn't perfect, but for tonight, it felt like enough.

Chapter 33

The Morning After
Natalie

I woke to the faint hum of hospital light, the steady beeping of machines, the shuffle of footsteps in the hallway, and the faint murmur of voices. My body ached from the unforgiving sofa, but the sight of Bebe sleeping peacefully in her hospital bed made it all worth it. She looked so small, her tiny frame swallowed by the blankets, but her color was better, and her breathing was soft and steady.

The nurse was at her bedside, checking the monitors. She smiled at me as I sat up.

"Good morning. Bebe is doing great. Her vitals are strong, and she's recovering beautifully. The doctor will be in soon, but if all goes well, she should be able to go home this afternoon."

I exhaled, relief washing over me. "Thank you," I said softly, my voice catching.

Jason stirred in the recliner by Bebe's bed, his hair disheveled and his movements sluggish. He rubbed his face, waking up slowly, then looked at me.

"Everything okay?"

"She's doing great," I said, my tone warm. "The nurse said she can probably go home today."

Jason nodded, his shoulders relaxing as he leaned back in the chair. "Good. That's a relief to hear."

Meredith swept into the room about twenty minutes later, juggling balloons, a bright stuffed yellow duck, and two steaming cups of coffee.

"Okay, who's ready for some sunshine?" she announced, setting the balloons down and the duck on the chair beside Bebe's bed.

She handed me one of the coffees, then offered the other to Jason.

"Figured you could use this, too," she said, winking at him.

Jason took it gratefully. "Thanks, Meredith. I appreciate this."

Meredith beamed, then turned her attention to Bebe. "How's my little warrior doing?"

"She's still sleeping, but she's doing really well," I said. "The nurse thinks she'll be able to go home later today."

"Good," Meredith said, settling into the chair. "She's a tough cookie."

Jason's phone buzzed, and he stepped to the corner of the room to answer it. When he hung up, he turned back to me.

"That was my mom," he said. "James is doing great. She said he had pancakes for breakfast and has been happily playing with his cars all morning."

I smiled, relieved to hear James was being well cared for.

"She asked if they should stop by the house today or wait until tomorrow," Jason said. "What do you think? Would it be too much for Bebe today?"

I glanced at Bebe, her little hand curled around the blanket Meredith had brought. "Let's give her a little space. They can come by tomorrow."

Jason nodded. "Makes sense. I'll stop by with them tomorrow morning before I drive my parents to the airport. My mom said she'd keep James at their hotel for another night if you're okay with that."

"That's fine," I said. "I think Bebe will need some quiet once we're home."

Jason's phone buzzed again. He stepped toward the door to answer it, his voice low. When he came back, he tucked his phone into his pocket.

"That was Brooke," he said, glancing at me. "She's bringing me a change of clothes. Is it okay if she stops by for a minute?"

I hesitated, but only for a second. "Of course. That's fine."

About a half-hour later, there was a soft knock at the door. Jason stood and opened it, stepping aside to let Brooke in. She entered cautiously, holding a small duffel bag and wearing a polite smile.

"Good morning," she said, her gaze flicking between me, Meredith, and Jason before landing briefly on Bebe. She handed the bag to Jason. "How's she doing?" Brooke asked quietly.

"She's doing well," I said evenly, keeping my tone polite. "The nurse said she'll probably be able to go home this afternoon."

"That's great news," Brooke said, offering a warm smile.

Jason gestured toward the recliner. "Do you want to sit for a second?"

Brooke shook her head quickly. "No, I don't want to intrude. I'll check in later."

Jason nodded, "Thanks for bringing this."

"Of course," Brooke said, her gaze flickering briefly toward me before she stepped back toward the door.

The door clicked softly shut behind Jason and Brooke, leaving the room noticeably quieter. Meredith stretched out in the chair, sipping her coffee.

"Well, that was... efficient," she said lightly, shooting me a knowing look.

I didn't respond, busying myself with smoothing the blanket over Bebe's legs. But as the quiet settled over the room, I instinctively reached for my phone on the side table.

Will: How's everything going?

Tapping a quick reply, I kept it short but honest.

Natalie: She's doing great. They're letting us go home this afternoon.

The message sent, and I set the phone back down, exhaling deeply. Will didn't overstep or press, and that steadiness was something I didn't know I needed until now.

Jason came back a few minutes later, carrying the duffel bag and looking a little more awake. He set it on the chair, then leaned down to check on Bebe.

"She's still out," he said quietly.

"She's been through a lot," I replied, glancing at the small rise and fall of her chest.

Jason nodded, running a hand through his hair before settling back into the recliner.

Not long after, Bebe's eyes began to flutter open.

"Mommy, I am sore."

"Hi baby, I know it hurts. You are doing great."

Jason stood up and walked over to Bebe and placed his hand on hers. "You were so brave, my little princess. We are going to get you home soon, okay."

There was a knock at the door, this time to the doctor entering with a clipboard and a warm smile.

"Good morning," she said, her tone cheerful as she crossed to Bebe's side, "How are you feeling today?"

Bebe nodded sleepily. "Okay. Just sore."

The doctor listened to her abdomen with a stethoscope, then gently pressed down on the bandages. Bebe winced but didn't pull away.

"That's totally normal," she assured Bebe, jotting down a quick note on the chart. "You are doing wonderfully. Vitals look strong, and your recovery's right on track." She turned to me. "We'll plan to discharge her this afternoon. I'll have the nurse bring in your instructions for home care."

"Thank you," I said, my voice steady but thick with emotion.

"You're very welcome," the doctor replied, then glanced at Bebe. "She's a tough little one. Let me know if you have any questions, but otherwise, we'll get her ready to go soon."

As the doctor left, I leaned back in the chair, relief washing over me.

Chapter 34

Home Again
Natalie

The car ride home was quiet, except for the hum of the engine and the occasional murmur from Meredith, who was narrating her mental to-do list as she drove. Bebe snuggled into Jason's side in the backseat, her head resting against his chest.

When we pulled into the driveway, Jason gently unbuckled Bebe and carried her inside while Meredith grabbed the balloons and the stuffed duck. I trailed behind, clutching the hospital discharge papers and bags, feeling the weight of the past twenty-four hours.

Jason set Bebe carefully on the couch, arranging the pillows around her and draping a blanket over her, her small body sinking into the soft cushions.

Jason lingered near the couch, shifting awkwardly. Finally, he cleared his throat. "Do you want me to stick around? I don't mind helping if you need it."

I straightened, turning to face him. "That's sweet of you, but I think we've got it. She's just going to be resting, and it's better if it's quiet."

Jason nodded, his shoulders relaxing slightly, though he still looked uncertain. "Alright. I'll call Brooke to come pick me up, then."

"Okay," I said softly.

He stepped outside, his phone already in his hand, and I glanced over at Meredith, who was making tea.

Meredith glanced up from the coffee pot, her sharp eyes catching mine. "You okay, Nat?" she asked, her tone casual but knowing.

I hesitated, smoothing the blanket over Bebe's legs even though it didn't need it. "Yeah, I'm fine," I said, a little too quickly.

Meredith glanced over toward the door that Jason was standing on the other side of. "It's okay if you're not. I mean, none of this is easy."

I looked up at her, startled. "It's not that," I started to say, but Meredith's expression told me she wasn't buying it.

"It's okay to feel weird about it," she said, her voice softening. "I mean, come on, Nat. You guys just got divorced, not that long ago. This stuff's going to sting a little. It's normal."

I let out a small sigh, my hands falling still in my lap. "It's just... I don't know. She's involved now, and I guess it does feel fast, you know?"

Meredith put her hands up in mock defense. "Okay, don't kill me but... Brooke seems alright, doesn't she?"

"Yes, annoyingly so." I admitted.

"But it is fast. And it's okay to feel some kind of way about it. You're allowed to feel weird about it."

I gave her a faint smile, appreciating her ability to read between the lines. "Thanks, Mer."

She shrugged, a small grin tugging at her lips. "What are sisters for?"

Meredith went to pour our coffees, my phone buzzed on the counter.

Will: How's everything going? Are you home yet?

A small smile tugged at my lips.

Natalie: Just got back. She's resting now. I think we're all just exhausted.

Will: I've got the kids today and for the next week. Let me know if you need anything, dinner, groceries, whatever. Ivy would love to see Bebe, but I know she probably needs to rest.

Natalie: Thanks. Maybe tomorrow? Just seeing Ivy would make her happy.

My chest felt lighter as I tucked the phone back into my pocket.

A few minutes later, Jason came back inside. "Brooke's on her way," he said, grabbing the duffel bag from where he'd left it near the door. "Let me know if you need anything," he said finally.

"Thanks, Jason," I said.

He nodded, glancing at Bebe one more time before stepping outside. I heard the faint sound of Brooke's car pulling up, and Jason's voice as he greeted her.

Meredith appeared beside me, her hands on her hips. "Well, that's that," she said.

I didn't know what to think of it all. I was just grateful Jason stuck around and was there for Bebe and maybe even for me.

We settled into a slow, quiet evening. Meredith poured us cups of tea and sat with me at the kitchen table, her fingers idly tracing the rim of her mug.

"So," she said lightly, giving me a pointed look, "your talk with Will must have gone well, I take it."

Heat crept into my cheeks. "I told him I was all in."

Her mug paused halfway to her lips. "All in?" she echoed, eyebrows lifting.

I gave a small nod, my throat tightening. "No more running, no more excuses. I meant it."

A slow smile spread across Meredith's face. "Wow. That's big, Nat. Really big."

I let out a shaky laugh. "Terrifying, too."

She leaned closer, her expression softening. "Terrifying usually means it's worth it."

Chapter 35

L-O-V-E

Natalie

The house was unusually quiet when I woke up the next morning. The soft light streaming through the windows gave everything a calm glow, a stark contrast to the chaos of the past few days. I went to check on Bebe who was still asleep, her tiny fist curled under her chin. Her cheeks had regained some color, and the deep furrow of discomfort that had settled on her face during the worst of it was finally gone.

I lingered for a moment, watching her breathe peacefully, then followed the scent of fresh coffee into the kitchen. Meredith was already awake, her hair pulled into a messy bun as she poured two steaming mugs.

"Morning," she said, sliding one toward me. "How's Bebe?"

"Still asleep," I said, wrapping my hands around the mug. "But she looks so much better."

Meredith nodded. How about you? How are you holding up?"

"I'm okay. Just... tired, I guess."

Meredith leaned against the counter, crossing her arms. "Well, then you'll be thrilled to know I changed my flight to Saturday. Figured you could use some extra hands."

"Aww, Mer," I said, my chest tightening with gratitude. "You didn't have to do that."

"Of course, I did," she said. "You're going to need someone to keep you sane. I've got some photo edits to finish, but I don't have any shoots until next Monday. I can handle it here."

I smiled, overwhelmed by how lucky I was to have her. "Seriously, you're the best."

"Obviously," she said with a wink.

A faint rustling sound came from upstairs. "I'm going to check on Bebe," I said, setting my coffee down.

Bebe stirred as I entered her room, her eyelids fluttering open slowly. She blinked up at me, her lips curving into a groggy smile.

"Hi, Baby. How are you?" I asked, kneeling beside her.

"Hi, Mommy," she said in a scratchy voice, rubbing her eyes.

"Are you hungry?"

"Kind of," she mumbled, still waking up.

"Okay. How about some oatmeal? Soft foods for a bit, okay?"

She nodded sleepily.

"Do you want me to put 'Bluey' on while you wait?"

"Yes, please, Mommy," she said, her voice perking up slightly.

"Let's have you brush your teeth and use the bathroom, and I will help you downstairs."

"Okay Mommy."

Meredith was already rummaging through the kitchen cabinets. "Jasper texted me earlier. He's dropping off some bone broth, soups, and meals for us."

"Wow, he's really going all out," I said, smirking. "Sounds like a smitten kitten."

She rolled her eyes. "He's just being nice."

"Uh-huh," I teased.

I finished making the oatmeal and brought it to Bebe, sitting beside her to make sure she ate slowly, spoonful by spoonful. Afterward, I tucked her back under the blanket, kissed her forehead, and headed upstairs to shower.

As I stepped out, my phone buzzed on the counter. A text from Will lit up the screen, and I noticed a missed call from Jason as well.

Will: Morning, babe. How's everyone doing? Are you up for some visitors? Ivy and I can come by tonight with dinner.

I smiled at the casual intimacy of his words, feeling warmth spread through me. Will had started talking to me like a real boyfriend lately. After months of sneaking around, it felt... normal.

I replied quickly:

Natalie: Hey, you. We'd love to see you both tonight. How about five?

Will: Works for us.

I tapped Jason's name and called him back.

"Hey, Nat," he answered. "How's Bebe doing?"

"She's good," I said. "She ate a little oatmeal."

"Good to hear. Can we stop by before I take my parents to the airport? Maybe in an hour?"

"Sure," I said.

"Oh, and I was thinking, why don't I keep James with me for the next few days? I'm not traveling next week, so I can check in on Bebe and help if you need anything."

"That would actually be great," I said, surprised by the offer. Jason wasn't known for taking time off, but it felt genuine. "Thanks, Jason."

"Of course," he said.

An hour later, Meredith opened the door, greeting Jason, James, and Jason's parents, Deb and Richard. James ran toward me immediately, throwing his arms around my waist.

"Mommy! I missed you so much!"

"I missed you too, buddy," I said, hugging him tightly.

James then approached Bebe on the couch, looking hesitant.

"Daddy told me I can't jump on you or the couch," he said solemnly.

"That's right, James," Bebe said, her voice soft but amused.

Deb handed me a bouquet of flowers. "Thought the house could use some color," she said, her tone surprisingly kind.

"Thank you," I said, graciously, as I took the flowers and set them on the counter.

Upstairs, as I packed James' duffel bag with his school uniform, Jason appeared in the doorway, leaning against the frame.

"Would you mind if Brooke and I took James to a movie tonight?" he asked casually, though there was something measured in his tone.

I paused, my hand frozen mid-fold. His question caught me off guard, and I was stunned by how I reacted. "Do you care if Will and Ivy come over tonight?" I asked, my voice sharper than I'd intended.

Jason straightened, his expression tightening. "I didn't even know things were serious with you and Will. You didn't bring it up to me and, honestly, I was surprised to see him last night. I was focused on Bebe last night but I wish I'd had some notice, Natalie." He paused, his jaw flexing. "I'm not going to make a big deal out of it, even though he fucked my wife."

I flinched at the bluntness of his words, my grip tightening on the shirt in my hands. "Jason," I said, my voice low but firm. "I get that I should've given you a heads-up. When you called about Bebe, I was with him. I needed him to take me to the hospital—I wasn't in any shape to drive."

Jason exhaled deeply, some of the tension in his face easing though not entirely. "I'm sorry," he said after a long pause. "I shouldn't have come at you like that. It's just...Will. You know what that feels like for me."

"I know," I said softly, meeting his eyes. "And I get it. But you had Brooke with you at the hospital, and I didn't say a word. It was not a situation any of us planned."

Jason sighed, dragging his hand through his hair as he leaned against the dresser. "Fair enough," he repeated, his tone softer. "I guess this whole situation is... a lot."

"It is," I agreed, folding the last of James's shirts and zipping the duffel bag closed. "But we're figuring it out. One step at a time."

Jason nodded, the tension in his shoulders easing slightly.

"Brooke seems to care a lot about you," I added after a moment, feeling the need to bridge the gap between us.

"She does," Jason admitted, his voice quieter now. "I'll admit, she's been patient with all of this. It's been a long week," he added with a faint laugh, though it didn't quite reach his eyes.

For a moment, there was no tension between us, just two people navigating a complicated new normal.

"I should get them to the airport," Jason said, straightening and grabbing the duffel bag.

"Here," I said, handing him James's uniforms on hangers.

"Thanks," Jason said, giving me a small nod.

We headed downstairs, where Meredith was entertaining the crowd like a pro. I caught a rare half-smile from Richard as he sipped his coffee, and Deb was unusually quiet, her attention focused entirely on Bebe.

After they left, the house fell blissfully peaceful. Bebe, Meredith, and I decided to watch "The Parent Trap." The cozy familiarity of the movie was exactly what we all needed. Bebe's giggles at the pranks warmed my heart, even as she held her stomach cautiously.

Jasper stopped by briefly to drop off the food he'd prepared for us. He didn't stay long, but Meredith followed him outside for a few moments. When she came back in, I couldn't tell what she thought of Jasper.

"Are you into him," I teased, leaning against the kitchen counter as she unpacked the containers.

"I do love the accent," she admitted with a grin. "I mean, I wonder what he can do with that tongue."

"Meredith!" I gasped, laughing as I threw a dish towel at her.

"What? I'm just saying!" she shrugged. "I don't know if I feel a spark, though. He might just be for fun."

"Just for fun, huh?" I gave her a look. "I'm surprised you are even using the word *spark*. I didn't think you did spark. Does this have anything to do with a certain other man you encountered this week" I quipped playfully. "Evan perhaps?"

She made a surprised face, and I could have sworn her cheeks blushed a little.

"I just realized, you're going to be here for the opening, aren't you? I completely forgot that's this week."

"Do you think Jason can stay with Bebe and James on Thursday so we can both go?" She asked.

"Yes, I'm sure he will," I said, though the thought of juggling so much with Bebe still recovering made me a little anxious.

"Relax, Nat," Meredith said, sensing my hesitation. "I'll be here. We'll make it work."

"You always come through for me," I said, meaning it with every fiber of my being.

Meredith suddenly broke into song, crooning *"L is for the way you look at me"* in a sing-song voice, her eyes fixed on me with a knowing smile.

"Meredith," I said, trying not to laugh as she swayed dramatically around the kitchen.

"Oh, come on, Nat. You know you want to join me."

I shook my head, but when she started singing louder, I gave in. Our voices tumbled together in a messy duet until we both dissolved into uncontrollable laughter.

Before I knew it, it was almost five, and Will and Ivy were due to arrive. A knock at the door came a few minutes later, and Meredith darted to answer it. I think she loved being the greeter.

"Hello, Will. And who do we have here?" Meredith asked in an exaggeratedly sweet voice.

"I'm Ivy," she said confidently. "Bebe's best friend. How do you do?"

Meredith laughed. "Well, well, I'm Meredith, Bebe's best aunt."

"I've heard of you," Ivy said matter-of-factly. "Bebe told me how cool and pretty you are."

"Did she?" Meredith replied, shooting me a sly look. "What a sweetie that Bebe is."

Ivy beamed as she skipped over to Bebe, carrying balloons and a small gift bag. Bebe's eyes lit up as Ivy handed her the items.

"These are for you," Ivy said proudly. "Is your scar like the red-haired girl in Madeline?"

"I don't know. I can't see it—it's covered with a bandage," Bebe replied, giggling.

Bebe opened the gift, revealing new pajamas, a Squishmallow, and a BFF necklace. Her face lit up as she hugged Ivy tentatively.

I turned my attention to Will, who was watching the girls with a smile.

"That was really thoughtful of you," I said, stepping closer to him.

He shrugged modestly. "Ivy picked everything out. She's very particular when it comes to her best friend."

"Very generous," I said softly, catching his gaze. "Their friendship is so pure. Do you think it'll stay that way?"

Will's hand brushed mine, sending chills up my spine. "I think they'd love to be sisters," he said quietly.

The depth of his words caught me off guard, but I didn't let myself overthink it. For now, I focused on the warmth of the moment.

The girls decided to watch "Spirit," and Will and I excused ourselves to the kitchen, where Meredith was setting out the sushi Will had brought.

"Okay, lovebirds, dinner is ready," Meredith teased, arranging the rolls on a platter.

I rolled my eyes. "Don't start, Mer."

Will grinned. "I don't mind. I've been called worse."

Meredith gave him a sly look. "Oh, I'm just getting warmed up."

We all sat down at the island, the soft hum of the movie playing in the background. Meredith poured us glasses of wine, her playful energy filling the room as she leaned into teasing me.

"So, Will," she said, leaning forward on her elbows. "How's life in the Parker household?"

Will chuckled, taking a sip of his wine. "Between Madison's high school drama, Ivy's very specific tastes in everything, and Carter and Chase turning everything into a sports or Nintendo competition, it's never dull," Will said with a grin.

Sounds like you've got your hands full," Meredith said, raising her glass. "Cheers to surviving it all."

Will clinked his glass to hers. "Cheers to that."

I couldn't help but smile as I watched them banter. Will's ease with Meredith felt like a glimpse of what life could be—blended, comfortable, and light.

After a while, Meredith excused herself to check on the girls. As she left the room, I got up to warm some soup for Bebe, just in case she wanted to eat later.

Will followed me to the stove, leaning against the counter as I stirred the pot. "This is nice," he said softly.

"What is?" I asked, glancing over my shoulder at him.

"Being here," he said. "With you. With your family. It feels... right."

The sincerity in his voice made my breath hitch. I looked at him, his eyes steady on mine, and for a moment, the room seemed to shrink around us.

"I wish I could kiss you," he whispered, his voice low and intimate.

A shiver ran through me as his words brushed against the air between us. "Me too".

Before the moment could deepen, Meredith's voice called from the living room. "Hey, no funny business in there! If you two need a room, go quick, I've got the girls covered!"

"Meredith!" I called back, my voice half-laughing, half-exasperated. "I'm heating up soup!"

Will smirked, leaning in just a fraction closer. "She's not wrong, though."

I shook my head, turning back to the stove. "Don't push your luck, Parker."

Meredith eventually wandered back into the kitchen, setting her phone on the counter with a knowing smirk. "The girls are in there giggling non-stop. 'Spirit' must be a comedy now."

Will chuckled, glancing toward the living room. "Ivy loves narrating that movie. She's probably explaining every scene to Bebe right now."

Meredith leaned casually against the counter, eyeing the sushi on the platter. "So, Nat, what's it like having a boyfriend who brings dinner and a daughter with perfect gift-giving skills?"

Will raised an eyebrow, his smirk teasing. "Boyfriend, huh? That's official now?"

I shot Meredith a look, though my cheeks warmed at the word. "Don't encourage her," I said.

Meredith grinned, unbothered by my protest. "Too late. You two are so smitten, it's painful to watch."

Will leaned toward me slightly, a playful glint in his eye. "Painful, huh? Guess I'm doing something right."

I rolled my eyes, ignoring the flutter in my chest. "Why don't we talk about your smitten status?" I countered, turning the spotlight onto Meredith. "How's Jasper's soup delivery? Thoughtful or flirtatious?"

Meredith groaned dramatically, tossing her hands up. "Oh, please. He's just being nice. The man can't help that he's a great cook and a good guy."

Will exchanged a look with me, his grin widening. "Definitely flirtatious," he said, nodding in agreement. "What about my guy, Evan? Is he still in the running?"

"Quiet, both of you!" Meredith said, though her laughter broke through. "You're not funny."

"Not even a little?" I teased.

She grabbed a dish towel and tossed it in my direction. "I hate you both," she muttered.

After finishing the sushi and wine with Will and Meredith, I grabbed the bowls of soup from the stove. "I'll bring these out to the girls," I said, carrying them into the living room where Bebe and Ivy were curled up under blankets.

"Bebe, honey, here's some soup," I said, setting the bowl on the coffee table. "Just take small sips, okay?"

Bebe nodded, her small hands reaching for the spoon. "Thanks, Mommy."

I set another bowl in front of Ivy, who gave me a big smile. "Thank you, Miss Natalie!"

"You're welcome," I said, brushing a strand of hair off Bebe's forehead. "

"They're good out there," I said, returning to the kitchen with the tray.

"Bebe looks good," he said, his voice soft. "You're doing a great job, Nat."

Thanks," I said quietly, leaning against the counter. His words, simple as they were, felt grounding.

Meredith joined us a moment later, refilling her wine and leaning casually against the counter across from us.

Before we could start another conversation, Will glanced at his phone and sighed. "I should probably head out. Madison's watching her brothers tonight, and I told her she could have her boyfriend over at eight if she held down the fort."

I raised an eyebrow. "Her boyfriend? That word is being tossed around a lot tonight."

He groaned, shaking his head. "Yep. I'm dreading it, but I figured it's better than her sneaking him in when I'm not there."

I laughed softly. "Parenting teenagers sounds... exciting."

"Let's go with exhausting," he said with a faint grin.

He turned back into the living room and crouched beside Ivy. "Ready to head out, kiddo?" he asked gently.

Ivy pouted dramatically but nodded. "Okay, Daddy." She turned to Bebe and gave her a gentle hug. "Feel better. I'll see you soon."

"Okay," Bebe said, her voice soft but happy.

I walked them to the door, letting Ivy step out first. Will lingered for a moment, turning back toward me.

"Good luck with the boyfriend," I teased lightly, crossing my arms.

He laughed, "I'll need it."

With one last look, he and Ivy disappeared into the evening, leaving me feeling both full and wistful.

Once Will and Ivy had gone, I returned to the living room to check on Bebe. She was still curled up on the couch, the blanket pulled tightly around her.

"Hey, sweetie," I said softly, crouching beside her. "Time for bed." I carefully scooped her into my arms. She rested her head on my shoulder, her body warm and surprisingly light. I could feel how tired she was as her little arms looped around my neck.

When we reached her room, I eased her down onto her bed, adjusting her pillow and tucking the blanket snugly around her. Her favorite stuffed animal was already waiting on the pillow, and I set it gently in her arms.

I leaned down and kissed her forehead. "I love you, Bebe. Good night."

"Love you too, Mommy," she said sleepily, her eyes already drifting closed.

Downstairs, Meredith was waiting on the couch, two wine glasses already filled.

I plopped down beside her, letting out a long breath. "Could you just move in?"

She laughed, handing me a glass.

"You really are a gem."

"We've always been each other's rock," she said, her big doe eyes soft, a small smile tugging at her lips.

I gave a small nod. "Through it all."

She tilted her head, giving me a knowing look. "Talk about smitten kitten—you are so far gone with Will. How are you going to tell all the kids?"

I sighed, swirling the wine in my glass. "I don't know. Now's not the time. Maybe after the holidays. It's the kids' first Christmas after the divorce..."

"Okay, excuses," Meredith interrupted, raising an eyebrow. "Your kids will be fine. They've already met Brooke. You're just worried about that teenager, aren't you? She's got you all freaked out."

I let out a soft laugh, shaking my head. "Madison is... complicated. I just don't want to push things too fast and make it harder on her, or on any of the kids. It has to feel like the right time."

Meredith gave me a long look before setting her glass down. "You've got a good heart, Nat. But don't let fear stop you from being happy. Will seems like he's ready to handle whatever comes your way. And honestly? I think your kids are, too."

I leaned back against the couch, letting her words sink in. "I hope you're right."

She smiled, leaning her head on my shoulder. "Trust me on this. You might get that picture perfect life with someone who you really love this time."

I leaned back letting her words sink in. *Is it possible to have a picture-perfect life with a blended family?*

We sat there in companionable silence for a moment before Meredith started to sing.

"L is for the way you look at me," she sang softly.

I laughed, joining in quietly. "O is for the only one I see..."

We sang the rest of the chorus together, our voices low so we didn't wake Bebe.

Meredith tilted her glass toward mine with a grin. "To being smitten. And to figuring it all out."

"To figuring it out," I agreed, clinking my glass with hers.

Chapter 36

My Girls

Will

After leaving Natalie's house, Ivy and I were in great spirits, singing along to the daddy-daughter mix we made. "My Girl" came on, and I smiled at her.

"This is our song now, officially," I told her.

"I love that, Daddy," she said, grinning.

When we pulled into the driveway, I spotted a light blue Hummer parked outside. My mood instantly shifted and clenched my jaw. Was that his car? It wasn't even eight yet. I must have missed my Ring notification when this kid decided to show up early. The buzz from the evening evaporated in an instant.

Under my breath I said, "Are you kidding me?" not meaning for it to slip out with a tone.

"What's wrong, Daddy?" Ivy asked, her little voice full of concern.

"Oh, nothing, sweetie. Madison and I just need to have a quick talk."

"Uh-oh. Is she in trouble?"

"Probably," I said. "I need you to be a big girl and head upstairs to get ready for bed on your own, okay? I'll be up to tuck you in soon."

"Sure thing!" she said, looking proud to handle it herself.

Inside, the house was quiet except for a faint glow coming from the theater room. The door was closed. My irritation grew as I approached, unsure what I might find. Without hesitating, I opened the door. "Goodfellas" was playing, and Madison and her boyfriend were under a blanket. I flicked the light on.

"Hi, Dad," Madison said, casually.

"Hi, Mr. Parker," the boy chimed in. "I'm Kellen."

"Madison, can I speak to you outside? Now."

"Uh... okay," she said, looking confused.

Once we stepped into the hall, I crossed my arms and leveled her with a look. "What happened to waiting until eight?"

"Well, he was already close by at Drake's house. It just made sense for him to come here," she said, defensive. "Did you want me to tell him to wait in his car until you got back?"

"Yes, Madison. That's exactly what I wanted. He shouldn't have stepped foot in this house until I was home."

"What's the big deal? Mom lets him come over when she's not home."

"Really?" I snapped. "Well, this is my house, and the rules are different here. No boys are allowed in this house unless I'm here. Do you understand me?"

"Geez, Dad. You're overreacting. I babysat the boys for you, and he's only been here for like twenty minutes. Check your Ring!"

"Madison," I said, my voice firm. "If you break the rules, Kellen won't be allowed over at all. And while he is here, the door stays open, the lights stay on, and there's no more sitting under a blanket. Got it?"

"Fine," she muttered, rolling her eyes.

"And he leaves at ten. No later."

"Ten-thirty?"

"Madison..." My tone warned her not to push me.

"Fine. Ten," she said, spinning on her heel. Her long blonde hair whipped around, a stark reminder of Kelly. The resemblance was uncanny, but the attitude... that wasn't like the Kelly I knew. Had our divorce caused this behavior in Madison?

I went upstairs to check on Ivy and the boys, needing a reprieve. Ivy was already tucked in, flipping through her *Madeline* book.

"Hi, Daddy! I brushed my teeth, washed my face, and got in my PJs all by myself. I'm growing up!"

I laughed. "You are, but slow down, okay? I want you to stay little for a long time."

She smiled, proud of herself. "I'm just reading about Madeline and how she got her appendix out, like Bebe."

"Yep, just like Bebe. But it's late. Time for sleep."

As I tucked her in and turned off the lights, she said softly, "I love you, Daddy. You know, it's okay if you like Miss Natalie. I like her too, and I love Bebe."

I laughed. Winning over Ivy was easy. I couldn't imagine what Madison would say about Natalie. She'd probably run off with Kellen in protest.

I went to check on the boys, who were spread out on the floor of Carter's room trading baseball cards. "Alright, time to wrap it up and get ready for bed," I told them.

They barely looked up, muttering, "Okay dad."

Watching them, I couldn't help but think how nice it was that they were so close, and still so innocent.

My phone buzzed.

Natalie: How's the boyfriend? Try to stay calm.

I smirked at my phone, grateful for her sense of humor.

Will: He showed up early. I'm livid. Madison said he was just around the corner, so it "made sense" for him to come here.

She responded almost instantly.

Natalie: Yikes.

Will: No kidding. I should've told him to leave, but she claims her mom lets him come over when she's not there. Either Kelly's doing things differently, or Madison's lying through her teeth.

Natalie: Hang in there, Papa Bear. Meredith is trying to get me drunk.

Will: I like drunk Natalie. When can we go on a date?

Natalie: I was going to ask if you have a date for the opening of Piers?

Will: Lucas' restaurant?

Natalie: And Jasper's. Be my plus one?

Will : A chance to make that handsome Brit jealous? I'm in.

Natalie: You're something else, Parker. Take it easy on Madison, okay? Remember what it's like to be a teenager.

I sighed, knowing she was right. But still, I wasn't going to make it easy for Kellen.

At 9:55, I went to the doorway and announced, "Madison, you've got five minutes."

"Okay, Dad," she said, annoyed.

I heard whispers and movement. A minute later, they emerged.

"Thanks for having me, Mr. Parker," Kellen said, polite but awkward.

I nodded stiffly. "Sure."

Madison walked him to the door, closing it behind her as they stepped outside. I stayed near the window, watching. A few minutes later, she came back in, her expression happy as she headed toward the stairs.

"Good night, Dad," she said.

"Wait," I called.

She turned, curious. "Yes?"

I hesitated. "I'm new to this, Madison. I want to keep an open line of communication. I love you, and I don't want anything bad to happen to you. You're still my little girl."

Her expression softened. "I know. I should've asked if it was okay for him to come early. He's a nice guy, though."

"I'll be the judge of that," I said. "Love you, kiddo."

"Love you too, Dad," she said, heading upstairs.

And just like that, we had a productive conversation. Small victories.

Chapter 37

Grand Debut

Natalie

It was the day before the opening of Pier and Table, and every muscle in my body felt like it was running on high alert. Weeks of preparation were about to culminate in a single night, and it needed to be flawless. This wasn't just a restaurant, it was the sum of vision and precision, each choice stitched together to mean something. From the lighting to the table settings, each element carried weight. I had checked, double-checked, and triple-checked the design, yet I still felt like something had slipped through my fingers.

The day stretched endlessly ahead, a blur of final walkthroughs, last-minute adjustments to the seating plan, and making sure each corner looked exactly as I had envisioned. Lori was already on-site, no doubt armed with another list of changes from her end, and I had a nagging feeling Lucas would appear soon to weigh in with his own touches.

Having Meredith here this past week had been an absolute lifesaver. She'd taken over helping with Bebe, keeping her entertained while I focused on the finishing touches for the restaurant. Bebe was finally on the mend after her surgery, but I still worried about her being home all day. Jason, to my surprise, had stepped up in ways I hadn't expected. He'd been taking James to school every morning while Meredith and Camille managed pickups. James would spend the afternoons at home with us, a welcome burst of normalcy in the middle of all the mayhem.

Jason had even joined us for dinner a couple nights. It felt like old times, it was... nice. Civil. We were finding a rhythm I hadn't thought possible. He'd leave with James in the evenings, giving me space to concentrate on my work. It felt good to have him close, even just as a co-parent. It was an odd comfort, knowing we were doing this part right, even if our marriage had fallen apart.

One evening, I decided to ask him for a favor.

"Hey, would you mind taking both kids tomorrow night? Just for the night, so I can focus on the opening and not worry about rushing home."

"Of course," he said, his tone surprisingly easy. "I could take them for the whole weekend to give you a chance to recover. You'll need it after a night like that."

I felt a wave of relief but also a twinge of guilt. "That would be amazing, but are you sure? Bebe still needs a little extra care."

Jason smiled. "I've got it covered. I'll work from home Friday and keep an eye on her. And I'm not doing it alone, the babysitter can come by to help with laundry and whatever else, and Brooke offered to bring dinner."

There it was—Brooke. I'd known her involvement was inevitable, but the mention of her name still caught me in the chest. Jason must have noticed the flicker of discomfort on my face because he added, "She's good with the kids, Nat. You don't have to worry."

I hesitated, swallowing my pride. "Okay. If it makes things easier for you, she can come. I just...want Bebe to feel taken care of."

"She will," he said firmly. "I promise."

After he left with James, Meredith found me sitting at the kitchen table, staring into my water cup.

"You, okay?" she asked, sliding into the chair across from me

"Yeah. It's just weird. Jason being so...helpful."

"And that's a bad thing?"

"No, it's not bad. It's just...new. I'm not used to him being so available. It's like he's trying to make up for all the times he wasn't, and it's throwing me off."

Meredith smirked. "Maybe he's finally realizing what he lost."

"I don't know," I said quickly. "He is being a good dad. He asked if Brooke can bring dinner. And honestly, I appreciate it. I need all the help I can get right now."

She tilted her head, studying me. "Well, it's big of you to let Brooke step in. But you know what's bigger? Telling your kids about Will."

I groaned.

"Nat, you're juggling a million things, and I get that, but you can't keep this part of your life in a bubble. They're going to find out sooner or later."

"I know," I admitted. "It's just...so much change at once. I'm trying to ease them into this new reality, but I don't want to overwhelm them."

Meredith reached across the table, squeezing my hand. "They'll be fine. You're a good mom. They know that."

The next morning, sunlight poured through the windows as I stood at the kitchen counter, running through my mental checklist for the day. The house was quiet, James was already at Jason's house for the week, and Bebe was curled up on the couch with her blanket and her stuffed duck, quietly flipping through a book. She was still moving slowly, her energy not quite back to normal yet.

Jason stopped by mid-morning, the familiar creak of the front door announcing his arrival. He stepped inside, set his keys on the counter, and glanced around. "I'm here for Bebe," he said.

"Thank you for being so helpful," I said, with sincerity. His assistance with the kids made me feel less guilty for being so focused on Pier and Table.

Bebe stirred on the couch, looking up when she saw Jason. "Hi, Daddy," she said, her voice soft but happy.

Jason walked over and crouched down next to her. "Hey, princess. You ready for a relaxing day?"

She nodded, clutching her duck closer.

"The babysitter is going to come by later to help, and Brooke's bringing dinner tonight. You just relax and let us take care of you."

I joined them, kneeling to Bebe's level and tucking her blanket around her for the car ride. "You'll have fun, sweetheart. Be good for Daddy, okay?"

"Okay, Mama. I love you."

"I love you too." I kissed her forehead and stepped back as Jason carefully scooped her from the couch and carried her to the car.

Once Bebe was settled in her booster seat with her duck and books, Jason turned to me. "I'll keep you posted on how she's doing. Don't stress about anything tonight, you've got enough on your plate."

"Thanks, Jason. For all of this. For being so... steady lately. It's nice to feel like we're a team."

Jason met my eyes, his expression serious but warm. "We are a team, Nat. I know I didn't always show that before, but I'm trying."

For a moment, I just stood there, taking in this new version of Jason. This wasn't the man I'd been married to, the one who was always rushing out the door or distracted by work. This version of Jason felt present and dependable. It wasn't the same as love, but it was something solid, and something we could build on for the kids.

"Call me if you need anything," I said.

"I will," he replied with a small smile. "Enjoy tonight." His tone was sincere.

As the car disappeared down the street, I turned back to the house. A strange mix of relief and gratitude settled over me. It was bittersweet to realize that Jason and I had finally figured out how to work together, when it was too late for us as a couple but exactly what we needed to be as co-parents.

With that thought, I grabbed my keys and my notebook. It was time to get back to Pier and Table for the final touches.

By the time I arrived at the restaurant, the space was already buzzing with activity. Staff moved through the dining room, polishing glasses, adjusting place settings, and preparing for tonight's soft opening. Lori was in the corner with her clipboard, her sharp voice cutting through the noise as she directed someone to rearrange the centerpiece on the bar.

I dropped my bag on a nearby counter and grabbed my notebook, ready to dive in. This was my last chance to make sure everything was perfect before the doors opened tonight.

"Natalie!" Lori called, waving me over. "We have a problem with the lighting in the private dining room. It's too harsh, it's killing the ambiance."

"On it," I said, following her through the room. I spent the next hour adjusting details: checking the lighting, testing the music levels, and obsessing over every table setting. I couldn't let myself relax, not when there was still so much to do.

Just as I was finalizing the arrangements for the outdoor seating, I spotted movement by the entrance. Will had walked in, looking handsome as always, but my stomach dropped when I saw who was with him. Lisa.

"Hey," Will said, walking toward me with a coffee in hand. "Thought you could use this."

"Thanks," I said, accepting the cup but keeping my tone neutral. "What are you doing here?"

"I had to finalize some details with Lisa," he said casually.

Lisa stepped forward, flashing a bright smile. "This place is stunning, Natalie. Really incredible work."

"Thanks," I replied, forcing a polite smile. "It will be fun to get moving on your space." I lied.

I tried to stay focused, but Lisa's gaze lingered on Will, and while I told myself it didn't matter, it still made me uncomfortable. Before I could say anything else, Lori and Lucas came over together, both carrying their usual energy and efficiency.

"Natalie, we've got an issue with the dimmers," Lori said, her words rapid-fire. "Lucas thinks the lights should be brighter for the opening, but I say it kills the mood. Thoughts?"

A wave of professionalism steadied me, like a lifeline. "Keep it low," I said, flipping open my notebook. "The lighting is layered to draw people in and make the room feel intimate. If it's too bright, you lose the warmth, and the energy falls flat. Everything has been designed to flow from the entryway to the last table, and the light sets the tone."

Will lingered nearby, but I pretended not to notice as I walked with Lori and Lucas toward the bar. The conversation moved to logistics, and for a while, I was able to bury myself in the details.

When I finally turned back toward the entrance, Lisa and Will were heading out. Lisa gave me a quick wave, her expression cheerful. "See you tonight!"

Will caught my eye before leaving, his voice low. "I'll pick you up at 5:30."

"I was just going to Uber with Meredith," I said, keeping my tone cool.

"Natalie," he said, his eyes steady, "Evan and I will pick you ladies up. See you then."

I nodded reluctantly, turning back to my notebook as they walked out.

Lori glanced at me with a raised eyebrow. "You two good?"

"We're fine," I said quickly. "I'm a hundred and ten percent focused on tonight."

Lucas flipped through his notes, then looked up. "Shall we take one more pass through the space?"

"Good idea," I said, following them toward the host stand, my eye catching on the entryway lighting and the alignment of the floral arrangements. Everything had to feel intentional the moment the first guest walked in.

By mid-afternoon, the restaurant was finally coming together. Each light glowed at just the right warmth, every table was set with precision, and the space carried the hum of anticipation. Lori, clipboard in hand, walked beside me through the dining room one last time, ticking off each element on her list.

"You've nailed it," she said as we paused near the front doors. "This place is going to blow people away tonight."

"Thanks, Lori," I said, exhaling a small sigh of relief.

"But" she added, turning to me with a critical eye, "you look like you've been running a marathon. Go do something about that hair."

"Will do," I said without hesitation.

"And I mean it—get out of here," she said, waving her clipboard at me. "You're done for the day. Go get fabulous."

"Alright," I said, smiling as I grabbed my bag. "See you tonight."

As I walked out of the restaurant, I felt a mix of exhaustion and excitement. Everything was perfect, and for the first time all day, I let myself relax. Now I just needed to make myself presentable.

When I got home, I dropped my bag by the door and headed upstairs. As soon as I stepped into my room, I spotted something unexpected, a stunning Galven London red dress hanging on the closet door. Next to it was a small note written in Meredith's bold handwriting:

This is exactly what you need tonight. Trust me. Mer xoxo.

I smiled, running my fingers over the fabric. Leave it to Meredith to find the perfect dress when I didn't even realize I needed one.

After a quick shower, I started blow-drying my hair, letting the noise of the day fade into the background. Halfway through, I noticed music growing louder, the unmistakable beat of Madonna's "Vogue" drifting closer and closer.

A moment later, Meredith appeared in the bathroom doorway, a Bluetooth speaker in hand and a wide grin on her face. She was in her silk Oscar de la Renta robe, her hair and makeup flawless.

"Okay," she said, setting the speaker down. "Let me do your makeup. You're not leaving this house until you look as perfect as that restaurant."

"I was doing fine on my own," I protested, but she rolled her eyes and motioned for me to sit.

"You were doing fine," she said, pulling out her makeup bag, "but you could do better. Now hold still."

I laughed as she started working, carefully brushing eyeshadow onto my lids and adding a pair of false lashes she somehow always seemed to have on hand. The whole time, she hummed along to the music, occasionally breaking into full-on lyrics whenever the mood struck her.

"Project complete," she said triumphantly when she was finished.

I turned to the mirror and blinked at my reflection. My eyes looked bigger, brighter, and my skin glowed like I'd just walked out of a professional studio.

"You're a magician," I said, standing to give her a hug.

"You look flawless," she said with a wink. "Now put that gorgeous dress on and meet me downstairs. We're having a glass of wine before the men show up."

"Yes, ma'am," I said, laughing as she swished out of the room, her robe trailing dramatically behind her.

I slipped into my red gown, smoothing the fabric down over my hips, and glanced at my reflection one last time. The woman staring back at me looked confident and in control—a far cry from the whirlwind of nerves I'd felt earlier. The dress was a knock out, but I also had to acknowledge how far I'd come in the last year: I'd found my footing after the end of my marriage, taken huge strides in my career, and was no longer living in the shadows of an affair. Was I finally stepping into my future?

When I headed downstairs, Meredith was waiting with two glasses of wine and a satisfied grin. "You look fabulous."

"Thanks to you," I said, taking the glass she offered. "You look stunning, as always."

She wore a black halter-neck jumpsuit with a plunging V-neck that revealed a tempting line of cleavage, making her look six feet tall, her toned shoulders on full display.

"Cheers," she said, holding up her glass.

"Cheers," I echoed, clinking mine against hers.

As we sipped, the house filled with easy warmth, the kind that only comes from being with someone who knows you better than anyone else. For the first time all day, I felt like I could let go.

As we sipped, the doorbell rang. Meredith smirked, setting her glass down. "I'll get it," she said, sashaying toward the door.

I heard the low rumble of male voices as I made my way toward the foyer. When I turned the corner, Will and Evan stood there, both looking ridiculously handsome. Will had a tailored navy suit with an open collar, his blonde hair gelled back just enough to look sinfully put together. Evan's hair had that intentional messiness that came with great genes. His dark gray suit and V-neck looked custom-fit, his grin already aimed at Meredith.

"Hello, boys," Meredith said, her voice laced with playful charm. "Don't you two clean up nicely."

Evan chuckled, his gaze lingering on her. "Not half as nice as you, darlin."

Meredith blushed and smiled.

Will's eyes locked on me, and for a moment, the world seemed to slow down. "Wow," he said softly, taking a step forward. "You look incredible."

"Thanks," I said, feeling a flush rise to my cheeks.

Will leaned in, his voice low enough for only me to hear. "Red is your color."

Meredith grabbed her phone and snapped a photo of the four of us. It was the first time Will and I were in a photo. No secrets. The real deal.

Evan looped his arm through Meredith's, "Shall we?"

I nodded, slipping my hand into Will's as we headed out the door.

I felt like everything was exactly where it was supposed to be.

When we pulled up to the restaurant, the glow of the lights from the windows spilled out onto the street, illuminating the gathering crowd of well-dressed guests. Lori had done a fantastic job organizing the evening, and the sight of people waiting to step inside filled me with pride and nerves all at once.

Will got out first, moving quickly to my side of the car. He opened the door for me, offering his hand.

"Ready for this?" he asked as I stepped out, his voice low and steady.

"As ready as I'll ever be," I said, taking a deep breath.

Will's hand rested lightly on the small of my back as he led me toward the entrance. His touch was reassuring, grounding me in the moment. Behind us, Evan offered his arm to Meredith, and she took it with a playful roll of her eyes.

When we stepped inside, the transformation of Pier and Table took my breath away. The soft glow of the chandeliers bathed the room in warm light, and the tables sparkled with crystal glasses and polished silverware. Servers moved gracefully between the guests, offering trays of champagne and hors d'oeuvres. The space was alive with energy, the buzz of conversation and laughter filling the air.

"Looks incredible," Will said, leaning closer to me.

"Thanks," I said, my voice in awe of the space around us.

Lori appeared like a whirlwind, clipboard still in hand, her sharp eyes scanning the room. "Natalie!" she called, stopping in front of us. "Everything's running smoothly so far. The first seating is almost ready, and Jasper says the kitchen is on schedule."

"Perfect," I said, feeling a wave of relief.

"Now," she said with a sly smile, "I have someone I want you to meet."

Without hesitation, I nodded and followed her as she led me toward a tall, distinguished man in his early fifties, wearing a perfectly tailored suit. His salt-and-pepper hair and confident demeanor immediately gave him an air of importance.

"Alan," Lori said, her voice warm but professional, "this is Natalie Bradford, the creative genius behind Pier and Table's design."

Alan turned toward me with an easy smile, extending his hand. "Natalie, it's a pleasure. This space is stunning, one of the most impressive restaurant designs I've seen in years."

"Thank you," I said, shaking his hand. "That means a lot."

"I've been in the design industry for over two decades," Alan said, his tone genuinely complimentary, "and I can tell when someone has a gift for creating not just a space, but an experience. You've nailed it here."

"That's very kind of you to say," I replied, feeling both flattered and slightly overwhelmed.

"Kind, but true," Lori interjected. "I told you Natalie was someone to watch."

Alan laughed. "You weren't exaggerating." He turned back to me. "If you're open to it, I'd love to talk more sometime. I have a few projects in the pipeline that could benefit from your touch."

My heart skipped at his words, but I kept my tone measured. "I'd love that. Thank you."

Alan handed me a sleek business card. "Let's connect soon. And enjoy your night—you've earned it."

As Alan and Lori moved on, Will reappeared at my side. "Is that who I think it is?"

"Alan Moore," I said, holding up the card. "Apparently, he's a big deal in the design world."

Will raised an eyebrow. "Yes, he is. And he's someone who knows talent when he sees it."

I smiled, tucking the card into my clutch. "We'll see."

Will leaned in closer, his voice warm. "I told you, you're the star tonight."

Before I could respond, a gentle chime rang out, silencing the hum of conversation in the room. The crowd turned toward a small platform near the center of the dining area, where Lori stood with a microphone in hand, Lucas standing just behind her.

"Good evening, everyone," Lori began, her voice clear and commanding. "Thank you all for being here tonight for the soft opening of Pier and Table. This restaurant has been a labor of love, and none of it would have been possible without an incredible team."

She gestured toward Lucas, who stepped forward, his polished British accent immediately drawing the crowd's attention. "I'd like to echo Lori's thanks," Lucas began, his tone steady and confident. "This restaurant has been a dream in the making, and seeing it come to life tonight has been nothing short of extraordinary. I'm deeply grateful to everyone who has worked tirelessly to make this happen—from our incredible chef, Jasper, and the kitchen team to the floor staff who have made tonight seamless."

A wave of applause spread across the room, and Lucas continued, "And, of course, this wouldn't be Pier and Table without the vision of Natalie Bradford. Her creativity and design expertise have made this space unforgettable. Natalie, thank you for bringing this dream to life."

The applause grew louder, and my cheeks burned as all eyes turned to me. Will nudged me lightly, murmuring, "Go on, take your bow."

I gave a small wave, too overwhelmed to do much more.

Lori stepped forward again, raising her glass. "Let's toast to Lucas, Jasper, Natalie and to the team. To the start of something truly special. Cheers!"

"Cheers!" the crowd echoed, glasses clinking throughout the room.

As the applause faded, Meredith and Evan appeared beside us, both holding glasses of champagne.

"Well," Meredith said, grinning as she took in the room, "look at you, Natalie. The toast of the town."

Evan raised his glass toward me dramatically. "To Natalie, the woman who can do no wrong. Except maybe choosing this guy as her plus one." He nodded toward Will with a teasing grin.

Will smirked. "Careful, Evan. That's a bold statement coming from someone who's spent most of the night following Natalie's sister around."

Evan chuckled. "Can you blame me? He turned to Meredith. "What's your secret?"

Meredith tilted her head, smiling slyly. "I don't give away my secrets. You'll just have to keep guessing."

"Fair enough," Evan replied, clinking his glass against hers.

The repartee between them was light, and I could see the beginnings of something playful and easy forming between them.

As the night continued, the four of us moved through the room, chatting with guests and sampling Jasper's hors d'oeuvres. At one point. Meredith pulled out her phone, snapping photos for social media. She turned her lens toward me and Will, tilting her head critically.

"Come on, you two," she said. "Stand closer. You're a team tonight, aren't you?"

Will slid his arm around my waist without hesitation, his hand resting lightly on my hip. "How's this?" he asked, his tone teasing.

Meredith snapped the photo, her expression satisfied. "Perfect. You two look like you belong together."

Evan leaned over to peek at the screen. "Not bad," he said with a grin. "But I still think you're going to need me to make these photos go viral."

"Nice try," Meredith said, slipping her phone back into her bag. "I've got it covered."

Later, as the evening wound down, the energy in the room softened, transitioning from lively buzz to a quieter hum. Guests began filtering out, full and happy, their faces glowing with the satisfaction of a memorable night.

Meredith, however, wasn't quite ready for it to end. "This place is amazing, but I feel like celebrating," she said, glancing toward Evan. "What's around here? I could use a nightcap."

Evan raised an eyebrow. "I know a great cocktail bar just down the block. What do you think, Will? Natalie? Up for it?"

I smirked. "You two have fun. I'm calling it a night."

Evan shot Will a glance. "What about you? You coming along?"

Will shook his head, his hand resting lightly on my lower back. "I'm good. You two go have fun. But, Meredith," he added, narrowing his eyes playfully, "don't let him get you into trouble."

Meredith laughed. "No promises, but I'll keep him in line."

Evan gave me a mock-serious nod. "I'll make sure your sister behaves herself."

Will grinned, shaking his head. "If anything, you're the one who needs babysitting."

Meredith rolled her eyes at them both. "All right, we're out. See you tomorrow, Nat!"

The car ride back to my house was quiet, the kind of comfortable silence that didn't need filling. Will's hand rested lightly on my knee, his thumb tracing small, absent-minded circles that sent warmth through me.

When we pulled into my driveway, he turned to me with a small smile. "You know," he said, his voice laced with humor, "Sarah and Todd might be my favorite people right now."

I tilted my head, confused. "Why's that?"

"They're playing house tonight," he said. "All four of my kids are over there, and I'm pretty sure Todd is regretting every decision he's made that led to this moment."

I laughed, shaking my head. "Sounds like they're getting a crash course in parenting."

Will grinned. "Yeah, and meanwhile, I've got the night off." His voice softened as he looked at me.

My heart fluttered, but I couldn't resist teasing him. "So, does this mean you want to sleep over?"

"Absolutely," he said, his tone steady and certain.

I smiled, my cheeks warming as we pulled in the driveway. Will came around to open my door, offering his hand as he helped me out of the passenger seat. He followed me to the front steps as I unlocked the front door. Outside, the night was quiet, the air cool and crisp, but inside, there was only the steady hum of something that felt like possibility.

Chapter 38

Minty Fresh
Natalie

The house was still as I closed the door behind us, the quiet hum of the evening settling in. Will rested his hand lightly on my lower back as I turned to face him, his blue eyes holding mine with a lock that sent heat rushing through me. His presence filled the space, warm and grounding, yet electric with anticipation.

"That was a big night," he said softly, his voice steady but laced with something undeniably intimate.

"It really was," I replied, a small smile tugging at my lips. "For the restaurant and the whole team behind The City Center."

"For us," he added, his words deliberate, his gaze unwavering. "Our first date."

The corners of my mouth lifted as his hand slid down my back, pulling me a fraction closer. The faint scent of his cologne lingered in the air between us, spicy and warm. "You're really counting tonight as our first real night out?" I teased.

"I am," he said, his voice dropping, the tension between us thickening. "But it wasn't just any night out. It was us, together. You and me. Like it should be. No hiding and sneaking around. The real deal."

My heart stuttered at his words, and the way his thumb brushed against the side of my waist sent a shiver coursing through me. The world outside seemed to fade, leaving only the quiet pulse of our breathing and the weight of what was unspoken between us.

"You're so sure," I murmured.

"I've never been more sure of anything," he said, his lips grazing the edge of my jaw, his breath warm against my skin.

Jillian Marie

The moment stretched, charged with a heady mix of anticipation and inevitability. Then suddenly, it snapped. His lips captured mine, fierce and consuming, and I sank into him, letting his hands and his touch pull me under.

Without breaking the kiss, he lifted me effortlessly, his arms cradling me as he carried me upstairs to my bedroom. The sound of my heartbeat thundered in my ears, each step he took feeling like an unspoken promise. The weight of the night, the applause, the conversation, it all melted away until there was nothing but us.

We stood next to the bed, his lips exploring the curve of my neck as his hands roamed over me, igniting a slow burn that spread through me like fire. Our connection only deepened as clothes slipped away, until there was nothing left between us but need.

The cool air against my skin sent a thrill through me as the fabric of my dress fell away. I felt his gaze on me, heated and reverent, as if I were the only thing that existed in the world.

"You're so damn beautiful," he murmured, his voice thick with reverence, and I felt a flush rise across my cheeks.

"You have a way of making me feel like I'm more than I ever thought I could be," I whispered.

His blue eyes locked on mine. "It's because you are. And I'll spend every chance I get making sure you know it."

His words undid me, breaking through every barrier I hadn't even realized I'd been holding onto. When his lips found mine again, all sense of anything but us melted away.

Every touch, every whisper, every kiss deepened the connection between us. His hands roamed over my body as if he was memorizing every curve, every reaction. By the time his fingers found me, I was already unraveling, my breath catching as I clung to him.

"I need you," I whispered, my voice trembling with want.

"You have me," he replied, his words heavy with meaning as he pressed his forehead to mine.

When he finally entered me, it was like everything in the world clicked into place. My breath hitched, and I clung to him, my fingertips digging into his back as a soft moan escaped my lips.

"It feels so right," I murmured, my voice breaking as he moved.

"Every time," he replied, his lips brushing against mine.

He had a way with my body that made it feel entirely his, like he had memorized every curve and every reaction. He moved with a rhythm made just for me, leaving me undone so many times that I lost count. The heat between us was all-consuming, and every touch felt like a promise that this moment would last forever.

When we finally collapsed together, the world blurred around the edges, leaving only the soft sounds of our breathing and the steady beat of his heart beneath my hand.

The next morning, I woke up in Will's cocoon. His warm body pressed against mine, his strong, lean arms draped over me. I stretched slightly, sinking deeper into the moment, feeling how safe and right it felt. My thoughts wandered, imagining what it would be like when six kids were running around the house.

"Morning," Will said, his voice rough with sleep.

"Morning," I said, turning over to face him.

"I love waking up next to you," he said, a slow, lazy smile spreading across his face.

"Me too." I hesitated for a moment before adding, "I've been thinking... how will we tell the kids about us?"

"Wow, Bradford," he teased, his blue eyes lighting up. "You're ready for the next step? I wasn't sure when you'd get to this point. With my scary teenager at home and all."

I tapped him playfully on the chest. "I'm still scared of her."

"Fair. Me too," he said with a chuckle. "We'll know when it's the right time. Maybe I should start with Kelly. Is it safe for me to tell her first?"

"I think so," I said, laughing. "I'm scared of her too. Jason already knows about us, thanks to that ER visit."

"Well, let's go back to cuddling then," he said, pulling me closer. His lips found mine, and before long, we naturally slipped into each other again. After we caught our breath, I slid out of bed, grabbing a robe.

"What do you want for breakfast?" I asked.

"I'll eat anything you make me."

"All right," I said. "Come down in a few. There's a spare toothbrush on the sink if you want to keep it here."

"Are you saying my breath smells?" he teased.

"No!" I laughed. "It's just...it's a big step for me, having you keep stuff here."

He smiled. "Thanks, babe. I'll take the toothbrush as a token of our official relationship." We both laughed as I headed downstairs.

The house was quiet, which meant Meredith was nowhere in sight. I checked my phone and found a text from her:

Meredith: I ended up staying at Evan's. Oops.

Shaking my head, I started making avocado toast. Will came downstairs as I poured coffee, wrapping his arms around me from behind and kissing my neck.

"I think that toothbrush works great," he said, his voice playful.

"You smell minty fresh." I said with a chuckle.

"Meredith stayed at Evan's," I said, turning in his arms. "Is it weird that they're hooking up?"

"A little," he admitted. "But nothing ever lasts with Evan."

"Same with Meredith," I said, laughing. "She never lets anyone get close. And she kind of blew off Jasper. She put him in the friend zone fast."

"She leaves soon, doesn't she?"

"Yeah, tomorrow. But she'll be back for Christmas."

"I love how close you two are," he said. "It's nice."

"You seem close with your sister too. And Evan. You two have that... closeness."

"Evan's like a brother to me. He is family."

I smiled, warmth tugging at my chest. I liked hearing him open up, collecting these little pieces of him as if they were mine to keep. The more I learned, the more I wanted, every detail that made Will, Will.

After breakfast, Will helped clear the dishes, much to my surprise.

"You don't have to do that," I said, watching him rinse plates. "I'm not used to a man helping in the kitchen."

"Hey, I'm divorced. I know how to do domestic stuff," he said with a smirk. "My maid only comes three days a week."

"Three days a week?" I teased. "You're fancy, Parker."

"My mom insisted. Otherwise, it would be her over five days a week." He said cringing.

We chatted about our upcoming schedules before Meredith walked in, clearly embracing the walk of shame. She wore what looked like Evan's boxers and one of his button-ups, her hair a chaotic bun. Somehow, she still looked like a Calvin Klein model.

"Head killing me. Need coffee," she groaned.

"Rough night?" Will asked, amused.

"Your friend is a bad influence," she muttered.

"That's my cue," Will said. He kissed me goodbye and left.

As I made Meredith breakfast, I couldn't resist asking, "So, how did Jasper lose out to Evan?"

"Jasper bored me. I set him up with Lisa. She's probably getting breakfast in bed from him right now," she said with a sly grin.

"You were bored? That fast?"

She shrugged. "It's not like Evan and I are serious. It's just fun."

Shaking my head, I handed her a plate and some ibuprofen. "You're a mess, Meredith."

She grinned. "Takes one to know one."

I laughed as I cleaned up the kitchen, grateful for the messy, imperfect people who made my life whole.

Chapter 39

Break On Through to the Other Side

Will

After I left Natalie's, I headed home for a shower and to get some work done. There was a note waiting for me on the kitchen counter.

Will,
The kids were great. Hope you had fun.
Love,
Sarah

I smiled at her neat handwriting, grateful for her help as always. Upstairs, I turned on the shower and stepped in, letting the hot water pour over me as I sorted through the day ahead. I needed to call Kelly and set up a time to meet. There was plenty we had to cover, starting with Madison having her boyfriend over when I wasn't home. We needed to be on the same page—no boys in the house without supervision. And then there was the harder part. I needed to tell her that Natalie and I were getting serious.

Once I was out of the shower, I dialed her number. She answered after a few rings.

"Hello, Will."

"Hey, Kelly, do you have time to meet up this afternoon before the kids get out of school?"

"Will, I just got back from our trip last night. But I do need to talk to you about something important, too. Let's plan to meet at the coffee house—say, around 1:00?"

"Great," I said. "I'll see you there."

After hanging up, I finished getting ready and headed to my office to work through some leasing details for The City Center. I had a stack of papers to review, including a few potential tenants for open spaces. Lori called me while I was working, her tone brisk and impatient as usual.

"Will, I've got a restaurant owner interested in another spot," she said. "Alan wants to work with Natalie on the design. He was impressed with how well Pier and Table turned out."

"That's great news," I said.

"Sure is. So, what's up with you and Natalie? I thought you were going to keep your dick in your pants," she added, half-joking but full of attitude.

"Lori, it's not just messing around. It's the real deal," I admitted.

"Oh, Will," she said with mock pity. "Well, it took me three tries to get marriage right, so who am I to judge? Now I'm married to the sweetest asshole around."

"Thanks for the pep talk, Lori," I said dryly. "Can you set up a meeting with Alan and the new possible tenant next week?"

"Will do. And bring Natalie. He values her input."

At 1:00, I arrived at the coffee house. Kelly was already seated at a small corner table, her planner open in front of her.

"Hello, William," she said, looking up briefly before returning her attention to her planner. "I ordered your usual, black coffee."

"Thanks," I said, sitting across from her.

She wasted no time. "While we were in Hawaii, Jeff proposed," she said. Her tone was even, but there was a slight edge to her voice. I haven't told the kids yet. I was planning to do it tonight."

"Wow," I said, keeping my tone neutral. "Congratulations. You seem happy." I meant it.

"Yes. We're planning to get married after the kids are out of school in June. We're taking them to Hawaii, it feels right to go back to where we got engaged."

"That sounds nice," I said.

Kelly flipped a page in her planner. "So, do you want to go over the schedule for the next few months?"

"Actually, I wanted to talk to you about two important things," I said, leaning forward. "First, Madison had her boyfriend, Kellen, over while I wasn't home.

I told her to wait until I got back, but she decided it was fine to let him over anyway."

"Yes, she told me," Kelly replied, her expression unchanging. "She also mentioned you were at Natalie's house with Ivy and left her to babysit the boys."

I frowned. "Madison is old enough to babysit, and I was gone for three hours. Don't turn this into something it's not."

"Why are you chasing after that woman, Will? You already ruined her marriage. She'll never make you happy. She's beneath you."

I leaned back, her words stoking the frustration I'd tried to keep at bay. "Really? Let me get this straight. I've supported you with Jeff, trusted your choices, and had your back. But you're more than okay with our teenage daughter having a boy over unsupervised than with me spending a few hours at Natalie's house with Ivy? I'm serious about Natalie. I was hoping you'd support me."

"You're serious about her?" Kelly's tone sharpened. "And spending time with her while you have our kids?"

"You're joking," I said, my voice rising. "I left for three hours and had Ivy with me the whole time. Real fair, Kelly."

I stood, my patience gone. "Thanks for the support. Good luck with your next husband."

I didn't wait for her reply. I turned and walked out, ignoring the stares from other customers as I left.

Driving along the PCH after leaving the coffee house I cranked up the volume as Jim Morrison's voice poured through the speakers. The haunting vocals and ominous rhythm felt like the perfect soundtrack to my mood. The salty ocean air drifted through the open window, but even the calming sound of the waves couldn't compete with the storm brewing in my mind.

I grabbed my phone at a stoplight and texted Evan.

Will: Can I come over?

Evan: Sure, I'm nursing my raging hangover. About to order burritos, want one?

Will: No thanks. I'll see you in fifteen minutes.

I knocked twice on Evan's door. I could hear Bear barking at my knock.

Evan opened the door, Bear greeted me.

"Bear, get down."

Evan was squinting against the sunlight. "Hey," he said, his voice hoarse. "You look like shit."

"So do you," I shot back.

He smirked, stepping aside to let me in. "Please, come in. Misery loves company."

I followed him inside, where he immediately flopped onto the couch and grabbed a bottle of water from the coffee table. "So, what's going on? You look like you're ready to explode," he said, popping a couple of Aleve into his mouth.

"It's Kelly," I said, sitting across from him. "I told her about Madison having a boy over when I wasn't home, and she twisted it into me being neglectful. Apparently, leaving Madison and the boys at home for three hours is some cardinal sin."

Evan raised an eyebrow. "Let me guess—you were at Natalie's?"

I nodded. "Yeah, Ivy wanted to visit Bebe after her surgery. It wasn't even a big deal."

"Wow," Evan said, shaking his head. "Kelly really knows how to make everything your fault, huh?"

"Yeah," I muttered. "And, she got engaged in Hawaii."

Evan whistled. "Well, that's rich. She's moving on, but you're not allowed to?"

"Exactly. She had a problem with Natalie from the moment she knew I was interested." I said, leaning back on the couch.

Evan walked over to the pantry and grabbed a bubbler, packing it with weed. "Will, you need to relax. Take a hit. You're too wound up."

I shook my head. "No thanks. I don't need to cloud my mind."

My phone buzzed, and I glanced at the screen. It was a text from Natalie.

Natalie: Hey, I just got the email about the meeting next week with the Italian tenant? The guy studied in Italy. I hope we get to taste test!

Will: I'm sure food will be involved at some point. Can I see you tonight?

Natalie: Sure. Any chance you can come here? Meredith's passed out on the couch. I hate to leave her on her last night.

Will: Is there anything I can bring?

Natalie: Your overnight bag. You could stay until Sunday. Meredith's flight is at noon tomorrow, and I have the day free.

"I'm going to head to Natalie's," I told Evan.

He raised an eyebrow. "Can I come, too?"

I shot him a look. "You just want to see Meredith, don't you?"

"Hey, what can I say? The woman's magnetic," he said with a grin.

"Let me ask her if it's alright," I said with a groan.

Will: Is it okay if I bring Evan? He's being a needy hot mess, and apparently, your sister isn't sick of him yet.

Natalie replied with a photo of Meredith sprawled out on the couch, her hair a wild mess, her face half-buried in a throw pillow.

Natalie: As hot of a mess as this?

I laughed and sent a photo back of Evan.

Will: Even worse.

"Go grab your stuff and clean up," I told Evan, rolling my eyes.

"Perfect," he said, standing up. "Give me ten minutes. Let me take the dog out and give him some food."

Just then, I felt my phone buzz again.

Natalie: Evan could bring Bear, so he doesn't have to leave him for long.

"She said you can bring the dog," I called after Evan.

"Sweet, I'll pack up his things."

We made our rounds and stopped at my house so I could grab my bag. On the way to Natalie's, I picked up Thai food for everyone, hoping it would help cure the hangovers.

When we arrived at Natalie's, Meredith was awake, her hair wrapped in a towel. Bear trotted straight to her, tail wagging like he just found his long-lost soul mate.

"He missed you," Evan said, unmistakable flirtation in his voice.

"I missed you too, Bear," her eyes locked on Bear but, presumably she meant this to Evan.

The attraction between them was impossible to ignore. I have never seen Evan like this before.

"You brought food, William. You're a saint," she said dramatically.

Natalie appeared from the kitchen, giving me a soft smile as she set out plates.

"How are you feeling, Evan?" Natalie asked, glancing at him as he unloaded his dog's stuff by the door.

"Like death," he admitted, rubbing his temple. Then, he added, "How are you feeling after your superstar night?"

She blushed, fiddling with the edge of a napkin. "Just tired and relieved it's over."

Bear wandered over to Natalie to greet her.

"Well, hello there." She said in a cooing voice.

We all sat down to eat, the comforting aroma of Pad Thai and drunken noodles filling the room. Meredith and Evan didn't even bother with small talk as they dove into their plates. After eating, the hangover twins disappeared outside to smoke, leaving Natalie and me alone in the kitchen.

"I talked to Kelly today," I said, leaning against the counter.

Natalie's face softened with concern. "Oh? How did it go?"

"Not great," I admitted. "She spun it around, saying I left Madison and the boys alone for you."

Her expression darkened. "I'm so sorry. That's not the response you were hoping for."

"And she's engaged," I added, shaking my head.

Natalie blinked in surprise. "Wow. You'd think that us dating wouldn't matter then."

"Yeah, you'd think," I said bitterly. "Whatever. I'm not going to let her dictate who I date. She's trying to control me."

Natalie didn't say much after that. Her posture shifted slightly, and I could tell the conversation made her uncomfortable.

"Want to watch a movie?" she asked, her tone lighter.

"Yes, we do," Meredith called out as she and Evan wandered back inside and plopped onto the couch.

We settled on "Once Upon a Time in Hollywood." Within twenty minutes, Evan was snoring, his head tilted back against the cushion. Meredith wasn't far behind him, her head propped awkwardly on his shoulder.

By the time the movie ended, Evan startled awake. "I should probably head out," he mumbled, running a hand through his hair. Bear lying on the ground beside him.

"You're welcome to stay," Meredith said, still half-asleep.

Evan glanced at Natalie. "You sure?"

"It's fine with me," Natalie said. "I'm heading to bed anyway. I'm wiped."

"Me too," I added, following Natalie upstairs.

She pointed toward the bathroom as we entered the room. "I left your toothbrush out for you," she said, her voice soft.

I stood beside her, brushing my teeth in comfortable silence. At one point, I slid over closer to her sink.

"I like your side better," I said, grinning at her through a mouthful of toothpaste.

She smiled back, her dimples peeking through, even as she finished brushing.

When we finally lay down in bed, Natalie turned toward me, her hazel eyes searching mine. "Are you okay? I know today was kind of a blow."

I let out a slow breath. "It's fine. It's typical Kelly. I just thought she'd be over it by now, maybe even a little supportive. But I do think we need to stay united on the no-boys rule for Madison. If we aren't strong together, she'll find a way to beat us down."

Her gaze softened, full of sincerity. "You're right," she said quietly.

"Thank you for not getting scared of this hurdle," I told her, brushing a strand of hair away from her face.

"I don't think this will be our last one," she replied.

I pulled her close, pressing a kiss to her forehead. She melted into my chest, fitting perfectly into my nook. We lay like that for a few moments, the weight of the day fading into the stillness of the night.

Then she kissed my cheek. It was a soft, fleeting gesture that sent a ripple through me. Her lips brushed mine next, and before I knew it, I was pulling her on top of me.

She moved over me, her hair falling in long waves around her shoulders, her body illuminated by the soft glow of the dimly lit lamp. Her tiny curves were perfect, her confidence intoxicating.

I held her hips as she moved, the rhythm between us building until I couldn't take it anymore. As I released, she fell forward onto my chest, and I wrapped my arms tightly around her, holding her close.

We didn't say anything as we lay tangled in each other. Sleep pulled at both of us, the steady rhythm of her breathing lulling me into calm.

I really could get used to this. Now, I just needed to get the four people who mattered most to me to be okay with it too.

Chapter 40

The Breakfast Club
Natalie

The next morning, with the sun creeping in, I turned to face Will, who was still sleeping peacefully. His long lashes rested against his cheekbones, making him look serene, almost tranquil.

I decided to surprise him with breakfast in bed. Carefully, I slipped out from under the covers, trying not to wake him. After brushing my teeth and washing my face, I tiptoed back through the room, only to hear his sleepy voice.

"Hey, pretty girl. Where do you think you're going?"

I walked over to the bed, leaning down to kiss him softly. "To make you breakfast," I said with a smile.

"Not so fast," he murmured, pulling me back onto the bed. I giggled as I landed against his chest.

Will laughed. "I should probably get up and brush my teeth, too, you're the teeth police," he said, though he made no move to leave.

I silenced his protest with a kiss, morning breath be damned. My lips trailed down his chest, then further over the ridges of his stomach, until I reached him. He drew in a sharp breath, his hands running through my hair as I took him into my mouth. The teasing was gone, replaced by a low sound that made me want to give him everything, to see him unravel for me.

When I finally came back up, his expression was tender, completely undone, as if I'd given him more than he knew how to hold.

"Good morning," I said.

"I'll say," he replied, his voice warm. "Breakfast in bed, huh? I think I could get used to Saturdays at the Bradfords."

By the time we both got up, I headed downstairs, expecting to start breakfast, only to find the coffee already brewing and the smell of bacon and eggs filling the air. Evan and Meredith were in the kitchen, cooking together. Meredith, wrapped in a robe, looked much better than she had the day before, and Evan looked just as refreshed. Were they... acting like a couple?

"Morning, you two," I said, pouring myself a cup of coffee. I grabbed another for Will and started putting together a breakfast tray—a tray we'd only ever used once before, years ago, on a Mother's Day when Bebe insisted on making me breakfast. That morning, I'd been served soggy cereal, burnt toast, and two sweet cards that made it all worth it.

As I thought about that memory, I wondered about the future. Would Will help my kids make breakfast someday? Was I thinking too far ahead? Or was it time to think about these things?

I pushed the thoughts aside and focused on the present, arranging our breakfast on the tray and adding a small vase of flowers for a nice touch.

"Breakfast in bed?" Meredith asked, her tone teasing.

"What time do I need to get you to the airport?" I asked, changing the subject.

"I can Uber, sweetie."

"Or I could take you," Evan chimed in. "I'll borrow Will's car."

"I'll take you, Meredith," I insisted.

"Okay, guys, no need to fight over me," Meredith said with a laugh.

I told her to just text me what she wanted to do as I headed back upstairs with the tray.

When I entered the room, Will was sitting up, scrolling through something on his phone.

"Wow," he said, smiling. "This looks amazing. I don't think anyone's ever done this for me before."

"Only once for me," I replied.

"Well," he said, "let's make a pact: we'll take turns making each other breakfast in bed."

"I can live with that," I said, sitting beside him.

We ate leisurely, laughing and talking. At one point, he asked, "So, tell me, what else do you love? What do you hate? What do you need from me?"

"Wow," I said, laughing. "You're really laying it on thick, Parker."

"I mean it. You weren't appreciated before, and I don't want to make that same mistake. I want to know what you want, what you need, how we make this work."

I paused, thoughtful. "I guess I haven't thought that far ahead," I admitted. "But I do like having my own space sometimes. And I think when the kids aren't with us, that could be our time."

Will nodded. "Makes sense. Bebe and Ivy already get along. Madison, though... well, she's not a monster every day. The boys all seem easy going if they can play some Nintendo or physical sports. Madison will come around. This is worth it, Natalie. What we have is worth figuring out the rocky stuff. Once we do, it'll get easier."

Before we could continue, my phone buzzed.

Meredith: Should we all drive to the airport? Evan wants to know if Will can drop him off after me.

I read the text aloud to Will.

"These two," he said, shaking his head with a grin. "What are they up to?"

"I'll text her back and let her know we'll be down in thirty."

Will got up to shower, and I couldn't resist joining him. "No funny business, Bradford," he teased, pulling me into a kiss.

We didn't make it out of the shower quickly, but eventually, we got dressed and headed downstairs. Meredith looked effortlessly chic in her matching ALO set, while Evan, casual with Bear by his side, couldn't stop glancing her way.

When we arrived at John Wayne Airport, Evan grabbed Meredith's luggage, and Will gave her a hug.

"Be good to my sister," she teased him.

"You know I will," he replied with a smile.

I hugged her tightly. "Thank you," I whispered. "I'll see you in two weeks for Christmas."

Meredith nodded, her eyes glistening. "I can't wait, wherever you are, you are my home."

I hugged her tight one last time.

Just before she walked away, Evan surprised us all by dipping her slightly and giving her a romantic kiss.

Once Meredith was on her way, we dropped Evan off and had time to ourselves.

"How about lunch and a walk on the beach?" Will suggested. "Have you been to Beachcomber Café?"

"I love that place," I said.

"Perfect. Let's go."

Chapter 41

Blissful Beginnings
Natalie

The salty breeze whipped gently across my face as I sat across from Will at a table outside the Beachcomber Café. The sound of waves crashing nearby mingled with the hum of happy chatter from other diners, creating the perfect backdrop for our lunch.

Will leaned back in his chair, a relaxed smile playing on his lips. "I could get used to this," he said, taking a sip of his drink.

"You mean the view or the company?" I teased, raising an eyebrow.

"Both," he replied smoothly, his eyes meeting mine with that mischievous glint that always made my stomach flutter.

The waitress arrived with our food, placing a grilled mahi sandwich in front of him and a vibrant salad in front of me. For a moment, we both focused on our meals, the silence between us comfortable.

"This feels unreal," I admitted after a few bites, setting my fork down.

"What does?"

"This," I said, gesturing between us. "Having time together in broad daylight. Just us. No kids, no interruptions. No hiding."

Will nodded thoughtfully. "It's nice, isn't it? Feels like we're finally getting to breathe a little."

I smiled, watching him as he ate, his movements unhurried, like he wanted to savor the moment.

After lunch, we wandered down the beach, shoes in hand. The sand was cool beneath my feet, the tide gently lapping at the shore. We walked side by side, close enough that our arms brushed every now and then.

"I've been thinking a lot about how we can make this work," Will said, breaking the comfortable silence.

"With our kids?" I asked.

"Yeah. I want this to feel...natural, you know? For everyone. But I also know we can't force it."

I nodded, appreciating his thoughtfulness. "I think we need to take it slow. The kids are still adjusting to everything. If we rush into this, it could backfire."

"Agreed," he said. "So, here's what I've been thinking: we line up our schedules. When I have my kids, you'll have yours, and when they're with their other parents, we'll have time to ourselves."

"That makes sense," I said. "Natalie and Will weekends. I like the sound of that."

He grinned. "We'll make the most of them. Lazy mornings, long walks, and plenty of time for..." He trailed off, raising an eyebrow suggestively.

"Time for what?" I asked, feigning innocence.

"Oh, I think you know exactly what I mean."

I laughed, shaking my head. "You're impossible."

"But you like me this way."

I bumped his shoulder lightly. "I do. And I like the idea of us not pushing the children too fast. Maybe we see each other a couple of times during the weeks when we have them, but we don't force the families together right away."

"That sounds right to me," he said. "And when it's just us..."

"When it's just us?" I prompted.

"Well, let's just say I plan to spend most of that time naked in bed with you."

I burst out laughing, the sound carried away by the breeze. "You're shameless."

"Just honest," he said, his tone teasing but his eyes serious.

We walked further along the shore, our conversation fading into a comfortable silence. The waves lapped at our feet, and the sun hung high in the sky, casting light across the water.

Out of nowhere, Will turned to me with a mischievous glint in his eye.

"What?" I asked, already smiling.

Without warning, he scooped me up into his arms, spinning us in a circle as I shrieked with laughter.

"Will!" I cried, clinging to his shoulders.

"You're too serious sometimes, Bradford," he teased, his grin widening.

He finally set me down, but before I could catch my breath, his hands slid to my waist, pulling me closer. His lips found mine in a kiss so soft and deliberate, it made my knees weak.

When he pulled back, his gaze locked on mine, and his voice dropped to a low murmur. "I've had a crush on you since the moment I saw you at the gate."

His words stole the air from my lungs. "Me too," I admitted softly, my cheeks warming. "I just didn't know what to do about it."

He smiled, brushing a strand of hair from my face. "I'm glad we figured it out."

"So am I," I whispered, leaning in to kiss him again, the waves crashing gently behind us.

We stopped by the market on the way back to my house, picking out fresh ingredients for dinner. Will carried the basket, tossing in items he thought would go well with the chicken I'd suggested.

"You're taking this very seriously," I said, watching as he inspected a bundle of herbs.

"I'm a perfectionist when it comes to cooking," he said. "You'll see."

Back at my house, we worked side by side in the kitchen. The air filled with the scent of garlic and rosemary as the chicken roasted in the oven. Will poured two glasses of wine, handing one to me before leaning against the counter.

"This feels good," he said, his voice soft.

"Cooking?"

"Being here. With you. Like this."

I met his gaze, my chest tightening at the sincerity in his expression. "It does," I said, my voice barely audible.

Dinner was simple but delicious, and by the time we'd finished eating, I felt relaxed and at ease.

"Let's take a bath," Will said as we carried the dishes to the sink.

I raised an eyebrow. "A bath?"

"Trust me," he said, his tone low and suggestive. Then came his signature wink. On any other guy it would have made me cringe.

The tub in my bathroom was big enough for two, the warm water swirling around us as we leaned back against the cool porcelain.

Will reached for me, his hands tracing slow, deliberate paths down my arms and along my sides. I leaned into his touch, my breath hitching as he kissed the curve of my shoulder.

Things heated quickly from there. The water sloshed against the sides of the tub as we moved together, our laughter mingling with gasps of pleasure. When we couldn't contain ourselves any longer, we shifted out of the tub, the cool tile of the floor a sharp contrast to the warmth between us.

A towel became our makeshift bed as Will hovered over me, his lips finding mine in a kiss that felt endless. His hands explored every inch of my skin, his touch both urgent and tender.

When he finally entered me, it was slow, deliberate, as if he wanted to savor every moment. We moved together, our rhythm building until we were both lost in the intensity of it.

Afterward, as we lay on the floor of my bathroom, the towel beneath us forgotten, I traced my fingers along his jawline. His breathing was still uneven, his body relaxed in a way that mirrored my own.

"You're dangerous," I teased, my voice soft.

"Why's that?" he asked, a lazy smile playing on his lips.

"Because you make me feel things I'm not sure I'm ready to feel," I admitted.

Will turned onto his side, propping his head on his hand. His dark eyes searched mine, and for a moment, I thought he might tease me. Instead, his tone softened.

"I love you, Natalie," he said quietly. The words hung in the air. I think I've been intrigued by you since the moment I saw you."

A lump rose in my throat, and my chest tightened. "I love you, too," I whispered, the words tumbling out before I could stop them. They felt right, like they'd been waiting for this moment to be spoken aloud.

He leaned down, brushing his lips against mine in a kiss that was more tender than anything we'd shared before. It wasn't urgent or passionate, it was filled with a quiet kind of certainty that settled something deep inside me.

We moved to the bedroom, falling into bed with the kind of ease that felt natural, like we'd been doing this for years. Will flipped on Seinfeld as we curled up together, my head resting on his chest, his arm draped around me.

"This was a good day," I murmured, my voice heavy with exhaustion.

"A great day," he replied, pressing a kiss to the top of my head.

The soft glow of the TV bathed the room in light, but my eyes were already closing. I fell asleep feeling completely at peace.

Chapter 42

Fourth And Goal

Will

The next morning came too soon. I wanted nothing more than to stay in bed with Natalie all day, putting her in positions only an acrobat could handle. But I knew she had plans. She was spending the day with James, something she'd been looking forward to since Bebe's surgery had taken up so much of her time.

Natalie groaned when she looked at the clock. "It's 7:30. I better get moving." She was curled up in my nook, her body perfectly spooned against mine. Every inch of her got me going, like some magnetic force I couldn't resist. I knew it was the same for her because, as soon as she felt me stir behind her, she slid her hand back to confirm what she already suspected.

Her fingers stroked me lightly, teasingly. "Okay, maybe a few more minutes," she whispered. Those "few more minutes" quickly turned into her straddling me, her body taking over as her breath hitched and her moans filled the air. I held her hips and met every movement until we both collapsed, out of breath and entirely spent.

She rolled out of bed, her naked frame disappearing into the bathroom. I watched her go, marveling at how she managed to be both graceful and devastatingly sexy. I was a man utterly, hopelessly in love with this woman.

I glanced at the clock. It was almost eight. I had plans with Evan to watch football around 10:30. Natalie stepped out of the shower, wrapped in a towel, her wet hair falling down her back. She picked out jeans and a long-sleeve sweater that hugged her in all the right places.

"You ready for a big day at the amusement park?" I teased as she finished getting dressed.

She laughed, shaking her head. "I'll meet you downstairs," she said, walking over to me. I was brushing my teeth, and she stood beside me, looking at our reflection in the mirror as though she couldn't quite believe it was real. I leaned down and kissed her.

"When can I see you again this week?" I asked.

She thought for a moment. "We have the Christmas concert on Thursday."

I grinned. "I'll save you a seat."

She rolled her eyes, laughing. "How about Tuesday at lunch? I'll come over."

"I think I can make that work," I said, rinsing my mouth. "By the way, Alan wants you at the meeting with his investor for the restaurant project. It's a big deal."

"Wow," she said, her face lighting up. "Count me in. Just let me know the details."

"Will do."

Natalie headed downstairs while I showered and got dressed. When I joined her in the kitchen, she was assembling a yogurt parfait. She handed me one along with a cup of coffee. I liked the way she took care of me, like it came naturally to her. It was a stark contrast to Kelly, who always made me feel like any effort on her part was a chore. With Natalie, everything felt easy.

Once breakfast was done, she packed snacks and water bottles for her and James, adding hats to her bag like she was mentally checking things off a list. "Okay, I think I have everything," she said.

We walked through her garage to the driveway, where my car was parked. I leaned in to kiss her goodbye, but a car pulled up just as I was about to. It was Jason.

He didn't look happy to see me.

Natalie noticed him immediately. "Jason," she said, her tone neutral. "I thought I was picking James up at 9:30."

Jason got out of the car, his expression cold. "I called and texted you. Bebe forgot a book she needs for her report. I thought I would pick it up and drop off James. He looked at me. "Enjoying my house, Will?"

Natalie stepped forward before things could escalate. "Jason, let's not do this with the children in the car," she said firmly.

Jason's jaw tightened, but he didn't argue. Bebe rolled down her window. "Is Ivy here?" she asked.

Natalie crouched down to her daughter's level. "No, sweetie. Ivy isn't here."

Jason raised an eyebrow, clearly waiting to see how Natalie would handle this. She opened the car door and said, "Why don't we all go inside for a minute?"

James looked confused. "Mommy, aren't we going to Legoland?"

"We are," Natalie said. "We just need to talk about something first."

Inside, Natalie gathered James and Bebe in the living room. Jason and I stood awkwardly to the side, waiting for her to speak.

Natalie knelt in front of the kids, her demeanor calm. "I love you both very much and you are my number one priority. You know how Daddy has a friend, Brooke?"

Bebe's face lit up. "I like Brooke! She sang to me the other night."

Natalie's smile faltered for just a moment, but she quickly recovered. "I'm glad you like her. That's what I wanted to talk to you about. You know how Daddy and Brooke spend time together because they're friends?"

Bebe nodded, her little brow furrowing slightly.

"Well, Will and I spend time together too, and he's very special to me. You're probably going to see him, Ivy, and her siblings a little more often."

James tilted his head. "Like...special how?"

Natalie hesitated, glancing at Jason, who remained silent but watchful. "He's more than a friend," she explained gently. "We really care about each other, and we enjoy spending time together. Does that make sense?"

Bebe looked thoughtful. "Does that mean Ivy and I will be sisters?"

"Not exactly," Natalie said with a small laugh. "But you might see her more often. You're still my number one priority, okay? That's never going to change."

Bebe's face relaxed. "Okay." She brightened suddenly. "Can Ivy and I have a sleepover here?"

Natalie laughed, glancing at Jason. "We'll talk about that another time. Right now, we're just figuring out how to spend time together as a family."

James shrugged. "Okay, can we go to Legoland now?"

"Almost, buddy. Just a couple more things to sort out first," Natalie said, standing up. "I'm just going to check Bebe's room for her book. Why don't you two spend a little time in the playroom while I look?"

"Yay!" James exclaimed, grabbing Bebe's hand as they darted out of the room.

As soon as the kids were gone, the tension in the room thickened. Jason turned to me, his jaw tight.

"I should punch you for fucking my wife," Jason said, his voice low and sharp.

I stood my ground, meeting his glare head-on. "You're right. What I did was out of line. I'd want to kill someone if they did that to me."

Jason's nostrils flared, but he didn't respond immediately.

The sound of footsteps broke the silence. Natalie returned, her brow furrowed. "What's going on here?" she asked, glancing between us.

Jason crossed his arms. "I'm not too happy about seeing both of you under my roof when I can't even get ahold of you."

Natalie sighed, running a hand through her hair. "Jason, I'm sorry. I know this is hard, and I should've been more on top of my phone. But we need to figure out a way to work together for the kids' sake."

I stepped in, keeping my tone calm and even. "Jason, I care about Natalie. I don't want to make things harder for you, Bebe or James. What I did was wrong, and I am sincerely sorry."

"Jason, you have Brooke and seem happy. Can you find a way to do that for me?" Natalie asked.

Jason's shoulders relaxed slightly. He looked at me, then at Natalie, and finally nodded. "I can try."

Natalie gave him a small smile. "Okay, now that we've gotten that out of the way... The book is nowhere to be found."

I spoke up. "I can call Kelly and see if Ivy has a copy we can borrow."

Jason glanced at me, looking uncertain. "If it's not a problem..."

"It's not," I assured him.

Natalie grabbed her bag. "I'm going to head out with James. I'm confident you two can figure this out," she said, her tone light but firm as she looked between Jason and me.

I stepped outside and called Kelly.

"Hello, Will," she said, sounding slightly annoyed.

"Hi, I was wondering if you had a copy of 'The One and Only Ivan' that Ivy is working on for her book report?"

"Why?" she asked, her tone sharper than I expected.

"Well, uh, Bebe can't find her copy. She may have left it at school before the break," I explained.

"Are you serious, Will?"

"Kelly," I said, lowering my voice so Jason and Bebe wouldn't overhear. "It's for Bebe."

"You mean Natalie," she replied curtly.

"Look, Natalie isn't here with me right now, I'm with Bebe's dad, Jason. Don't punish Bebe because you're upset with me about my relationship with her mom."

"Relationship?" Kelly said, her voice rising slightly. "I thought I made myself clear about how I feel about her."

"Kelly, if her ex-husband can accept this, then you can try too. Please, Kelly. Do the right thing here."

"Don't patronize me," she snapped. "I'll have Madison drop it off at your house."

Before I could even offer to come pick it up myself, she hung up.

I went back in the kitchen to find Jason. "My daughter, Madison, is going to bring the book to my house. You are welcome to come over and wait for it or I can drop it off."

"I'll follow you over to your house," he said, sounding uncomfortable.

Jason held his car door open for Bebe, while I climbed into mine. As we pulled out of Natalie's driveway. It was a strange dynamic—one I never thought I'd be part of—but here I was, leading Natalie's ex and her daughter to my house to borrow a book.

Halfway to my house, my phone buzzed. It was Evan.

"Hey," I answered.

"Where are you? I'm at your place. Door's locked, alarms are on... Did you forget about our plans?"

I groaned inwardly. "Sorry, I got caught up. I'm on my way. Just go in through the garage, I'll disarm the alarm remotely."

Evan hesitated. "Caught up with what? Are you with Natalie?"

"No, Jason and Bebe are coming over to grab a book for her report. Madison's stopping by too," I said quickly, hoping to keep it brief.

Evan laughed. "Jason, as in Natalie's ex? And Madison? Sounds cozy."

"Evan," I said, my tone sharp. "Don't be a dumbass."

"Relax, William. I'll be on my best behavior."

I hung up thinking about how this was not the day I thought I would be having.

Before I knew it, we were at my house, I turned into my driveway. Jason pulled in behind me, helping Bebe out of the car as I walked over to greet them.

"Come on in for a beer and some apple juice while we wait for Madison," I said, trying to make Jason feel comfortable under the circumstances.

Jason hesitated for a moment, clearly uneasy, but eventually nodded. "Alright."

We walked inside, and Evan was already in full football mode, with four different games on the big screen.

"Hey, Jason, this is Evan. Evan, Jason.

Jason extended his hand. "Hey, man. Nice to meet you. What's going on? Did the Bears just kick a field goal?"

Evan grinned and nodded. "Yeah, Santos nailed it. Right down the middle."

Jason stood by the couch, still looking a little unsure but loosening up as the game went on. I handed him a beer and gave Bebe an apple juice.

"Can I go play in Ivy's room?" Bebe asked after a while.

"Absolutely," I said. Ivy's room had a Barbie dream house that I knew she loved.

I stood as we watched the game. As a quarter went by, I noticed Jason coming in closer toward the couch, eventually we both sat down.

We started to talk about our fantasy football lineups, and Evan, never one to miss an opportunity, made a few jokes about Jason's picks. Jason held his own and shot back about his tight end choking this season.

Right before halftime, we heard the garage door open. Madison walked in, dressed in her riding gear, her boots clicking against the tile.

"Hi, Maddie," I said, standing up. "Thanks for bringing the book."

I motioned toward Jason. "This is Jason, Bebe's dad. He needed the book for her report."

Madison's brows furrowed slightly, but she quickly recovered. "Hi," she said politely to Jason, before turning to Evan. "Hi, Uncle Evan."

Evan grinned, leaning back on the couch. "Hey, don't you want to hang out? We're a lot of fun."

Madison smirked faintly, shaking her head. "No thanks, I'm heading to the barn."

Jason nodded at her. "Nice to meet you, and thanks for dropping this off."

Madison said, "You're welcome. Nice to meet you, too."

She headed out quickly, still looking a little confused.

Jason glanced at the clock. "I'd better get Bebe back to the house so we can work on this," he said, standing.

"You're welcome to stay," I offered, meaning it.

He looked touched by the offer but shook his head. "It's all good. I appreciate the beer and the book, though."

"No problem," I said.

"Bebe!" Jason called, his voice echoing through the house.

As we waited for her, I saw Jason glancing around the living room. I could tell he was taking in the details, the furniture, the decor. Natalie had done it all, and it was obvious he knew that. He stayed composed though, not letting his emotions show.

Bebe came bouncing down the stairs. "Ready, kiddo?" Jason asked.

"Yup!" she said cheerfully, heading toward the door.

I followed them out.

As Jason closed the car door behind Bebe, I hesitated before speaking. "Jason,"

He turned, waiting.

"I'm sorry," I said simply.

Jason looked at me for a long moment before giving a brief nod. "Take care," he said, then climbed into his car and drove off with Bebe.

I stood there watching them go.

"Well, that wasn't too awkward," Evan said, coming up behind me. "He's actually pretty cool."

I exhaled, shaking my head. "Yeah, but I still feel like a dick. I was at his house this morning. With his ex-wife. I slept with her in this house while they were married. She decorated my house, and he knows it."

Evan gave me a look. "Didn't you say he cheated on Natalie? Obviously, their marriage wasn't exactly thriving, or she wouldn't have given your lame ass a second thought."

"He didn't have a full-on affair like Natalie and I did. They could've worked it out. They might still be together if it weren't for me."

Evan rolled his eyes. "Don't beat yourself up about it. Sounds like he's moved on. He's got a girlfriend, right? If they're both happier apart, then so be it. Now can we get back to the game? Enough of this Hallmark Channel crap."

I laughed despite myself. "You're something else, man."

"Damn right," Evan said with a grin.

"Thanks for listening," I added, meaning it.

Evan smirked. "Anytime. Now grab us another round. The second half is starting."

Chapter 43

I Saw Daddy Kissing Mrs. Clause

Natalie

It was Tuesday, and I was headed to Will's for lunch and to prepare for a meeting with Alan and his investor about another restaurant going into The City Center. The concept was exciting—an upscale Italian dining spot led by a chef who had studied in Italy for years. I was already visualizing an open kitchen where customers could view the pasta being made by hand. I couldn't wait to work on this project, especially under Alan. It was an incredible opportunity.

When I arrived at Will's, I let myself in through the garage, the door shutting softly behind me. He'd given me the code, a small but meaningful gesture that made me smile.

Will was in the kitchen on the phone, leaning casually against the counter. He glanced up as I walked in, his eyes lighting up. He mouthed, sorry, and I nodded, setting down the sandwiches and pasta salad I'd brought and grabbing plates to set up for lunch.

When he ended the call, he came straight over, pulling me into a kiss that left me breathless.

"Hi, you," he said softly.

"How long has it been since I've seen you?" I asked, smiling.

"Too long," he said, his hands sliding to my waist.

I laughed lightly, shaking my head.

His lips trailed down my neck, making me shiver. "Do we have time for a quickie?" he murmured, his voice low and teasing.

"What about the food?" I said, though my resolve was already crumbling.

"It can wait. I can't."

His hands moved to the buttons of my blouse, and before I knew it, I was completely caught up in him. His lips brushed over my collarbone, his hands pulling me closer as he slid my blouse off. His touch was deliberate, confident, and I melted into him.

He guided me to the couch, his mouth never leaving my skin. As he laid me back, his hands moved over me with purpose. I felt his lips press against my collarbone, trailing down to the edge of my bra, and a shiver ran through me.

My hands tugged at his shirt, pulling it over his head as his fingers found the button of my jeans. He unfastened it with ease, the moment his fingers brushed over me, I lost all control. My hips arched into his touch, a soft moan escaping my lips as he teased me.

"You're so ready for me," he murmured, his voice rough with desire.

I tried to respond, but all I could manage was a gasp as he slipped a finger inside me, curling it just enough to make me grip his shoulders. My breath hitched, and my hands tangled in his hair, pulling him closer as the tension in my body built.

When I thought I couldn't take any more, he pulled his hand away, leaving me aching for more. He shifted, tugging his pants off in one swift motion. I reached for him, wrapping my hand around him, and the low groan that escaped his lips sent a fresh wave of heat through me.

He leaned down, his mouth capturing mine in a searing kiss as he positioned himself. Then, with one smooth movement, he pushed inside me, and I gasped, my nails digging into his back. He paused for a moment, his forehead resting against mine as we caught our breath.

And then we moved. Together, our bodies fell into a perfect rhythm, his hands gripping my hips as if he couldn't let go. Every thrust pushed me closer to the edge, and when the tension finally broke, it hit me like a wave, leaving me breathless and trembling beneath him.

He followed soon after, his body shuddering against mine as he let out a low, guttural sound that sent shivers down my spine. Our breaths were heavy, and my heart was racing.

But the moment didn't last long. Will glanced at the clock on the wall and groaned. "We got to get moving," he said, brushing his hand through his hair.

I laughed, still catching my breath. "Maybe you should've thought about that before you attacked me in the kitchen."

He grinned, leaning down to kiss me one last time before standing. "You didn't exactly resist."

"Fair," I said, quickly pulling on my blouse and straightening my jeans. "Now, come on. We've got work to do."

We managed to finish lunch quickly, the conversation shifting to Friday's meeting.

"You've got to be top of your game with Alan," Will said, leaning back in his chair. "He's tough and ruthless, but I think you will be able to handle it."

I smiled, nodding. "I'm ready. What's the investor like?"

"From what I hear, he's the kind of guy who doesn't waste time. If he's not impressed, he's out. No second chances," Will said, his expression serious. "We really have to blow him away, so he locks up the deal."

"No pressure," I teased, but I felt the weight of what he was saying.

After we finished reviewing the details of Friday's meeting, I glanced at the time and realized I had to leave soon for school pick up.

"So, Thursday," Will said, leaning forward slightly. "Should I come pick you and the kids up and take you to the Christmas Concert? Or is that too bold?"

I chuckled, shaking my head. "I think we probably need to meet there. We should take it one step at a time."

He nodded, his grin softening. "Fair enough. But I'll be looking for you as soon as I walk in."

"You won't miss us," I said with a small smile. "We'll be in Room 3C—Bebe and Ivy's classroom."

"So, when do you think you're going to tell your kids?" I asked, shifting the conversation.

"Friday," he said without hesitation. "I'll have them starting after school, and I want to talk to them face-to-face. They deserve that."

I nodded. "That's a good idea. I told Bebe not to say anything until you've had a chance to talk to them. Madison's going to be tough, though."

He let out a long breath, running a hand through his hair. "Yeah. I know. But I'm ready for it. I'll make sure she sees how much this means to me—to us."

"Hopefully, she'll come around," I said gently. "It's not going to be easy. I don't want her to hate me."

He reached across the table, his hand finding mine. "She won't hate you," he said firmly, holding my gaze. "This is worth it—you're worth it."

I felt my chest tighten with warmth, the sincerity in his voice cutting straight through me.

"Speaking of schedules," he said, his tone lightening as he leaned back, "let me know your plans for Christmas and New Year's. Maybe we can line up some time together."

"Jason and I are supposed to meet next week to finalize everything," I said. "Once that's sorted, I'll let you know. But I'd love to spend some time with you."

He grinned. "I'll send you my kid-free weekends. I'd love to take you away somewhere. Just us."

"I'd love that too," I said, already picturing it.

"See? Things are going to work out," he said confidently.

"We haven't jumped all the hurdles yet," I said.

"She'll come around," he said again, though there was a flicker of hesitation in his voice.

Glancing at the time, I stood and reached for my bag. "I really need to run to get Bebe and James."

Will walked me to the door, pulling me in for a long, lingering kiss that left my heart racing. That kiss stayed with me, warming my thoughts as I drove to school.

The next few days went by quickly, and before I knew it, it was Thursday evening and time for the Christmas concert for the elementary students. The kids were all dolled up in their holiday outfits, Bebe in a plaid Christmas dress from Janie and Jack with gold ballet flats and a gold bow to complement the details.

James in his little tux that had a plaid bowtie. The excitement in the house was contagious.

Lauren had called earlier in the day to ask if we could ride together. Her husband was at an away game, and with both our kids involved in the concert, it made sense. I agreed, and we coordinated pickup times.

When we arrived at the school, the parking lot was already packed. Thankfully, we found a spot and made our way inside, dodging parents dressed to the nines and kids buzzing with energy.

The moment we walked in, I spotted Jason and Brooke near the front lobby. Jason waved and stepped forward.

"Daddy!" James exclaimed, running to him.

Jason scooped him up with a grin. "Hey, buddy, you clean up nice."

"And how's my princess?" he said, turning to Bebe. "You look absolutely gorgeous."

"Thank you, Daddy," she said, wrapping him in a big hug.

"I'll take James to his class," Jason offered, nodding toward him.

"Thanks," I said, leaning down to kiss James on the cheek. "Break a leg, buddy."

Brooke gave me a polite smile. "Hi, Natalie."

"Hi, Brooke." I returned the smile. We weren't friends, but we'd find neutral ground.

I was in such a good place with Will, I didn't feel the need to hold on to any lingering resentment. If she was good to my children, that was all that mattered.

Lauren and I walked the girls toward the third-grade classroom, weaving through parents chatting in the hallways.

When we arrived, Will was standing in the back with Ivy, his tall frame relaxed yet somehow commanding the space.

Charlie and Bebe raced over to hug their friend, and the girls dissolved into a fit of giggles, complimenting each other's outfits.

Will turned toward us and smiled, saying hello to Lauren and me. For a moment, it looked like he wanted to lean in and kiss my cheek, but he stopped himself, his restraint almost endearing.

"Crazy to think how much has happened in a year," he said quietly, his voice just loud enough for me to hear.

"I know," I said, my gaze meeting his. "I was thinking the same thing."

"Would it be crazy to sit together tonight?" he asked, his tone half-teasing but with a hint of sincerity.

I considered it for a moment before nodding. "I guess we could."

Lauren chimed in, snapping me out of the moment. "Ready to head to our seats? I think Camille has some saved for us."

"Of course, she does," I said with a laugh.

We said goodbye to the girls, leaving them in the classroom, and headed back to the gym where the concert was taking place.

Camille waved us over, her seats perfectly situated in front and center.

"Camille, is it ok that I have one more person crashing in on your seats?" I asked her.

"Of course, sit, sit, everyone." She responded.

Camille introduced her husband to Will. "This is Tate," she said.

"Hey, nice to meet you," Will said, shaking his hand.

As we settled in, I noticed Will's gaze drift across the room, landing on Kelly, who was sitting with Jeff and Madison.

"I'm just going to go say hi to Madison," he said, standing up.

"Alright," I said, watching as he made his way over.

While he was gone, Camille and Lauren leaned in.

"So, how are you doing with Brooke here?" Lauren asked quietly, her tone cautious.

I glanced toward Jason and Brooke, who were sitting a few rows back. "It's all good," I said honestly.

"Wow, divorce looks so good on you, darling," Camille said, grinning.

I laughed.

"Well, she's clearly happy with the most eligible bachelor in all of Orange County," Lauren added with a wink.

Camille leaned closer, her voice dropping to a whisper. "So, are you two official?"

"I think so," I said, smiling. "I told Jason. Bebe and James know too. He told Kelly, but it didn't go over well. He is going to tell his kids Friday."

"The ex will get over it." Lauren said. "Didn't you say she is engaged?"

I nodded, "She is."

"Oh, honey, I'm so happy for you," Camille said. "That man is head over heels for you."

Will returned just as the lights dimmed. He slid into the seat next to me, leaning in close.

I glanced toward Madison, who was sitting with her mom. Her expression darkened the moment she saw us together. Her eyes locked on mine, and I felt her glare like a laser.

"Will," I whispered, "did you tell Madison?"

"No," he admitted, his tone quiet but firm. "I didn't tell her anything yet."

I let out a small sigh. "Maybe it was a bad idea for us to sit together."

The gym buzzed with excitement as the lights dimmed, and the sound of shuffling feet filled the room. Parents whispered to one another, craning their necks to get a better view of the stage.

The concert began with the kindergarteners, their sweet voices barely audible over the hum of the crowd. When their performance ended, the first graders were called up, and I leaned forward in my seat, scanning the line of kids until I spotted James.

"There he is," I whispered to Will, pointing toward the stage.

James looked confident as he walked to his spot, his gelled hair perfectly in place and his little bow tie straight. When the music started, I couldn't help but smile. He was singing his heart out, his voice louder than most of the kids around him.

"He's a natural," Will whispered, leaning closer to me.

"He always brings energy," I said, beaming.

James gave a quick wave toward our section at the end of the song, and I waved back, my heart swelling with pride.

After the first-graders took their bows and walked off the stage, the second graders followed, and then it was finally Bebe, Ivy and Charlie's turn. By this point, the room was filled with applause and anticipation.

The girls beamed as they took their places, scanning the audience until they spotted us. Bebe waved excitedly, and I couldn't help but wave back.

"They look great up there," Will said quietly, his voice warm.

"They are adorable," I said, smiling.

The class launched into their rendition of "Jingle Bell Rock," complete with a few adorable missteps that had the crowd chuckling. It was impossible not to feel the joy in the room, though I couldn't help but glance over at Madison every so often. Her body language screamed irritation, and she hadn't clapped once.

A few minutes later, out of the corner of my eye, I noticed her lean over and whisper something to Kelly. Madison stood, adjusting her dress, and walked down the aisle toward the back of the gym. I assumed she was going to the bathroom, but when the next group, fourth grade, finished their song, she still wasn't back.

By the time the fifth graders took the stage, her seat was still empty.

I leaned closer to Will, keeping my voice low. "Do you think Madison left?"

He frowned, shaking his head. "No, she wouldn't do that."

"She's been gone for a while," I said.

Will sighed and pulled his phone out of his pocket. I watched as he quickly typed out a text, his expression tight.

Will: Where's Madison?

He stared at his phone, waiting for a response. A minute later, his screen lit up with Kelly's reply.

Kelly: I thought she was with you. She said she was going to sit by you after the bathroom.

Will's jaw clenched, his hand gripping his phone tightly.

"If she's not sitting with me and hasn't come back yet," he muttered under his breath, "I wonder if she left."

"What do you want to do?" I asked, feeling the tension rising.

He exhaled sharply, standing abruptly. "I'm going to find her."

"Do you want me to come with you?"

"No," he said, shaking his head. "Stay here for the kids. I'll handle it."

I stayed in my seat, my stomach twisting as he walked briskly toward the exit.

The rest of the show continued, but I struggled to pay attention, clapping absently for each performance while my thoughts remained on Will and Madison.

Camille leaned over, her brow furrowed. "Everything okay?"

"Will went to check on Madison," I said quietly, not wanting to draw too much attention.

The concert continued, but the knot in my stomach refused to fade.

Chapter 44

Chasing The Runaway

Will

I stood up and headed out of the gym, my heart pounding as I weaved through the rows of chairs and slipped into the hallway. The sound of applause and muffled chatter from the pageant echoed behind me. I walked quickly toward the girls' bathroom, stopping at the door and knocking firmly.

A woman stepped out, her expression curious. "Can I help you?"

"Is there a young girl in there? I'm looking for my daughter."

She shook her head apologetically. "Sorry, no one's in there."

I thanked her and stepped outside. A faint breeze brushed against my face as I scanned the parking lot. Parents were still inside the gym, but a few had started trickling out to their cars. Madison was nowhere to be seen.

I pulled out my phone and dialed her number for the third time. Straight to voicemail. She'd turned off her location.

"Damn," I muttered, typing out another text.

Will: Where are you?

No response.

The knot in my chest tightened as I heard the principal's voice inside, wrapping up the program. A loud round of applause followed, signaling the end of the pageant. I couldn't wait any longer, I needed to move.

I texted Natalie.

Will: Can you check the ladies' bathroom again for me? I'm going to head out before traffic gets bad and start looking for her. Tell Ivy I'm sorry.

Then I called Kelly. She picked up immediately, her voice tight with worry.

"Did you find her?" she asked.

"No," I said, trying to keep the frustration out of my voice.

"She probably saw you with her and got upset," she said.

"Kelly, this isn't a time for blame," I said firmly. "Do you know Kellen's number? Or any of her friends? Any idea where she might've gone?"

"I'll send you his number," she said quickly. "I'll start calling some of her friends."

"Thanks. Let's stick together on this. This is about getting Madison back safe."

"Agreed," she said. "Keep me updated."

I glanced at my phone again.

Natalie: No sign of her anywhere. Let me know what I can do.

I called Natalie.

"Hey," I said, my voice tight. "I've got to go find her."

"Do you want me to go with you?" she asked. "Jason and Brooke are taking Bebe and James home, so I'm free."

"No," I said after a pause. "I think that might upset her more. Hang on, Kelly's calling me."

I switched over. "Hey."

"I just talked to another mom," Kelly said. "She said there's a house party on Summit in Ridge North. Apparently, her daughter mentioned it earlier today."

"I'm on it," I said, already walking to my car.

I hung up and immediately called Natalie back.

"Kelly gave me a lead about a house party," I said. "Can you head to my place, just in case she shows up there?"

"Of course," she said without hesitation.

I sped through traffic, my jaw tight as I focused on the road. By the time I reached Summit, the street was lined with cars, music thumping faintly from a nearby house.

I parked and headed toward the house with kids coming in and out of, weaving through clusters of underage teenagers holding red cups. Inside, the living room was hot and stifling, the smell of cheap beer hanging heavily in the air.

I started asking random kids if they'd seen Madison. Most of them shrugged or avoided eye contact until finally, one girl spoke up.

"Yeah, she was here," she said. "She left like ten minutes ago with some kids from Saint John's."

"Kellen?" I asked.

"Yeah, him," she said.

"Do you know where they went?"

She shook her head. "Sorry, no idea."

I left the party and got back into my car, anger bubbling just beneath the surface. I called Kellen's number as I pulled out onto the road. It rang several times before going to voicemail.

"Kellen, this is Madison's dad," I said, my voice sharp. "Call me back immediately. I need to know where Madison is."

I hung up and texted him as well:

Will: Kellen, this is Madison's father. I am looking for her. Please have her call me.

No response.

I called Madison again, but her phone was still off. My frustration was starting to morph into panic. I couldn't stop replaying her behavior earlier—how she sat stone-faced during the pageant, her crossed arms and pointed glares in Natalie's direction.

My phone buzzed, and I grabbed it, relief flooding through me when I saw the name on the screen.

Natalie: I found her.

I exhaled sharply and immediately called her.

"You found her?" I asked, my voice rough.

"She's at your place," Natalie said. "I just pulled into the driveway, and she was getting out of a car. I will see you when you get here."

"Thank God," I muttered. "I'll be there as soon as I can."

I texted Kelly quickly.

Will: She's safe. Natalie found her at my house.

Kelly: Thank God. Call me when you get there.

I drove back, relief washing over me in waves. But as much as I was grateful that she was safe, I knew this wasn't over. Madison couldn't keep acting out like this, and I had no idea how to fix it.

Chapter 45

Not So Different
Natalie

The street was quiet as I sat in Will's driveway, my phone in my lap and my thoughts racing. Jason had taken Bebe and James home without hesitation, offering me a small smile and a quick, "Good luck." I took this as a sign of us being united. Now it was just me, waiting at Will's house.

The faint rumble of an engine broke through the silence, and I straightened in my seat. A Hummer pulled up to the curb, its headlights cutting through the dark. My chest tightened as I watched Madison climb out, her shoulders hunched and her head down.

The driver, who I assumed was the boyfriend, Kellen, glanced toward me briefly, guilt etched across his face. He didn't say a word before driving off, leaving Madison standing alone on the sidewalk.

I stepped out of my car, walking toward her cautiously.

"Madison," I called softly.

She froze, her body tense, before turning to face me. "What are you doing here?" she snapped, her voice sharp.

"I'm waiting for you," I said, keeping my tone steady.

She let out a bitter laugh. "Well, you found me. You can leave now."

"I'm not going anywhere," I said, taking a step closer. "What happened?"

She crossed her arms, her voice cracking as she muttered, "Nothing."

"Madison," I said gently, "you wouldn't have gotten out of that car looking like this if it was nothing."

She glanced away, her jaw tight. "Fine. Kellen dumped me, okay? Happy now?"

Her words hit me harder than I expected, but I kept my expression neutral. "Why?"

Her voice broke as she said, "Because I wouldn't sleep with him. He said I was immature, and then he just... left."

I closed the distance between us, my heart aching at the pain in her voice. "Madison, I'm so sorry," I said softly.

She shook her head, her hands trembling. Tears starting to form. "It doesn't matter. Nothing matters. My dad is with you, my mom's with Jeff, and now Kellen's gone. Everyone's moving on, and I'm just stuck."

I swallowed hard, her words pulling at a part of me I hadn't thought about in years. "I know how it feels to think everyone's leaving you behind," I said quietly.

She scoffed. "You don't know anything about how I feel."

I hesitated, then made a decision. "When I was your age, my parents divorced too. My dad remarried quickly, and I hated his new wife. Her name is Veronica. She made me feel like I didn't belong—like there wasn't room for me in my own dad's life anymore."

Madison's glare softened slightly, her arms loosening around herself.

"I was so angry at them, at everything," I continued. "There was this boy I was dating at the time. He wasn't kind, but I didn't see it then. I was so mad about Veronica, so lonely, that I..." I paused, the words catching in my throat.

"You what?" Madison asked, her voice quieter now.

I took a deep breath. "I lost my virginity to him. Not because I wanted to, but because I was angry and desperate to feel like someone cared about me. The truth is that it only made me feel worse. I didn't have anyone to talk to about it, and I felt even lonelier afterward."

Madison's face softened, her gaze dropping to the ground.

"I'm telling you this because I don't want you to feel like I did," I said. "You have so many people who love you—your dad, your mom, your siblings. And I know I'm not your favorite person, but I care about you, too."

Her eyes filled with tears, and she blinked quickly, trying to hold them back. "It's just... everything feels different now. My mom's getting married, you and my dad are together, and it's like no one cares what I think."

"I know it feels that way," I said gently. "But I promise you, your dad cares. He worries about you so much. And your mom—she loves you more than anything. They're not moving on from you, Madison. They're just trying to figure out how to be happy again. That doesn't mean they don't need you."

Madison swiped at her eyes, sniffling. "I just... I don't know."

"It's okay to feel like this," I said. "It's okay to be upset and confused. But you're not alone in this, no matter how it feels right now."

She nodded slowly, her defenses beginning to crumble.

"Can I walk you inside?" I asked softly.

She hesitated, then nodded again.

We walked into the house together, and she slumped onto the couch, hugging a pillow tightly to her chest. I grabbed a bottle of water from the kitchen and handed it to her.

"Thanks," she murmured, her voice barely audible.

"Of course," I said, sitting across from her.

The sound of a car door closing outside drew our attention, and Madison stiffened as the front door opened.

Will walked in, his gaze locking on Madison immediately. Relief flooded his face as he took her in.

"Madison," he said softly.

She stood abruptly, clutching a throw pillow to her chest. "I'm fine," she said. "You don't have to act like you care."

Will stepped closer, his voice calm but firm. "Madison, I've been driving all over looking for you. Of course, I care."

Her lower lip quivered, and she glared at him. "Then why didn't you tell me about her? Why did I have to see it for myself at the concert?"

Will paused, his shoulders stiffening.

"I'm not a little kid, Dad," she continued, her voice breaking. "If you want me to be honest with you, then you have to be honest with me."

"That's fair," he said after a long pause, his tone heavy with regret.

I stepped forward quietly, touching his arm. He glanced at me, his eyes filled with uncertainty.

"Not right now," I whispered. "Don't let this turn into a fight. She needs to know you love her."

He nodded, his gaze softening as he turned back to Madison. "You're right, Maddie," he said. "I should've told you sooner, and I'm sorry. I love you, and I didn't want to hurt you. I know this is hard, but we'll figure it out together. I promise."

Her face crumpled, and for a moment, she looked so young, so vulnerable. Will stepped closer, hesitating before pulling her into a hug. She didn't resist, her arms wrapping around him tightly.

I stepped back, giving them their moment, but I couldn't help feeling a flicker of hope. Maybe tonight wasn't just about finding Madison—it was about something that may have been lost and was starting to heal.

Chapter 46

Madison In the Meadow
Will

After Madison had calmed down, she wanted to head upstairs, take a shower, and lie down. She looked emotionally drained but more at ease than she had been earlier.

Before she went up, she walked over to Natalie, who was rearranging a few books and pieces of decor in the dining room. She couldn't help herself.

"Hey, thanks for being so cool tonight," Madison said, her voice soft but sincere.

Natalie smiled and stepped closer, her tone gentle. "Anytime you need anything, I'll be there."

Watching them, I felt a knot I hadn't realized I'd been holding loosen. Of all nights, somehow the bridge between them had started to form.

Something about Madison's demeanor told me she had shared more with Natalie than she had with me. Whatever it was, she respected Madison's privacy, and that made me love her even more.

Madison looked at us both and said, "Goodnight."

"I'll be up soon," I told her, and she gave me a small, tired smile before climbing the stairs to her room.

"I'm going to head out," Natalie said quietly, glancing at me. "I'll see you both soon."

I walked her to the door and then out to her car. The night air was crisp, carrying the faint scent of the sea.

When we reached her car, I opened the door for her. A strand of hair fell in front of her face as she turned, and without thinking, I tucked it behind her ear. My fingers lingered for a moment.

"I don't know what happened between you two," I said softly. "If you want to keep it between you, I respect that. But can I just say... you're amazing."

She hesitated, then replied, "She's hurting right now. Sometimes when the world feels like it's spinning out of control, you grab onto the wrong things, hoping they'll steady you. But they never do."

Her words carried more weight than the moment required, and I had a sudden flash of insight. Natalie's dad had remarried. She'd hinted before that he'd pulled away after that. She didn't talk about her parents much, only mentioning Meredith as her family. This was why she'd been so scared of stepping into this role with Madison because she understood it too well.

"You're such a good dad," she added, breaking through my thoughts. "Don't let her forget that."

I took her hands in mine, squeezing them lightly. "I love you," I said, the words falling naturally.

Her hazel eyes softened as she smiled, her hand brushing my cheek. "I love you too."

Leaning in, I kissed her, a slow, lingering kiss that seemed to erase the chaos of the night.

"Text me when you get home so I know you're safe," I said, stepping back reluctantly.

She chuckled lightly, giving me that smile I'd come to rely on. "Okay. Goodnight, Will."

I watched her drive away, the red glow of her taillights disappearing into the night.

Back inside, I headed upstairs to change. Madison's shower was still running as I walked past her room, but when I came back, her door was open, and she wasn't there. The faint light leading downstairs gave her away.

I found her in the kitchen, sitting at the island with a bowl of ice cream.

"Can I join you?" I asked, grabbing a spoon from the drawer.

She smirked, the same expression she'd been making since she was two years old. "Sure."

I sat across from her, letting the silence stretch comfortably for a moment before speaking. "What do you say you and I have an evening to ourselves soon? I will see if your mom will let you stay with me on one of her nights. Anything you want. If you don't mind hanging with your old dad, that is."

She raised an eyebrow. "I mean, you're not that old. A lot of my friends think you're hot, which is so gross."

I laughed. "Where am I taking you?"

She grinned. "How about California Adventure? We haven't done Guardians of the Galaxy in forever."

"It's a date," I said. "And you know what? I'll even let you miss first period so you can sleep in. I'm feeling generous since you called me 'not that old.'"

We both laughed, the sound filling the quiet house in a way that made it feel warmer.

Her expression softened as she licked her spoon. "Dad...I'm sorry if I made things hard for you and Natalie. She's not bad. Actually, she's... good. Way better than that big-boob, blonde you brought around for a bit. She was desperate."

"Okay, that was a rebound. Not my best judgment," I admitted, chuckling.

Madison smiled. "I can tell you really care about Natalie."

I nodded, meeting her gaze. "I do. But that doesn't take away my love for you or your siblings. You guys are my number one. Always. You're my girl, Maddie. My firstborn. There's nothing I wouldn't do for you."

She looked down at her bowl, her voice quieter now. "I know. It's just... sometimes, it's hard."

"I know it is," I said. "Let's promise to communicate more, okay? I'll trust you more, and you'll have more freedom. But that doesn't mean boys are allowed here when I'm not."

She rolled her eyes. "Don't worry. Kellen dumped me tonight."

"Want me to kill him?" I asked, only half-joking.

She gave me a look. "Dad, no. He's a jerk, but not worth you going to jail for."

"No one would know," I said with a smirk.

"You're not a Soprano," she shot back.

I laughed, leaning into a terrible Italian accent. "Those who want respect, give respect!"

She burst out laughing, the sound so genuine it made my chest tighten. "That was the worst Soprano's impression."

"Fair," I said.

We cleaned up our bowls and headed upstairs. As I got into bed, I felt something I hadn't in a long time, peace. For the first time in months, I wasn't weighed down by doubt or tension. Madison was okay. Natalie was okay.

And somehow, so was I.

Chapter 47

The Right Kind of Home

Natalie

Time had moved quickly. The school year was winding down, and summer was just around the corner. The kids were buzzing with end-of-year excitement, and everything had started to fall into place in a way that still amazed me. After Christmas and New Years all the kids knew about our feelings for each other and our interactions became open and comfortable.

Will and I had settled into a rhythm. Some nights at my house, others at his, depending on where our kids were. The transition had been smoother than I could have imagined. James adored Carter and Chase, who let him join in on their games. Ivy and Bebe had gone from best friends to practically sisters. Even Madison had embraced my children.

Madison and I had taken our time, but our relationship had started to flourish. She and Meredith had grown close, bonding over fashion and New York, and we were even planning a girls' trip this summer. The biggest surprise, though, was that Kelly and I had managed to build a friendship, learning how to work together for the kids.

Once Madison and I connected, we realized we had more in common than we ever expected. I had fallen in love with all of Will's kids. Ivy had been easy from the start, she was just darling. Carter and Chase were quieter, but I'd learned they were night owls who loved sleeping in on the weekends and devoured my French toast and muffins. Chase was heading into high school next year, which felt like a big transition. James looked up to the older boys so much, and it was heartwarming to see. Carter, on the other hand, was already a little heartbreaker. Will had told him one day he'd meet a girl who would stop him in his tracks, and he wouldn't be able to chase her if he was busy chasing everyone else.

Sarah and I had grown close too, so much that she had asked me to be a bridesmaid at her wedding. She included my kids in her wedding too, which was so sweet. Ivy and Bebe were flower girls together and James was the ring bearer. It was a perfect day, made even more special when she and Todd announced that they were expecting. A baby was coming in the fall, and the kids were already excited about their new cousin.

Jason and Brooke had just gotten engaged and had bought a house together, a beautifully renovated four-bedroom in Dana Point, painted all white with a baby blue door. It was big enough for several kids, which I suspected was in their plans, to continue to grow their family. Their wedding was set for the winter, and Bebe and James were excited about it. They were going to be a flower girl and ring bearer once more.

Meredith was visiting as much as she could, and her relationship with Evan was growing. He was even flying to see her. They weren't calling it exclusive, just *fun*, according to Meredith. But from the way Evan had her as his date to Sarah's wedding, I had my suspicions it was getting serious.

Kelly's wedding was coming up in June. They were flying to Hawaii for a small, intimate ceremony, just her kids and Jeff.

One afternoon, Will and I were walking through town, coffee in hand, when I mentioned, "Your mom actually asked me about our summer plans the other day."

Will huffed, taking a sip of his drink. "See? She's warming up."

I shot him a look. "You really believe that?"

He shrugged. "She didn't insult you. That's something."

I laughed, shaking my head. "You have a very loose definition of 'warming up.'"

Will just smirked. "Give it time."

That evening, just before dusk, with the kids at Jason's for the weekend, Will turned to me, his eyes dancing with mischief. "Come on. I want to show you something. Let's take a drive."

We drove inland listening to Sonny and Cher sing "I Got You Babe," until he pulled into the driveway of a large white colonial-style house. The black shutters needed work, but the house had character. A giant tree with a swing stood in the front yard. The landscaping was beautiful, with manicured grass and vibrant flowers. A porte-cochère led to a five-car garage.

I turned to him, suspicion creeping in. "Will, what are we doing here?"

He stepped out of the car, motioning for me to follow. "Just come inside."

I hesitated before trailing him up the steps. He unlocked a keypad and took the key out. The moment the door opened, my mind spun into designer mode with ideas—black-and-white checkered tile in the foyer, a wrought-iron staircase, warm sconces along the walls.

In the back, there was a pool, a half-court, and a swing set. Beyond the property, the land opened to a breathtaking valley view, where the sun was just beginning to dip toward the horizon.

I stopped in my tracks, taking it all in.

He turned to me, his expression serious yet full of hope. "Is it something you could picture living in? With me. With our families."

My heart stilled.

"I know my house isn't your style, even though you designed the interior. And I know you love your house. But it doesn't have the space for all of us. I want to live with you, Natalie. I want to wake up next to you every morning. I want this house full of love, laughter, and the chaos of six kids running around—maybe even a seventh." He smirked at me as I shot him a look.

"Okay, six is enough," he laughed, pulling me into a kiss. "Keep in mind, it'll need your touch."

I glanced at him suspiciously. "How did you get access to this place?"

"This off-market gem?" He grinned, dangling a set of keys. "I'm in real estate, baby. It has its perks."

We toured the rooms—spacious living and dining areas, an office, a large open-concept kitchen and family room. Everything needed updating, but that was my favorite part.

"This could be Meredith's room," Will suggested when we found a bedroom downstairs. "We could turn the dining room into an extra office for you, and the front living room into a theater or game room."

Upstairs, we found five more bedrooms. A loft sat in the center, and over the garage was another large room.

"I think Carter and Chase could share this one," Will mused. "The loft could be a playroom, with desks for homework. Bebe and Ivy can take the Jack-and-Jill room. Madison can have this smaller one, she'll be off to college soon. And James can take this one."

Finally, we stepped into the master bedroom. The floor-to-ceiling windows faced the stunning valley view. The sunset painted the room in warm gold.

"This," Will said, turning to me, "is where we'd wake up together. Every day. And, you know, do all the other things." He raised an eyebrow playfully.

I laughed. "Don't be cute."

He stepped closer, his voice suddenly softer. "What do you think?"

I looked around, already envisioning every detail I would design. "It's timeless," I admitted.

Then, without warning, he dropped to one knee. His blue eyes locked on mine.

"Natalie Rose Bradford," he said, his voice steady but full of emotion. "I wanted you when I wasn't supposed to. Every part of me was drawn to you, no matter how hard I tried to resist. Whatever this pull is between us, it has only brought me love and happiness. I want you to be my wife. Will you marry me?"

Tears blurred my vision as I looked down at the man I loved.

"Yes, Will," I whispered. "I would love to marry you."

He stood up and slid the ring onto my finger—an oval-cut diamond on a rose gold band, sparkling like the sunset.

I stared at it, then at him. "Did Meredith help with this?"

He smirked. "Hey, give a guy some credit. But, okay, yes, she did."

Will stood, wrapping me in his arms. Kissing me deeply, sharing all the love he has for me in this one kiss.

"So, what do you say? Let's put in an offer. Once we close, you can run free with your design plans."

I laughed against his chest, feeling utterly happy. "Let's do it."

Will picked me up and hugged me tight, kissing my nose.

I let out a deep breath, feeling the weight of everything settle in, the life we were building, the home we were standing in, and the future we were stepping into together.

Chapter 48

The Right Kind of Imperfect
Natalie

Will and I had quietly decided we were going to elope—just the two of us—this coming spring. We didn't want the stress or spotlight of a wedding. Cabo was the plan, and Will would take care of the details. We'd tell everyone once we got back. We were still debating whether to include Meredith and Evan, but we figured we'd decide closer to the date.

It was Christmas Eve, and we were hosting the holiday at our new home. We had Will's kids with us this year, while Bebe and James would be spending the night at Jason and Brooke's—but everyone was coming over for dinner. It would be my first Christmas morning without them, which tugged at my heart a little. Still, I was so grateful to have Will's kids this year.

It was Kelly's first Christmas without her children, too. We were all doing our best to show up for each other and navigate this blended version of family. I told her she was more than welcome to come by in the morning, even though I had a feeling she wouldn't. But tonight, she'd be here. Everyone would.

When the renovations were finally complete, we each sold our homes. Thankfully within a day, thanks to the California market, so we didn't have to live through the construction phase.

Letting go of my house was bittersweet. It had been my home with Jason. But the kids were genuinely excited about the new place, which helped ease the transition. James was thrilled about the basketball court and about having brothers. Bebe and I had decorated her room together, complete with a little vanity, a ballet barre with a mirror, and a window seat piled with big pillows and bookshelves behind it. It was her cozy little hideaway.

Ivy and I worked on her room too. She loved art, so we set up an easel by the window where she could paint in the natural light. She said it made her feel grown-up.

In Madison's room, we hung the large horse portrait above her bed and arranged her ribbons. She had a bulletin board with photos of her friends and one of us. It was from the horse show I went to with Will, the one she'd won. He had taken the picture, and I was genuinely touched that she'd put it up.

The boys weren't particularly interested in decorating, but they gave me a few ideas. They were all into sports, so I tied that into each of their rooms. Carter and Chase didn't seem to mind sharing, they had their own space and were genuinely easy going about it.

The kitchen was a dream. White cabinets, two glass-front fridges, one stocked with food, the other with drinks. I told Will we'd need to keep them pretty since everything was on display.

In the family room, I added a wood beam to the ceiling to give it warmth. The fireplace sat at the center of the room, cozy and inviting, and our oversized sectional fit our large, wonderfully chaotic family.

We'd built a small pool house in the backyard that doubled as our guest room—also known as Meredith's room. The downstairs guest bedroom had become my office, which meant we were able to keep the dining room intact. Tonight would be our first time using it.

Kelly and Jeff were coming. So were Brooke and Jason, Will's parents, Meredith, Evan, Sarah, and Todd. Sarah was five months pregnant and glowing, and the kids were buzzing with excitement over their soon-to-be cousin.

I had the table set beautifully. I was proud of it. Since our group was so big, I set up a kids' table in the foyer next to the dining room so we could all be close and in the same space.

When Will came downstairs and saw everything, he grinned.

"Watch out, Martha Stewart," he said.

"Thank you, 'Home & Garden' magazine," I replied.

We'd given Bebe and James their gifts the night before and had a cozy evening watching "Home Alone," just the four of us. We told them Santa would be visiting their dad's house this year.

Meredith and Evan had dinner together last night, and she stayed at his place. They didn't arrive until nearly four.

"Hello, you two," I said when they walked in.

"The couple in denial," Will teased.

Evan shot him a look.

"Okay, fine," Meredith said. "We've decided to go steady."

I laughed. "Steady? Are you going to prom together?"

"Oh stop." She huffed. "But seriously, is it weird?"

"It's practically perfect," I said.

"Just don't screw it up, Evan," Will added. "Or things will get really awkward at family gatherings."

"We've thought about that," Meredith said. "But we can't seem to stay apart. Even when we try. The distance is hard, but...we're going to see where it goes."

"Well then, you have our blessing," I said, smiling.

"To the happy couple," Will said, handing everyone a glass.

Just then, Will's mom walked in.

"Hello, everyone! I bring gifts."

Bebe and James ran over to her.

"Hello, darlings," she said, hugging them.

Will's mom had always been warm to my kids, which was a relief. Brooke's parents had embraced the kids as well. They were loved in so many directions, and I was grateful.

Brooke and Jason arrived next. She looked a little heavier, and I couldn't help but wonder, was she pregnant?

Then came Kelly, Jeff, and the children. That's when the house truly came to life. Laughter, chatter, and kids everywhere.

Kelly leaned in to me and whispered, "Brooke's looking a little...plump. You don't think—"

"That she's on the wrong diet?" I asked, smirking.

"No," she said. "Pregnant."

I shrugged. "Maybe. If she is, then I'm happy for them. I know Brooke wants kids of her own."

Kelly looked at me. "Would you and Will want another one?"

I laughed. "I think this *Step-by-Step* clan is big enough. You know they had a baby and then the show got canceled."

We both cracked up as we carried dishes to the table.

When it was time to eat, everyone gathered around. Will stood up with his glass raised.

"I'd like to propose a toast," he said. "To family. Not all families look the same—and ours might be the most unique of them all. But it's full of love, chaos, and unity. And to my future wife, who pulled off this amazing night."

"To family," everyone echoed.

It wasn't picture-perfect. But it was ours, beautiful, messy, and imperfect in all the best ways.

And I wouldn't have it any other way.

Acknowledgments

Writing, for me, is loving something so much that I can't wait to get back to it. I love getting lost in these stories, sometimes for hours. None of this would be possible without my husband, Matthew, who lets me slip away on Saturdays when I need to disappear into the world of my characters. To bring them to life, I have to fully immerse myself in their world. Thank you for always encouraging me and being my rock.

To my readers, thank you for coming back for another story. I still can't believe we're here with book two. I hope the ending of Will and Natalie's journey gave you exactly what you were waiting for. Indie authors wouldn't have a voice without readers like you—those who take a chance on something new and then return for a second chance. Your support, reviews, and excitement mean more than you'll ever know.

To all the amazing people who helped shape this book:

Hilari Conen, thank you for always pushing me to dig deeper, especially as I explored more of Natalie's past in this story.

Liza Illuzzi, for helping me pull everything together and guiding me as I wrapped up this world.

Ceri Marsh, words can't express my gratitude for stepping in at the last minute when my hands were so sore, and for combing through every last detail with such care.

To Aura Lewis, thank you for creating another stunning cover. From the gate to the construction site, your talent has been such a gift.

To Ashley Stevenson and my team at Love Story PR, thank you for cheering me on and reminding me that it truly takes a village to bring a book into the world.

To my incredible ARC readers, your early support and enthusiasm give these stories their voice. You are the reason they find their way into readers' hands.

To my dad, who has always believed in me and taught me that "no risk, no reward."

To my mom, who loves me without judgment and lets me be fully myself, no matter how silly the dream may be.

To my daughters, who let me be more than just their Uber driver—you inspire me every day. Seeing you make your own little books is the sweetest reminder of why I do this.

To my sister, Haley, for always believing in me.

P.S. Thank you for reading my chapters from the Notes section. You've taught me that the bond between sisters is something truly special. Natalie and Meredith's relationship was inspired by the love and all the laughs we have shared over the years.

To my friends, thank you for the endless encouragement, the coffee runs, the late-night pep talks, and for helping with my kids when deadlines took over. The love and support surrounding me through this second book have meant more than words can say. Writing is such a vulnerable thing to do, and knowing I have all of you in my corner makes it a little less scary and a lot more meaningful.

To everyone who helped make *The Right Kind of Wrong* possible, thank you. The support I've received since the first book has been unreal, and it's what keeps me going on this wild, beautiful adventure. Here's to taking chances—and second chances—on love, on stories, and on ourselves.

Lindsay Adams Photography

About the Author

Jillian Marie fell in love with romance novels for the same reason she writes them: to get lost in imperfect love stories that still find a way to feel perfect. *The Right Kind of Wrong* is her second book, continuing Natalie and Will's story that began in *The Wrong Kind of Perfect*.

She lives in Southern California with her husband and three daughters, whose love, laughter, and just a little bit of drama inspire her every day.

Sneak Peek:
Never Would I Forever

Chapter 1
Meredith

I told myself it was for the best.

The thing is, I don't fall for people. I don't let it get that far. Once was enough—and I promised myself I'd never do it again.

So I should've known better than to get involved with a sexy surfer who lived halfway across the country. The kind of man who made everything feel easy until it wasn't. Evan and I were a slow-motion train wreck from the start. Distance, timing, too many ghosts between us. Two people raised on divorce trying to prove we weren't built the same way.

The subway jolted, pulling me back to the present. I was two stops from my East Village loft when my phone buzzed—Natalie. My older sister.

I let it go to voicemail. There was no way I could reach my pocket without ending up in the lap of the sixty-something-year-old man beside me, who was holding a cat carrier that smelled faintly of tuna.

When the train screeched to a stop, I climbed the stairs and stepped into one of those rare spring days that make New York feel almost kind. The kind where you can actually feel the vitamin D soaking in, the sun kissing your skin in the most perfect way, and you know summer is just around the corner.

My stop left me a few blocks from home. I passed a café that knew my order, a record shop that never seemed open when I had time, and a mural that always changed but somehow stayed the same.

My building was a narrow walk-up on East Ninth, rent-controlled and stubbornly standing against time. My corner loft had the same mismatched decor I'd pieced together over the years, plus a few of Natalie's "finds" to make it look less tragic. Like the brass lamp that gave off the softest glow next to my forest-green reading chair—the one place I could breathe.

That's where I dropped my bag and called her back.

"Hey, Mer," she said, her voice muffled as a door clicked shut behind her.

"Hello my loving sister, you called earlier."

" I was checking to see if you really can't make it for the Fourth this year. We rented a lake house in Coeur d'Alene—plenty of room for you."

"I already told you—I've got Jack's got a new boyfriend so his all-white party in the Hamptons has to be extra. It's our thing."

"Last year, we were your thing."

"Last summer was different."

"I know," Natalie said softly. "I really thought you two were going to be it."

What she said stuck in a place I didn't want to touch.

My natural reaction is just to bury every piece of him.

I'd spent the past year convincing myself I was fine. That what happened with Evan was just a mistake. That I didn't need anyone. I'm best alone.

And then, as if the universe were listening and wanted to test me, my phone buzzed again.

Evan's name lit up the screen.

www.ingramcontent.com/pod-product-compliance
Lightning Source LLC
Chambersburg PA
CBHW020421110726
47899CB00006B/2081